THE TREASURE OF PARAGON BOOK 7

HIDDEN DRAGON

USA TODAY BESTSELLING AUTHOR

GENEVIEVE JACK

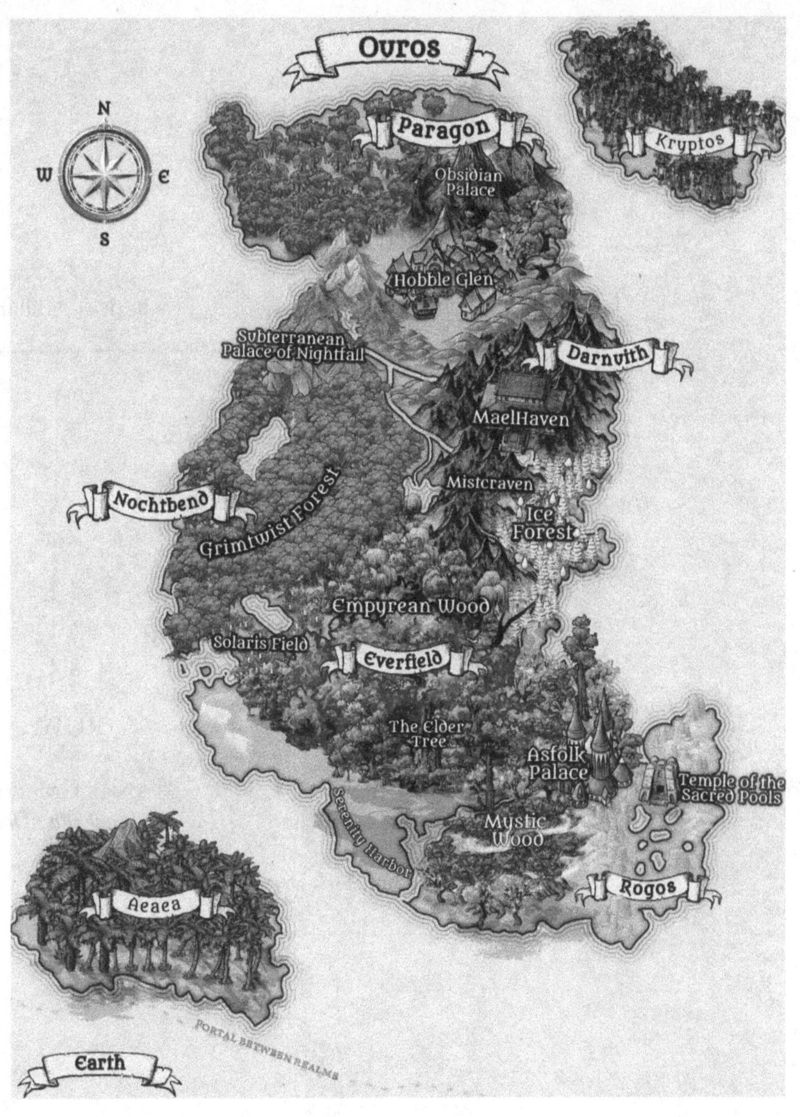

Ouros
Paragon
Obsidian Palace
Hobble Glen
Kryptos
Subterranean Palace of Nightfall
Darnvith
MaelHaven
Mistcraven
Ice Forest
Nochtbend
Grimtwist Forest
Empyrean Wood
Solaris Field
Everfield
The Elder Tree
Asfolk Palace
Temple of the Sacred Pools
Serenity Harbor
Mystic Wood
Rogos
Aeaea
PORTAL BETWEEN REALMS
Earth
N
W   E
S

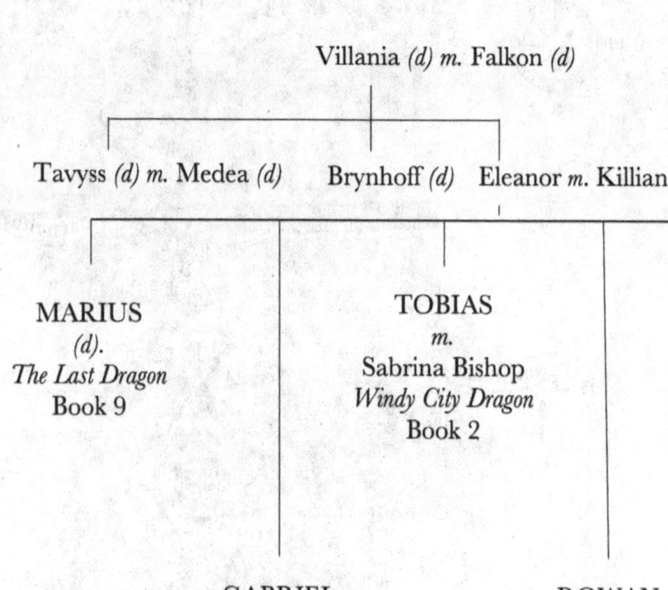

Villania (d) m. Falkon (d)

Tavyss (d) m. Medea (d)   Brynhoff (d)   Eleanor m. Killian (d)

MARIUS
(d).
The Last Dragon
Book 9

TOBIAS
m.
Sabrina Bishop
Windy City Dragon
Book 2

GABRIEL
m.
Raven Tanglewood
The Dragon of New
Orleans
Book 1

ROWAN
m.
Nick Grandstaff
Manhattan Dragon
Book 3

The Treasure of Paragon

FAMILY TREE

ALEXANDER
m.
Maiara
The Dragon of Sedona
Book 4

XAVIER
m.
Avery Tanglewood
Highland Dragon
Book 6

COLIN
*The Dragons of
Paragon*
Book 8

NATHANIEL
m.
Clarissa Black
*The Dragon of Cecil
Court*
Book 5

SYLAS
m.
Dianthe
Hidden Dragon
Book 7

AUTHOR'S NOTE

Dear Reader,

Love is the truest magic and the most fulfilling fantasy. Thank you for coming along on this journey as I share the tale of the Treasure of Paragon, nine exiled royal dragon shifters destined to find love and their way home.

There are three things you can expect from a Genevieve Jack novel: magic will play a key role, unexpected twists are the norm, and love will conquer all.

The Treasure of Paragon Reading Order

The Dragon of New Orleans, Book 1

Windy City Dragon, Book 2,

Manhattan Dragon, Book 3

The Dragon of Sedona, Book 4

The Dragon of Cecil Court, Book 5

Highland Dragon, Book 6

Hidden Dragon, Book 7

The Dragons of Paragon, Book 8

The Last Dragon, Book 9

Keep in touch to stay in the know about new releases, sales, and giveaways.

Join my VIP reader group
Sign up for my newsletter

Now, let's spread our wings (or at least our pages) and escape together!

Genevieve Jack

ABOUT THE BOOK

Her gift was to see...

Dianthe's second sight has always been both a blessing and a curse. She can't control her visions, yet they're unerringly accurate... until an erroneous prophecy results in the destruction of her homeland. The revelation crushes her spirit and endangers her role as an officer in the rebellion to take back the kingdom of Paragon.

Until their future was hidden.

Sylas, dragon shifter and exiled prince, is the leader of the rebellion, but he can no longer rely on his mate Dianthe's psychic powers. His inner dragon is secretly pleased to relegate her to the sidelines. Even if his decision temporarily drives her away, he'd rather have her angry than dead. Or worse.

No one ever promised forever would be easy.

When changing circumstances accelerate the rebellion's plans, Dianthe's fairy roots make her the only one who can perform a dangerous and necessary task. Her need to prove herself soon collides with Sylas's desire to protect her and strains their connection to the breaking point. Dragon mating bonds are eternal, but if Dianthe and Sylas don't find a way back to each other, not only will their marriage fail, their mission to reclaim Paragon will as well.

CHAPTER ONE

Every time Sylas thought of his wife, Dianthe, he pictured her in the kitchen. When the light poured through their cottage window and caught the flecks of gold—color that had shed from her wings like glitter—on her mahogany skin, everything in his world felt right. Something about watching her bent over a bowl or inspecting a freshly baked tray of cookies proved to his soul that the world was good. How could tragedy befall anyone surrounded by the smell of warmed cinnamon?

Not that Dianthe's talents were limited to the domestic arts. On the contrary, her healing powers were legendary among her kind, and her second sight had proven invaluable to the resistance. Before he'd even known who the Defenders of the Goddess were, Dianthe had been a high-ranking officer and an integral part of the formation of the rebellion.

Their relationship had taken root on the island of Aeaea where he'd hidden after he and his siblings had been scattered to the four winds following the murder of his eldest brother, Marius. One of Dianthe's visions had led the Defenders of the Goddess to the same island for the purpose of establishing a base camp. Once she'd discovered who he was, a Treasure of Paragon, one of eight remaining heirs to the kingdom, she had been the one to tell him the truth about his wicked mother. In Eleanor's bottomless thirst for power, she and his uncle Brynhoff had murdered Marius. Dianthe was the reason he had joined the rebellion and risen through the ranks, finding his purpose in the cause.

She was a warrior even if her only weapon was her mind.

Still, after so long away from home, picturing her in the kitchen had become his way to ground himself. Dianthe always seemed happy there. All the muscles of her face and shoulders relaxed, the tiny lines of tension loosening around her eyes and mouth. Her pupils grew large, the amber irises focused evenly on her task, completely empty of worry, completely content. In the kitchen, she was above it all. Nothing could touch her.

That's how he chose to think of her. There was too much blood, too much violence, to see her as she truly was, a fairy who'd chosen a life fighting by his side, fighting his evil mother's lust for power and risking her life to defend the five kingdoms. She'd chosen the fight before they met, but he'd always recognized it was his fucked-up family that had brought darkness into her life.

Now he joined her at the kitchen table and dipped his finger into the batter inside the powder-blue bowl she worked over. He stole a taste. "Mmmm. You're making crizzle rolls. My favorite."

"Sylas!" Dianthe smacked his shoulder. "That's for the party tonight. You don't want to show up at Elder Tree empty-handed, do you?"

"They won't miss a mouthful." He smacked his lips. "There's something different."

"I added a little lemon and fever fruit. Trader's spice."

He scooped up another dollop and popped it in his mouth. "Yes, the trader's spice makes it," he mumbled around his finger.

"Goddess have you, Sylas, I'm serious! Get your hands out of my bowl." She turned the full weight of her heavily annoyed stare on him.

He took it as a challenge. "Hmm. If I can't have the batter, what can I do to keep my mouth busy?" Reaching for her, he traced along the skin of her shoulder with the back of his nails.

She lowered her chin and stared up at him through impossibly thick lashes. "If I hadn't known what I was getting into mating a dragon, I'd tell you to go suck an egg." Wings fluttering, she allowed the spoon to clink against the side of the bowl. She wrapped her arms around his neck. "Lucky for you, I knew exactly what I was getting into mating a dragon, and I have far better uses for that naughty mouth."

A deep, vibrating purr rumbled in his chest when her mouth met his, her full lips tasting of crizzle batter and the remains of her smile. He hoisted her up his body, felt her legs wrap around his hips. The world melted away. All his responsibilities, the horrors he'd seen over his years leading the rebellion, all of it retreated to the back of his mind and pure joy filled his heart. Goddess, he wanted her. Wanted to bury himself in her for days. Wanted to taste every inch of her.

He pushed the bowl aside and lowered his mate to the table, reaching for the buttons of her dress.

"Sylas, stop. Wait." Dianthe's lashes fluttered.

Sylas froze. Her eyes rolled back in the way they did when she was seized by a vision; her stomach tensed rigidly. A tremble rattled her body. He supported her with his arms as the magic rolled through her.

"What is it? What do you see?"

Her eyes widened in terror, her entire body quaking under him.

He held her tighter. "I've got you. I've got you. Tell me what you've seen."

"Everfield... on fire. The Obsidian Guard is coming."

"When?" He stood up and lifted her from the table, placing her on her feet.

A tear cut along her cheek and her voice shook as she blurted, "Now."

Screams cut through the cottage from the forest outside and Sylas inhaled deeply, then cursed. He smelled smoke. "Mountain help us."

He ran to the door and peeked out. Fire. Chaos. Fairies screamed as they fled from dragons in black-and-red uniforms who were kicking in doors and dragging people from their homes before they set those homes on fire.

He closed the door. "They're burning Empyrean Wood."

"Oh goddess, Sylas. What can we do?" Dianthe began to weep in earnest.

Taking her by the shoulders, he denied his instinct to comfort her. They'd both known this was a possibility. Dianthe could fall apart. He couldn't. He had to follow the plan and get her out of there.

He grabbed the bags he'd packed for just such an emergency and handed one to her. He strapped the other onto his back. "We go together, out the back, hand in hand. I'll cloak you in invisibility. Don't look back."

Dianthe stared at the backpack in her hands. "When did you pack these?"

"You know when."

She frowned. "We can't just leave, Sylas! People will die. The Obsidian Guard is here. They're showing no mercy. You have to shift. We have to fight!" She clutched the strap of the bag until her fingers turned white.

He shook his head. "I'm not strong enough to face the Guard alone, and calling on the rebellion now would undermine everything we've worked for. They're not ready. We'd lose and all would be for nothing."

When she didn't move, he hoisted her bag onto one shoulder. If she wouldn't carry it, he would.

More screams filtered through the walls, closer now. A knock came on the door, followed by the voice of a young fairy. "The Guard is coming. Save yourself. Run!"

Sylas grabbed her hooded cloak off the rack and wrapped it around Dianthe, dressing her as if she were a child. He thanked the Mountain she was still wearing her boots. "Out the back." He tugged her toward the rear door.

She pulled up short of the exit and glanced woefully at the healing branches of the tree that grew at the center of their cottage. "Sylas, the zum zum! It's one of the last of its kind."

It was much too large to move, big enough to support the body of a full-grown male now and capable of curing fairies of most ills. Dianthe had healed many friends, neighbors, and community members in that tree, as well as the one fairy he'd begged her not to heal—Aborella.

Dianthe had claimed she'd seen a vision of Aborella fighting on the side of the rebellion, but her visions were open to interpretation. That one was exceptionally nebulous. But when they'd come across the fairy, gravely injured and buried alive outside the palace walls in Paragon, he'd allowed Dianthe to talk him into bringing her here. His mate had spent days painstakingly caring for and healing the fairy. But once she was healed, Aborella went straight back to the Obsidian Palace. He was almost certain she was behind this raid. Why else would the Guard be in Everfield now?

He gave Dianthe a mournful look. "We have to leave it. There's nothing we can do."

"Sylas—"

"Shhhh." He made them both invisible before throwing open the back door and ushering her out onto the path.

All fairy homes were built from living materials, and their cottage was no exception. The walls consisted of tightly woven branches, creating a large, leafy dome completely integrated into the forest. Outside, the scene of utter chaos that met them turned his stomach. The entire north side of the Empyrean Wood was on fire. Everyone was evacuating. Those not fast enough to flee found their faces plunged into the dirt by soldiers wearing the black-and-red uniforms of Paragon. Blood flowed. Everything was on fire.

He tried to cover Dianthe's eyes to save her from the sight.

"Don't bother. I saw it in my vision." She shoved his hand away. "I'll be seeing it in my nightmares for as long as I live."

He tugged her forward, breaking into a run when he saw a guard at the neighboring cottage, kicking down the door.

"By order of the empress of Paragon, I am here to exact punishment for aiding a fugitive of the crown." The guard's pronouncement came through a haughty grin before he charged into the abode.

Sylas heard the screams of their elderly neighbor, Wynter.

"Oh my goddess, Sylas. What will they do to her?"

"I don't know. Keep moving."

"We have to help!"

He repositioned the bags, yanked her against him with his free arm, and spread his wings, taking to the air. The position of the bags and uneven weight set him off-balance, and it took his best effort to climb above the trees and soar beyond the limits of the village. It was a relief when Serenity Harbor came into view.

"Sylas, answer me!" Dianthe sobbed. "How could you just leave her there to deal with those... those cretins alone?"

He landed on the docks and swept her toward the sailboat he'd kept at the ready. He tossed in both bags, then turned to his mate. "Get in."

"Not until you talk to me."

He swept her under his arm and carried her onto the boat, then went about untying it from the dock. His oread, Indigo, appeared beside him, and together they pushed off the dock and rowed out to open water.

Indigo readied the sail. "To Aeaea as planned?"

Sylas nodded.

"Aeaea?" Dianthe asked. "We're going back to Circe's island now? What about Everfield?"

"There's nothing we can do, Dianthe. There're too many of them. Any attempt to help would reveal our identities. We'd both be in the dungeon by nightfall." Sylas's throat was thick and gritty. He'd held back his emotions from the first sniff of smoke. Just a few more minutes. He couldn't allow himself to break, not until he knew they were safe.

Dianthe looked back the way they'd come and broke into deep, wrenching sobs. Even though Sylas told himself not to, he looked back too. Flames engulfed Everfield, licking over the trees and turning the entire sky red and hazy. Fairies gathered on Serenity Beach, holding each other as their homes burned. He thanked the Mountain for every single one he saw. At least they were alive.

His mate grabbed his arm as if she were holding on for dear life.

"We'll be safe soon." The words sounded hollow, completely inadequate.

Her sobs abated. A far darker emotion moved in,

clouding her eyes and causing her lips to peel back from her teeth. "Safe? You think I'm worried about being safe! How could you just leave them like that? We could have helped. We might have saved Wynter from whatever fate befell her at the hands of *your* people!"

That was it. Sylas could abide no more. Heat flooded his face, and all the muscles in his back tensed. "Wynter would be fine if you hadn't invited a viper into our home."

Dianthe pushed away from him, hugging herself against his words.

"Why do you think the Obsidian Guard was there? Didn't you hear them say this was retribution for taking in a fugitive? Who do you think told them there was a fugitive in Everfield? Who is the only other person who knows who I really am and that I've been living with you there?"

"No. It can't be. I saw... I saw her helping us." Dianthe shook her head vehemently.

"Your vision was wrong. Don't you get it?" He pointed a hand at Everfield in flames. "You made a mistake, Dianthe, and Everfield paid the price!"

She gasped as if he'd slapped her.

"I'm sorry to put it so bluntly, but you knew there was the possibility. You told me yourself that visions are open to interpretation. People have free will. They can change their minds."

"Yes, but I befriended her. She's changed. She was kind."

"Give me a break." Sylas held his head. "She was

kind when you were giving her what she wanted! When she needed you! I told you she was evil."

Dianthe's already red eyes began to tear again.

"You gave her information. I know you did. Not a lot, I'm sure. But you wanted to endear yourself to her. I know you, Dianthe. I know you had good intentions. But if you'd seen her face when I told her we knew who she was. If you'd seen how quickly she fled... Everfield is burning because of Aborella."

Dianthe's knees seemed to give out and she sat down hard, her hair blowing in the saltwater breeze. All light drained from her eyes and her mouth gaped. Beyond the stern, the ever-reddening sky over Everfield was thick with smoke from the active fires. How long would Empyrean Wood burn? Would there be anything left by the time they put it out?

"You think Everfield is burning because of Aborella, and Aborella was there because of... me." Dianthe grimaced as the truth set in.

Sylas wished he could tell her she was wrong, but he'd known this would happen. Aborella was as evil as they came. She couldn't be trusted. "It's not your fault. You've always been able to trust your visions in the past. It's just now..."

"Now what?"

Every part of Sylas felt heavy and bone weary. He didn't have the heart to tell her that Aborella might have infected her or polluted her gift with a dark curse. He didn't know for sure, but he suspected they could not trust Dianthe's visions any longer. Not right away. Even tonight's prophecy had been far too late to be of much help. She was off her game. They'd have to be cautious.

He couldn't tell her now though. Not like this. Not when her homeland was burning and she had no idea if the community she'd grown up in, the people she loved, were well and safe. He sat beside her and slid his hand into hers.

"Nothing. We're safe. I'm here. This is the best we can do for now."

He was relieved when she seemed to accept it. She laid her head on his shoulder and watched helplessly as the forest of her childhood and the home they'd built together blazed.

CHAPTER TWO

Aborella stood at the window of her ritual room, scanning the forest beyond the Obsidian Palace for any sign of her familiar, Abacus. Days ago she'd tied a note of warning to the leg of the silver bird, commanding her to fly to Dianthe. Abacus had never returned. Worse, when she'd attempted to call the bird to her using their magical bond, she'd been met only with emptiness where there'd once been a connection. She was beginning to fear her dear pet was dead.

Surely Dianthe wouldn't have harmed the bird. Sylas perhaps, if he'd thought she was using it to spy, but she doubted it. His mate would never allow it. Still, she hadn't slept well since. Something was wrong. Something that was too close to her to see.

After searching the sky one more time, she turned to the dark crystal she sometimes used for scrying. She rested her fingers on the smooth surface.

"Show me Abacus," she whispered.

Cloudy images flitted through the reflection in the

stone. Shapeless masses. Nothing she could discern. Nothing helpful. But then an easily recognizable feeling overcame her. Like being dipped in ice water, she sensed evil pressing in around her, nipping her skin. She was sinking, being swallowed by absolute darkness.

With a gasp, she removed her fingers from the stone. *Oh, Abacus. What happened to you?*

Three sharp knocks came on the door. Strange—normally no one bothered her here. They were all too afraid of disturbing her work for the empress. She didn't get a chance to ask who it was. Without any invitation on Aborella's part, Eleanor, empress of Paragon, entered like an arctic wind.

Aborella stood and bowed. "Empress, to what do I owe the pleasure?"

"Have you found the child yet?" Eleanor demanded. She was dressed in red velvet today, in a gown that might have hung on the wall as its own work of art. The stiff neckline circled her shoulders and folded around her body, giving the appearance that she was wrapped inside the head of a rose. The effect was striking... until the empress smiled. Then all Aborella could think was that she'd found the thorn.

"Unfortunately, no." Aborella did her best to feign disappointment. "My visions are unclear. I suspect Raven and her sisters are blocking me. I'll keep trying. I'm bound to find a crack in their protective magic with time."

The empress grunted and paced into the room, her fingers trailing over the herbs and magical objects on the shelf. Aborella bristled as Eleanor's nails passed the shadow-mail candle she'd stolen from Sylas and Dianthe. If the empress ever found out she'd used it to warn Nathaniel of the empress's plans to destroy the child, she'd likely kill Aborella. Or worse.

"And what of the rebellion," Eleanor asked slowly. "Has your sight been effective at tracking their whereabouts?"

Aborella knew better than to try the same trick twice. Eleanor's expectations must be appeased. "Yes, I see them in Rogos. I believe they're sheltering near the sacred pools of Niven."

Eleanor's brows arched toward her intricately braided dark hair. "The pools of Niven? Smart of them to hide in the only place on Ouros where the water is deadly to dragons. I wonder though how they managed the elves. After all, their leader, Lord Niall, told me only yesterday that they were committed to neutrality. I doubt he'd suffer a band of rebels on his most holy ground."

Aborella spread her hands. "My visions are always open to interpretation."

"Hmmm. Yes. And lately all interpretations seem to lead nowhere." Eleanor walked to the window, crossed her arms, and stared out at nothing in particular. Her already dark eyes seemed to grow darker despite her face turning toward the sun. Aborella remembered when those eyes shone silver.

Eleanor had changed over the past months, lost weight and grown exceedingly pale. Her eyes were now the color of onyx and seemed to absorb the light rather than reflect it. It was the blood magic. That type of magic demanded a price, and it showed in Eleanor's hollow cheeks and skeletal arms.

"I will redouble my efforts," Aborella promised. "I haven't tried an amplification spell yet. With the right magic, I know I can get you what you need."

"I expect more from you." Eleanor turned from the window and glared at her.

Icy shards of fear speared through Aborella's torso, and the hair on the back of her neck stood on end. What had happened? What did Eleanor know that she wasn't sharing?

"And you will get it, my empress. For as long as we've been friends, I've taken pride in teaching you magic and advocating for you through your many trials, all in support of your goal to unite the five kingdoms. I won't stop now. We will find answers. We'll find the child and the rebels." Aborella thought the lie sounded perfectly believable to her ears, but with every word, Eleanor's face distorted with building rage.

"Yes," she snapped. "You will find answers, Aborella, or things will get... difficult for you." Hands planted on her bony hips, Eleanor called toward the open door. "Ransom, please show Aborella what you showed me."

A dragon with a chiseled jaw and thick wavy hair strode into the room. She'd long suspected that Ransom, captain of the Obsidian Guard, was serving the empress in another capacity than her head of security. She'd caught the empress's fingers lingering on his arm and encountered him in the hall outside her chambers late into the evening. The dragon was handsome but both a coward and a fool. She never welcomed his company.

He had a bag in his hand. Whatever was in it stank like rancid meat. Aborella shivered from the stench. "What is that?"

He reached a hand into the bag and retrieved a dead animal. Dead for days by the looks of it. With abject horror, she realized it was a bird, dangling from his fingers by its legs, its feathers stained with blood. Oh goddess, it was Abacus! Dead, rotting. She stank of decay. Her once bright silver color had dulled in her death. Her silvery voice had silenced for evermore.

An arrow of pain shot straight through Aborella's heart, shattering it. She stumbled back a step, clutching her chest. Small sips of air were all she could manage as she tried her best not to cry. Nothing good would come from Eleanor seeing her cry.

"What have you done?" she rasped. The symbols in her dark purple skin came alive, her magic itching to teach Ransom a lesson.

"Don't," the empress warned Aborella. "I will fry you where you stand."

Aborella shot daggers at Eleanor. "What is the meaning of this?"

Eleanor nodded at Ransom, who withdrew a strip of rolled parchment from the bag. Aborella's heart stopped. The message she'd sent to Dianthe, it was there in his hand.

To her dismay, he unrolled it and read her message aloud. "Beware. The forest has eyes. Don't lose faith. I will help you."

"Ransom saw the bird fly from your window the very day you returned to us. Who will you help, Aborella?

Which forest has eyes? What exactly should they beware of?" Eleanor took a step toward her, unblinking, like a tiger moving in for the kill.

"I have no idea who wrote that—"

"I shot the bird from the air directly." Ransom stared down his nose at her. "No one else could have written it but you."

"It was your familiar, Aborella. The note is in your handwriting. Do not play games with me. Haven't you learned yet that I make the rules, I hold all the pieces? You are either on my side or no side. Do you under-stand?" Eleanor barked the words, striding closer until she was towering over Aborella, her teeth bared. "Now tell me the truth! Who was the note intended for?"

Aborella allowed the first lie that popped into her mind to slip off her tongue. "Merely a girl in the village who I promised to teach magic. Her father does not approve. We've been using the forest to practice."

Eleanor shook her head. Before Aborella could take her next breath, the empress's magic coursed over her skin like liquid lightning, holding her in place. Talons gripped one of her wings. Sharp pain cut into the place the silver gossamer met her back.

"I am so disappointed in you, Aborella. Do you know what I think? I think the time you spent in Everfield recovering has corrupted you. I think that message was meant for the friends you made there. I think you are helping the rebellion."

Helpless in the grip of Eleanor's magic, Aborella's panicked gaze pleaded with Ransom, but the guard barely looked at her. He seemed bored. His gaze drifted toward the window, the body of her familiar still dangling from his fingertips. There would be no help coming from his direction. There would be no help coming at all.

"I haven't told you the best part." Eleanor's voice was eerily quiet. She whispered the words through her teeth, directly into Aborella's ear. "Since we couldn't trust you and we weren't sure who got into your head, we simply burned down the entire Empyrean Wood. Even as we speak, your home kingdom of Everfield is in ashes."

Hot, prickling tears stirred in Aborella's vision. Was Dianthe okay? What about all the people, the children who'd danced around the fire during the waning festival the last night she was there? Were they all homeless now?

"I am a generous empress," Eleanor said through a fake pout. "I offered to annex Everfield and devote all of Paragon's resources to rebuilding the territory, but alas, Chancellor Ciro is hell-bent on retaining their independence. I imagine it's only a matter of time though before the population is so hungry they will beg to become ours."

Aborella felt the magic noose around her throat loosen by a fraction, and she gasped to cover a sob. "Eleanor, there's been a mistake. It's not what it seems."

"Then tell me now, Aborella. Where is the child?"

Aborella closed her eyes. Days ago she'd seen where Raven and the others were heading, but she'd kept the vision secret, trying her best to protect the heirs until they reached safety. But now she had to convince Eleanor she was on her side. She fluttered her lashes and rolled her eyes back in her head, imitating what happened to her when she was seized by a vision.

"I see the babe now. The family is on a ship, a sail-boat traveling from Crete to the island of Aeaea. They have not arrived as of yet."

"Circe's island?"

Aborella nodded. "If my vision is correct, they have not reached the island's shores. If you go now, you will intercept them."

Eleanor gave a divisive snort. "The one thing we know is we can't count on your visions to be correct, can we?" Eleanor moved her talon from Aborella's wing to her throat. "Ransom, take her to the dungeon. The back. The hottest cell."

"No! Please, I can't help you without access to my magic!" Aborella spoke frantically. The dungeon was incredibly dark and hot, torture for a fairy such as herself. She'd do anything to avoid that fate.

But Eleanor showed no mercy. "If you've told me the truth and my children are in fact on a ship to Aeaea, your visit to the dungeon will be short. We'll follow up on this vision of yours. Pray I find the child. If I don't, there will be hell to pay."

Ransom clamped cuffs around her wrists and shoved her out the door, her protests falling on deaf ears. Even as they descended to the place she'd personally seen prisoners go to die, she prayed—for Dianthe, for the Treasure of Paragon. Goddess help them. They were going to need it.

CHAPTER THREE

"I think I see it!" Raven bounced her daughter, Charlie, on her hip and searched the horizon for the island of Aeaea, their promised sanctuary from those who wanted them dead, namely her mate's mother, Eleanor, empress of Paragon. She'd only now noticed a jagged dark line on the horizon, far off in the distance. She stroked the blond curls back from Charlie's forehead. "What do you think? That looks like a nice place to stay for a while, doesn't it?"

Charlie returned her smile, her blue eyes dancing in the sunlight. How the babe could smile after so many days and nights on the move, she had no idea. Their journey from London to Aeaea had required traveling by car, train, cruise ship, plane, and now a rickety wooden sailboat captained by Rowan's mate, Nick, who thankfully had a sliver of experience sailing, although never a vessel like this. The ship appeared to be several hundred years old, a necessity in order to reach the island if the oreads on Crete were to be believed. Apparently Circe was wary of modern technology, and this boat increased their odds of being granted sanctuary by the goddess.

"It shouldn't be too much longer now." Gabriel sidled up to her and handed Charlie a piece of lamb they'd brought from Crete. The babe grabbed the piece in her chubby hand and tore off a bite.

Raven groaned. "I'm still not used to the idea that my newborn eats meat and that she prefers it raw."

Gabriel grinned. "Perfectly natural. You must remember, Raven, Charlie is a baby dragon—"

"She's also a witch."

"Normally our young learn to walk and then to fly in the first weeks outside the egg. Her development will far surpass that of a human child."

"Considering she was born less than a week ago but is developmentally equivalent to a six- or seven-month-old baby, I'd say that's pretty obvious. It's a lot for a new mother to adjust to."

He kissed her soundly on the cheek. "I think you are handling all this like a goddess. No dragon could ask for a better mother to their child."

Gabriel's confidence in her exceeded what she had in herself, but she was determined to do her best, one day at a time. She kissed her daughter on the head. "Whatever you do, Charlie, it will be perfect, and I plan to cherish every moment."

Avery strode in their direction with fire in her eyes. "Not to interrupt what is obviously a beautiful family moment, but do you see that?" She pointed at the water between their boat and the island. A dark shape lingered under the surface.

"It's huge. Is that a rock?" Raven asked.

Shaking her head, Avery led them to the side of the ship for a better view. "That is no rock. It's moving. I have a bad feeling about this."

"Maybe it's a whale," Raven said hopefully.

"Gabriel!" Tobias called from the other side of the ship. He pointed east. "We've got trouble."

Raven followed her mate's line of sight to see two dragons in the distance, one solid gold against the azure sky, the other silver like a fish. She swore with an intensity that made her want to cover Charlie's ears. "Is that who I think it is?"

"Mother." Gabriel removed his jacket. "Apparently killing Charlie was important enough to her to come herself. And I'm betting that's the worm Ransom by her side."

Ribbons of terror wrapped around Raven and squeezed. She darted a glance toward the island, still too far away—the dragons were closing in fast. "How fast can you fly? If you get us to the island..."

"Not fast enough. Besides, until we have Circe's invitation, we won't have her protection. It's not enough to make it to shore." He frowned. "We'll have to hold Eleanor off." He unbuttoned his shirt and cast it aside. She noticed his brothers and sister were doing the same. "Stay on the boat. Watch Charlie. We'll take care of this. There are six of us and two of them."

"Be careful, Gabriel. Don't underestimate her or her magic." Raven was a powerful witch, but she hadn't yet learned the limits of Eleanor's dark abilities. Worse, she might not be able to help without physical proximity to the battle.

Nathaniel piped up as he tossed his clothes aside. "Try to keep her in her dragon form. She can't perform magic as her beast. We stand a bloody better chance at winning this if we can stop her from using it."

"Let's fly." Gabriel's hands stretched toward the deck, scales shingling along his skin. He dove from the ship, finishing his transformation in midair. His black-and-emerald dragon swooped over the water and headed straight for his mother.

Raven's skin tightened and her jaw clenched. Six against two didn't seem good odds when one of the two was a narcissistic psychopath. And if Aborella had helped Eleanor, who knew what wicked magical booby trap waited in store for her mate. With the fairy seer on Eleanor's side, the empress knew what was coming. It was an unfair advantage.

Tobias kissed his mate, Sabrina, who huddled in the cabin's shade. As a hybrid, the vampire could be awake during the day, but the sun burned and weakened her quickly. She gave Raven a sympathetic look from the shadows as Tobias dove overboard, transforming into a silvery-white dragon that followed Gabriel into battle. Rowan's fiery red scales followed, her mate, Nick, swearing fiercely at the ship's wheel. Alexander's turquoise beast flew next, his mate Maiara scaling the mast with superhuman speed and drawing an arrow from her quiver. She lowered it quickly, however. No arrow, no matter how well aimed, could reach Eleanor, let alone pierce her dragon hide.

Xavier took Avery by the shoulders, his eyes twinkling. "Use that piece of metal on yer back if ye need to, woman!"

Avery touched the hilt of the sword she called Fairy Killer. "Bring her close enough and I'll use it to pry out her citrine heart."

He gave her a firm kiss on the lips. "That's my *curaidh*." He dove overboard, transforming into his amber-and-blue beast and beating the air to catch up with the others.

On Raven's hip, Charlie fussed, probably picking up on her growing anxiety. She bounced her and patted her back as she made her way across deck to Clarissa, whose mate, Nathaniel, had followed the others into battle, his amethyst scales glinting in the sun.

"How fast can you get us to shore?" Raven asked her sister.

"I'll have you and Charlie on the island before that bitch can think her own name." She turned in the direction of the sail, opened her mouth, and sang. A gust of wind filled the sail, powered by her voice. The boat jerked and picked up speed, careening toward the island and the dark figure between them and it.

Charlie's whines turned into full cries. Raven tried her best to soothe the babe while keeping one eye on Gabriel and the pack of dragons that would collide with their mother at any moment. Avery swept in. "Here, give her to me. Maybe she wants her aunt Avery."

Raven handed over the baby to her sister. "If we make it to shore, maybe the three of us can perform a spell together to knock that bitch out of the sky."

Avery frowned, her eyes drawn back to the darkness under the water. "I don't think the empress is the only thing we have to worry about." Charlie cried harder in her arms. "That's not a whale."

Raven's skin prickled as she watched the thing undulate under the surface, not far in front of the boat. "What is it?"

"I'm not sure, but I thought I saw... I mean, it looked like..."

"Spit it out, Avery!" Raven demanded.

In the distance, Gabriel and his mother collided and grappled in midair, his brothers and sister backing him up. Avery was distracted as Xavier's claws sank deep into Ransom's shoulders.

"Fuck," Avery murmured. "The fight is on."

Beside them, Clarissa stopped singing. The boat slowed. "Did you see that?"

Raven tore her eyes away from her mate to look at her oldest sister. "See what?"

"Tentacles. I think it has tentacles." Clarissa's face went chalky white, and she pointed toward the dark blob ahead of them. "I hate tentacles."

Avery released a trepid moan. Charlie was positively inconsolable in her arms. "We're almost on top of it. You don't think that a Greek goddess's island would be protected by a Greek monster, do you?"

Raven felt her eyes stretch wide. "Oh hell no—"

A monstrous tentacle drove straight up out of the water and slapped down across the deck of the ship between where Raven and her sisters stood and where Nick controlled the wheel. The creature's suction cups clung to the wood and halted the ship's progress. The ship groaned, threatening to come apart in the monster's grip.

Nick swore. "It's going to take us under!"

Above them, Maiara howled and released an arrow into the tentacle, but it had no effect. The thing had to be twenty yards long and three feet in diameter. How big was the monster it was attached to? In a blur, Sabrina rushed from the belly of the ship, tore the tentacle from the deck with vampire strength, and tossed it over the side. It took several chunks of wood with it, but they were freed. Nick banked hard to the left.

From under the hood of a dark cloak, Sabrina glared at Raven and her sisters as they all shifted their weight to counter the hard turn. "Okay, witches, time to fire up that three-sisters' magic. I don't have the energy for much more in full light."

Charlie screamed and pointed her chubby finger. The monster's head and body rose from the water to their right as Nick desperately tried to steer around it. Raven resisted competing with Charlie for the loudest scream.

A round, bulbous head covered in stringy seaweed towered above them, or was that its hair? She didn't plan to get close enough to find out. Three rows of eyes stared down at them from over a gaping maw sporting row after row of razor-sharp teeth. No discernible nose marred the face, but what appeared to be gills worked behind the open mouth. The chinless jaw melded into the torso. The rest of it disappeared beneath the surface and controlled a number of tentacles that now emerged all around them.

Maiara drew her bow and let arrow after arrow fly.

Her aim was true. One sank directly into the thing's eye. The monster roared.

"What's she doing? She's just pissing it off," Avery yelled.

"I've got this!" Raven concentrated. Unfortunately, she'd sacrificed her emerald ring as an offering to the Goddess of the Mountain when she'd escaped Paragon months ago. Without it, she had nothing to focus her raw power. She took a deep breath and did her best without it, throwing the first spell she could think of at the thing. "*Pagoma!*"

An intense ripple of magic plowed into the beast. Even without her ring, Raven was well practiced with the petrification spell. The monster halted, frozen in the water.

"There, I—"

The monster lifted and thrashed the deck in retribution. The wood railing cracked, a piece breaking off and falling into the water. At this rate, it would either tear the ship apart or swallow it whole.

"I'm not strong enough!" Raven cried. "My magic won't last."

"It must be resistant," Avery yelled. "Clarissa, try using the water around it rather than attacking it directly."

"Leave it to me." Clarissa opened her mouth, releasing a barrage of powerful notes.

A tower of ice erupted between the boat and the thing's teeth. She kept singing, and the ice formed a dome around the creature, thickening, caging it in. The tentacles retreated. Behind the ice wall, the monster roared and thrashed against its enclosure.

Raven gripped Clarissa's hand. She couldn't keep this up forever. She was already running out of air. The note gave out, and Clarissa gasped for breath.

"Maybe it will hold!" Raven prayed it would, but it wasn't to be. The ice shattered. The enraged creature thrashed itself free, reared, and reached for the ship again. A tentacle slapped the bow, sending pieces of wood flying. How were they even remaining afloat?

Avery handed Charlie back to Raven and drew her sword. "Raven, levitate me over it! I'll use my power to drain its magic. Then you two attack."

It was a good idea. If Avery was brave enough, Raven could be brave too. Raven drew a symbol in the air with her hand and sent her sister flying over the monster. For one harrowing moment, she pictured the thing tipping its head back and snapping Avery right out of the air. Thankfully, the creature didn't seem capable of moving that way. Avery landed on its grotesque head and thrust her sword into the top of its skull. She clung to the anchor as the beast swayed and roared, then placed her hands on its eel-skin flesh.

"Which spell?" Raven yelled to Clarissa. She had to yell to be heard over Charlie's wailing.

"Do we try to freeze it again? Or tear it apart?" Clarissa asked.

"I'm afraid if we eviscerate the monster, we'll potentially hurt Avery. She's immune to our magic, but the fall might kill her. The thing has to be fifty feet tall."

"Then we freeze it. You hit it in the gut, and I'll sing."

"Ready!" Avery's voice came on the ocean breeze.

Raven raised both hands, centering her energy and directing it at the monster. "*Pagoma*."

She'd just spat the word out when another tentacle slapped down on the wooden ship. It was too much for the ancient vessel to bear. The wooden hull splintered in two, and Raven dropped into the sea. She gripped Charlie, terror's icy fingers digging in where the cold water left off. They descended into dark blue. Above her, the light of the sun danced on the surface of the water. She kicked hard and swam with one arm, but the weight of her jeans was dragging her down, Charlie still gripped tightly to her side. Oh dear goddess, Charlie! She had to get to the surface.

She closed her eyes, searching her memory for any spell that could help. It came to her from the cobwebs of her brain. "*Fysallída*."

They rose like a bubble in a straw. Hungry for air, she gasped when they broke the surface. Little Charlie coughed over her shoulder, her wings working uselessly on her back.

Raven bobbed on the surface in a bubble of her magic, but she knew it wouldn't last. She eyed a floating beam and reached for it. Thankfully it was large enough to hold Charlie, and she laid her on her stomach and patted her back. At least she'd stopped crying. Imminent drowning overcome, she turned her attention to the next crisis.

Slowly Raven became aware of Clarissa's singing. Her sister had done it! The monster stood before them, a giant ice sculpture. Avery waved to them from its head.

Sabrina was nearby with Nick and Maiara, floating in what appeared to be the ship's dinghy. As Raven watched, Avery sheathed her sword and dove into the water, swimming safely to their boat.

"Let's get to shore, baby," she said to Charlie.

Although she was drained from overusing her magic, she forced herself to kick, navigating around the remains of the creature and praying it did not come to life again. She could see the island now. Closer. Closer.

A colossal splash behind her turned her head. Rowan's dragon popped up among the waves. She shifted back into her *soma* form and started swimming toward her. Raven was relieved when she realized her feet could touch bottom. Scooping Charlie into her arms, she walked toward shore, feeling like a waterlogged mess. Clarissa was already there, staring at the battle overhead.

Rowan stumbled out of the water, shaking her head. "By the Mountain, the bitch stunned me!"

Behind her, Alexander's dragon collided with the surface, then Tobias's. Gabriel, Nathaniel, and Xavier still battled above, bending and snapping around Eleanor and Ransom.

Sabrina, Maiara, and Nick rowed up.

"Thank fuck Sabrina was able to free the dinghy in time," Nick said, pulling Rowan into his arms. "I would have been fish food."

An exhausted Sabrina stumbled to meet Tobias as he reached the shore. She collapsed in his arms. Alexander met Maiara halfway. He held her as she rambled out the story about the monster and he comforted her with soft words. Together, they all turned to watch the battle still going on above them.

"What do we do?" Raven asked Avery and Clarissa. "It doesn't look good up there."

Flashes of dragon fire exploded in the sunny sky.

"No spell we put out from here is going to help them up there. It's too far away," Clarissa said.

"Her claws..." Rowan worked to catch her breath at Nick's side. Raven noticed her wing was torn and a wicked bruise was growing across her cheek. Raven hadn't known a dragon could bruise like that. "They're enchanted. It's like being hit by a Paragonian grenade every time she touches you. I'd go back up, but I have nothing left to give."

Alexander held up his arm, torn deep but healing slowly. "She got me too."

Tobias rubbed the back of his neck. "My ears are still ringing from the shock she gave me. I can't shift yet. So much for the theory that she can't use magic in her dragon form." Tobias squinted. "Wait a minute... What's that?"

Raven's human eyes saw what Tobias's sharper vision had picked up a few seconds earlier. A dragon the color of rich garnet was heading straight toward Eleanor and the others, coming up directly behind her. "Who is that?"

"Sylas!" Tobias cheered.

"Sylas! Of course! He must have seen us from the island." Rowan squealed. "Go get 'em, little brother!"

Sylas was the reason they were all here. Nathaniel had left him a shadow-mail candle after rescuing him from the dungeon. After Charlie was born, a message had come through the candle, warning them to evacuate Nathaniel's home, Mistwood Manor. Although the message had simply said that Eleanor was coming and to run, Nathaniel had assumed it was from Sylas and thus had led them to Aeaea. Sylas had mentioned hiding here before. Without any formal communication though, they hadn't known for sure he'd be here. Now it seemed clear they'd made the right move.

Sylas collided with Eleanor, digging his talons into her back and shifting his weight, throwing her off-balance. Gabriel dodged and Xavier used his hold on Ransom to turn the gray male. In a clever, coordinated move, the two thrust Eleanor and Ransom into each other. There was a flash of purple as Eleanor's talons, sandwiched between their bodies, stunned both Ransom and herself. The two dragons fell from the sky into dark waters.

Raven cheered along with the others and was relieved when Gabriel, Nathaniel, Xavier and Sylas made a beeline for her. Before long, they stood triumphant on the beach. She pulled Gabriel, bruised and battered, into her arms while Nathaniel and Xavier reunited with their mates beside her.

"Oh my goddess," Raven muttered. Her hand flowed over Gabriel's face, his shoulders. "Are you in one piece?"

"Fine." Gabriel kissed Charlie's head.

When Raven raised her eyes again, Sylas was speaking to a slender woman draped in a silver toga, her irises so pale they looked white and her hair blond with streaks of green.

"Greetings, travelers," she said, her silvery voice ringing like a bell.

"A water sprite," Nathaniel whispered beside her. "Favored companions of Circe."

A beautiful dark-skinned fairy seemed to appear out of nowhere and fluttered to Sylas's side. She threaded her fingers into his.

"Sylas and Dianthe of Everfield seek asylum with the goddess along with our family." He gestured toward the rest of them.

"Welcome back. Circe will be pleased you have returned to us." Other sprites arrived with clothing for the dragons. "Dress quickly and follow me. I'll take you to her." The sprite turned and led the way into the forest bordering the beach.

Clarissa elbowed her side. "Did I hear her right?"

Raven raised her eyebrow. "It sounds like we're going to meet the goddess herself."

CHAPTER FOUR

All Dianthe wanted to do was curl into a ball and sleep. After watching Everfield burn and then having her mate have to battle his wicked and deadly mother all in the same day, it was all she could do to set one foot in front of the other. Hollow and exhausted, she fell in line behind Sylas as they climbed the path toward Circe's forest temple.

Circe's palace wasn't a white-pillared monstrosity like the ones portrayed in pictures of Mount Olympus. On top of the hill that rose near the center of Aeaea, her sacred house was a massive ivy-enshrined wood cottage covered in blooms. The natural materials reminded Dianthe somewhat of the homes in Everfield, only it was far larger and made from cut wood rather than living branches. Still, it was clear the goddess loved to live among the wilds.

They reached the oversized doors of the entrance and found them open. Illith, the water sprite, welcomed them inside. Dianthe accepted a hug from her old friend as she passed into the homey temple. A fire blazed in the grate in front of a set of comfortable chairs and a spinning wheel that took up an entire corner. The room was otherwise filled with plants, drying herbs, and the sound of wind chimes from a set that hung in the open window.

"Goddess, I bring you weary travelers asking for asylum on your shores," Illith announced.

The growl of a wildcat cut through the temple and Circe appeared, flanked by two golden pumas that eyed them as if they might be their next meal. Dressed in a white toga, the goddess glowed, her black hair wild around her shoulders.

Dianthe had met Circe before when she was last here with the rebellion, but she didn't expect the goddess to remember her. An immortal such as herself could hardly be expected to remember a few short encounters. But when Circe's eyes met hers, the goddess gave her a knowing smile of recognition.

"Captain Dawn?" the one she'd heard called Avery asked from beside her.

Dianthe hadn't yet been formally introduced to the others, although she felt like she knew them from Sylas's stories.

The goddess ignored Avery's question and asked, "Who speaks for you?"

Sylas squeezed her hand and stepped forward. "I do, my goddess."

"Sylas and Dianthe, welcome back." Circe tilted her head. "What has brought you to my island?"

"Relations with Paragon have grown far worse," Sylas

said. "Eleanor, empress of Paragon, has burned Everfield, the entire Empyrean Wood, to the ground."

At that news, Circe scowled in a way that bolstered Dianthe's soul. She saw in the goddess's expression the same hatred for Eleanor that Dianthe felt in her heart. It was comforting to be back here, under her protection.

"Do you still lead the rebellion?"

"Yes."

"And what of your latest mission?"

"I await the return of our emissary to Rogos."

"You are welcome here, Sylas." Circe turned her attention to Dianthe. "It is good to see you, Dianthe, as well."

Dianthe bowed low. "My pleasure, as always, Goddess."

"I sense your second sight will be useful to the resistance. You are welcome here." Circe smiled.

Sylas cleared his throat. "Dianthe's gift of sight has proven unreliable as of late. She is here as my mate, not in her former role."

All the air rushed from Dianthe's lungs. If Sylas had turned around and stabbed her in the heart with his own talon, she would not have been more shocked or hurt by his comment. Her ears grew hot with embarrassment and her eyes prickled. Why would he say that in front of the goddess? Even if he believed it to be true! She blinked rapidly against the onslaught of tears.

By a small miracle, the goddess did not react to his insulting comment but turned her gaze to his brothers. Dianthe was relieved. She wasn't sure she'd survive any scrutiny into what Sylas had said.

"My brothers Gabriel, Tobias, Alexander, Nathaniel, and Xavier, and my sister Rowan," Sylas announced. They each stepped forward and bowed as he introduced them. "And their mates, Sabrina, Maiara, Nick, Raven, Avery, and Clarissa. They are all here to aid the resistance."

Everyone but her, Dianthe thought. Sylas's comment burned in her torso. She couldn't wait to get him alone. How dare he undermine her position in the resistance?

The goddess tipped her head and focused on Raven, Clarissa, and Avery. "You are the three sisters, my descendants."

Dianthe raised her eyebrows, distracted from her anger by the revelation. Did she say descendants? Sylas had told her about his time with Raven in the dungeon and how she was a powerful witch, but a descendant of the goddess herself? Her skin tingled at the thought.

Raven smiled, Charlie laughing on her hip. "Yes, Goddess."

"And this child?" The goddess stepped forward, taking in the blond babe.

"Charlie," Raven said. "My daughter, with Gabriel."

The goddess beamed. "The progeny of a dragon and a witch. No wonder Eleanor wants you dead."

"Thank you for saving me after I delivered her. I—"

Circe raised one finger. "You must be mistaken, my dear Raven. I am not allowed off this island. There are rules even gods must follow."

Raven bowed her head.

Dianthe got the distinct impression the goddess was lying but couldn't fathom about what exactly. Had she left the island before? Or perhaps used sorcery to appear to leave?

"I would like to offer my sincere admiration for how you and your sisters handled the trap Hera set for you beyond the shores of my island. It is the rare group of witches who can face a sea monster of that magnitude and live to tell the tale." Circe gazed at the three proudly.

"Hera?" Raven repeated.

"Hera," Circe confirmed.

Their eyes met and Dianthe wondered at the goddess's words. Why was Hera sending sea monsters to stop the siblings? It was well known that Aitna, the goddess of the mountain, created the first dragons from the fabric of the universe. Circe, though, was credited with giving dragons the ability to shift into their *soma* or two-legged form. The only link that Hera had to her mate and the rest of the treasure of Paragon was that Aitna had once had an affair with Zeus. To protect her from Hera's wrath, the king of the Gods made it so that Hera could not set foot on Ouros nor see it in her scrying mirror or interfere with its environment. But it had always been thus, for as long as Dianthe could remember. It seemed a little late for Hera to be exacting her revenge against Zeus by targeting Aitna and Circe's creation. Dianthe had a hunch there was something more, some secret that Circe and Raven shared.

The goddess backed away, trailing her fingers over the head of one of the great cats. "I hereby grant you all sanctuary and the use of my island. I am sorry I cannot do more. My sentence here forbids my involvement in the spectacle that is the lives of men. Be well."

In the blink of an eye, she disappeared.

Finally, Dianthe thought she could confront Sylas about his comment, but she never got a chance.

He wasted no time taking charge. "If you will all follow me, the rebellion has a base camp in the valley. I'll show you where you're going to stay."

⁂

"SYLAS, ARE WE GOING TO TALK ABOUT WHY YOU embarrassed me back there?" It had taken all of Dianthe's strength to wait until each of the mated couples had found an appropriate tent in the rebellion's compound to talk to Sylas. The way he'd treated her in front of the goddess burned like a coal in her stomach. When he'd denied her abilities as a seer, he'd denied who she was, down to her soul.

"I don't know what you mean." Sylas strode away from her, out of the compound.

"You do so. You know exactly what you did." She hurried to keep up when he walked faster. "Where are you going?"

"To the hot spring. I thought I'd soak before dinner. I think I pulled every muscle in my body fighting Eleanor. We're all lucky to have survived it."

Dianthe crossed her arms against a wave of guilt for bringing up how he'd hurt her considering what he'd endured today. But this conversation needed to happen. She wouldn't sleep tonight without clearing the air. "I'll come with you."

She followed him along the narrow path away from

camp. This part of the island was both familiar to her and more beautiful than she remembered. Bright, multicolored birds called overhead while lush green leaves surrounded her, decorated with silky magenta blooms. Flowers the color of freshly churned butter lined both sides of the path. It was difficult to hold on to her anger in this paradise. Even the scent of the air—ocean water mixed with fragrant blossoms—seemed designed to soothe. Romantic memories of when they'd first met flooded her brain.

Maybe she should let it go.

She *couldn't* let it go.

They reached the hot springs, and Sylas peeled the borrowed white tunic from his body and then reached for the string ties of his pants. Although they'd been mated for decades, she never grew tired of seeing him naked. His body was a thing of beauty. Broad shoulders tapered to a trim waist and tight buttocks. His chestnut hair had grown out since his last haircut and curled at the base of his skull. She allowed her gaze to travel lower and had to glance away quickly to keep herself from becoming completely distracted. She was torn between wanting to thank the goddess or curse her as he sank into the hot spring, concealing his body below the waist.

"Well," he said, "aren't you going to get in?"

"I want to talk about what you said to Circe." Dianthe refused to let him sidetrack her.

His gray eyes locked on to her with an intensity that made her heart flutter. He released a deep sigh. "Get in and we will."

At least now he wasn't denying it. She stripped out of her dress and dipped a toe in. Hot. Very hot.

"Go slow. You'll adapt."

"I remember." She sat on the side and eased herself inch by inch into the water. At first it was uncomfortable, but as she remained in the heat, her muscles loosened and her wings sagged. She spread her arms along the edge and leaned her head back. "Mmmm. Okay, yes, this was a good idea."

"I thought so."

Eventually though, the wound he'd opened in Circe's temple began to ache again and she gave him a somber stare. "Why did you tell Circe that my gift was unreliable?"

"I thought that would be obvious. We talked about it on the way here. Aborella."

Her breath hitched. He couldn't possibly think that one misinterpretation would mean all her visions were unreliable, could he? She decided to take a different tack. "Do you remember the story of how I learned I was a seer?"

"You predicted the death of your mother," he said softly.

Her throat tightened as long-suppressed emotions began working their way to the surface. "I was three. Just a child. I kept having fits. My parents thought they were seizures, but the healer could find nothing wrong with me. Every time it would happen, I'd see my mother dropping out of the sky. I told my father about the visions, but he assured me my mother was fine, completely healthy, and would be with me for a long, long time. He was wrong."

"No one should lose their mother so young," he whispered, looking truly sad now. "Or their father."

"She was shot out of the sky by an Obsidian guard who claimed his arrow had slipped during target practice. He blamed her for flying too close to their encampment. She died and the guard was never punished. My father died of a broken heart a few years after."

"You've often said their deaths were the reason you decided to join the rebellion."

"One of many. But that's not my point. My point is that seeing has been part of who I am for as long as I can remember. It's as much a part of me as my eyesight or my hearing."

"Dianthe..."

"When you denied my abilities, you denied who I am!" Her voice rose, sounding pinched.

His face remained impassive, but Dianthe got the impression he was holding strong emotions at bay. When he spoke, the words came slowly. "I couldn't allow the goddess to believe we could rely on your abilities. Not after what happened."

"Why? I'm still a seer, Sylas. Just because I misinterpreted one vision—"

"You spent hours with her, Dianthe." His face crumpled into an awful expression of sympathy that made her skin crawl.

"I had to. I was healing her. I cared for her. Of course I spent time with her."

Sylas frowned. "Aborella is the most powerful fairy

sorceress that ever lived. You didn't just get it wrong about her. You didn't see the attack on Everfield coming until the Guard was upon us. Your visions have been few and far between since you healed her."

"I—" He was right. Usually an attack of that magnitude would trigger a vision when it was planned, not when it was executed. The rebellion had thwarted many initiatives in the past based on her early visions. She had no explanation for why her abilities had failed her this time.

"You don't know why."

"No... Yes... Maybe. It could be because it was too personal for me to see clearly. Or... things have been tense between us since you came home. My gift doesn't work well when I'm under emotional stress."

He scoffed. "You think this is my fault?"

"I didn't say that."

"What if it was *her*, Dianthe? Aborella could have cursed you or somehow diluted your power. You probably didn't even know it was happening." He shook his head. "She's evil. She's an abomination."

Dianthe shook her head. She knew Aborella had done evil things in the past, but she'd felt a real connection to the fairy by the end of their time together. "I don't think that's true. I don't feel any different."

"No. You wouldn't. She'd want you to feel the same. Think about it. Pretend you are her and you wanted to use a talented fairy to your advantage, what would you do? If she hurt you, she'd hurt only you. But if she planted visions in your head, or worse, planted a spell so she could control what you see..."

Tears broke the dam of her eyelids. This was too frustrating. "You think she cursed me so that she could plant visions in my head?"

"Who knows? We don't know what she did or what she told Eleanor. You spent days with that snake within striking distance."

"I don't think it's true. I feel fine." She was trembling now, raw emotion tangling up inside her and forming a lump in her throat.

"Be that as it may, I am the leader of the Defenders of the Goddess. It is my responsibility to ensure the safety and effectiveness of our missions. Which means, until we can prove you haven't been cursed, you can't participate as an officer of the rebellion."

She gasped. "You're removing me from my position?"

He looked away from her. "I have to. It's too dangerous."

"I was an officer in the DOGs before you even suspected that your mother killed Marius! I brought you on, Sylas. You can't do this!"

He reached for her, but she pulled away, lifting herself out of the water and snagging her dress from where she'd left it.

"I have to, Dianthe. I know you. You might be angry at me now, but you'd never want to put anyone in danger."

What he said made sense. If Aborella had planted some sort of enchantment in her head, the sorceress had violated her in the worst possible way. But even as she considered that possibility, she just couldn't accept it. Was she stupid for still believing that when she'd looked into Aborella's eyes, she'd seen true friendship there?

"How can I prove to you that I am not cursed and regain my position in the rebellion?" She pulled her dress over her head, no longer comfortable being naked in his presence.

He sighed. "I thought we could ask Raven to examine you. She's a very powerful witch. Perhaps she'd have some ideas."

Dianthe bit her lip. As a fairy, her dealings with witches were few and far between. The citizens of Darnuith kept to themselves, and she hadn't had the opportunity to get to know the few who were involved in the rebellion. Their powers seemed strange and unpredictable. Still, if everything Sylas had told her about his time in the dungeon was true, Raven could be trusted. And if allowing her to scan her body for curses was the only way to prove Sylas wrong and regain her proper role in the resistance, that's exactly what she'd do.

She nodded. "Okay. I'll find Raven. You'll see, Sylas. I'm not cursed. You're mistaken."

"Dianthe..."

But she was already striding back toward camp, anxious to prove him wrong.

CHAPTER FIVE

The last thing Sylas wanted to do was to hurt Dianthe. As she stormed off, his instinct was to go after her. He longed for simpler times when he could sweep her into his arms and spend the rest of the afternoon making love to her in their tent. He longed to tell her everything would be okay and mean it.

But his decision was for the best. What magical poison might have infected his mate? Could Aborella see everything Dianthe did? Hear everything she said? Could she influence his mate's thoughts? Her mind? It was too risky to assume anything less.

Besides, wasn't it time for her to be away from the front lines of this damn war? Even if she wasn't cursed, Aborella had seen her face. She knew Dianthe's identity now. Hadn't she earned a break considering her previous service? Sylas had no choice but to fight. It was his mother after all who was the cause of the problem. His kingdom that must be stopped. Dianthe could rest. She could grieve what happened to Everfield. She could be content being his wife.

On this island, as his mate, not as an officer of the rebellion, she'd be safe.

Sylas climbed from the hot spring, the island air feeling cool against his body from the abrupt change in temperature. Dianthe might hate him in the moment, but did it matter as long as she was alive to hate him?

Everything *wouldn't* be okay, not until they overthrew his bloodthirsty mother. She wouldn't stop at burning Everfield. She wouldn't stop until the five kingdoms fell under the heel of Paragon.

He dressed and hurried back to camp, hoping some of Dianthe's anger might have dissipated. The group of tents at the base of the island's central mountain had been there for years thanks to Circe's support of their campaign. There was one central tent, large enough to serve as both a mess hall and a gathering place, a command center of sorts for their work across the five kingdoms. Residential tents surrounded that central locale, smaller in size and meant to house one to four adults.

The island itself, bolstered by the magic of the goddess, provided more than enough in the way of natural resources to keep a contingent of rebels fed and clothed until they could safely rejoin their communities.

As he neared the mess hall, the smell of roasted pig met his nose and he was pleased to find the sprites had cooked up a buffet worthy of a family reunion. That's what this was. He hadn't spent any significant time with his siblings in centuries.

Dianthe was waiting for him outside. "We should go in together. We can't make our problems the rebellion's problems."

"I agree." He put an arm around her waist and pulled her into his side. Thank the goddess she'd chosen to listen to reason. She didn't look happy necessarily, but definitely resolved. Good enough.

"Only Colin is missing," Dianthe noted once they entered. "Have you heard anything from him?"

He glanced down at her, then intentionally changed the subject. "There's Raven. Let's grab a plate and follow her to a table."

Dianthe nodded, clearly distracted by the opportunity to talk to the witch about helping her determine if Aborella had cursed her. The redirection worked like a charm. The truth was Sylas knew exactly where Colin was. His brother was on a mission for the rebellion. But his whereabouts were top secret, and given Dianthe's current predicament, he refused to give up Colin's locale.

He ushered Dianthe through the line and loaded his plate with roasted boar, roots, and fresh fruit, then hurried to follow Raven to her table of choice. He settled across from her, Dianthe taking the bench beside him.

"I see you've convinced my brother to do his fair share," Sylas said, noting that Gabriel had Charlie at the buffet.

Raven laughed. "He's better at choosing what she'll like. I'm still getting used to her having a dragon's diet." The witch took a hungry bite and then glanced between Sylas and Dianthe. "I have to say it's a pleasure to see you without an iron grate between us, Sylas. But I get the sense you sought me out for more than a post-dungeon reunion."

Sylas glanced at Dianthe, then lowered his voice to just above a whisper. "We were wondering if you knew a spell to detect if someone has been cursed or carries negative magic within them."

Raven leaned back in her chair and sipped her wine. "I don't need a spell for that. It's built in. I'm a walking, talking curse detector."

"Excuse me?" Dianthe tipped her head.

"My inherent ability is to absorb magic. I don't know if all witches have innate talents, but that is mine. If I touch a person who's been cursed, I'll be able to feel it. Taste it. Discern its nature." Raven gave a sheepish smile. "I can't necessarily break the curse though. That's a different matter entirely."

Dianthe grew visibly excited, her back straightening and the corners of her mouth lifting. "You've done this before then?"

Raven nodded, her gaze searching their faces as her expression turned curious. "With my own husband when his ring was cursed. What's going on? Who's cursed?"

Gabriel and Charlie arrived then, the second smiling around a face full of something red and meaty. "What am I missing? Your faces look far too serious."

Thankfully, Raven was discreet enough not to disclose their conversation. "Just revisiting our days in the dungeons of Paragon."

"Hmm. I'd think happier conversation was in order considering we are all lucky to be alive today," Gabriel said. "I think we all owe you extreme gratitude for what you did for us, Sylas."

Sylas assumed he was talking about his auspicious arrival. The truth was, he'd enjoyed the chance to sink his talons into Eleanor's back, but before he could tell Gabriel so, Rowan ran into the tent.

"Sylas!" She beckoned him with her hand.

Popping out of his seat, he motioned for Dianthe to stay where she was, then followed his sister out the flap and to the place Nick waited. "There's someone headed down the hill from Circe's temple. Nick and I noticed the fires in the palace were burning. There were two silhouettes, a man and a woman. Are you expecting someone?"

"Not exactly." Sylas frowned. If it was who he thought it was, something had either gone terribly wrong or terribly right.

"You don't think Circe would allow Eleanor and Ransom sanctuary, do you?" Rowan asked.

"Never."

Leaves rustled as the new visitors drew near. A commotion behind him announced the arrival of all his siblings and their mates, who had taken it upon themselves to gather in the mouth of the tent, staring in silence at the path to the temple. Dianthe was there too. Why couldn't she just stay where he told her to?

Still, he didn't want to cause a scene, not when the new arrivals were so close to revealing themselves. In the falling twilight, a man and a female elf broke from the forest and stood smiling before him. The man, his twin, his confidant, and the rebellion's long-hidden weapon, spread his arms.

"Colin! Welcome home!" Sylas strode forward and embraced his brother.

DIANTHE STARED AT HER MATE AS HE EMBRACED HIS twin, marveling at their identical features. To be sure, Colin was the larger of the two, not in height but in overall size. The male looked as if he snacked on full-grown elderbeasts between meals. Also different was his hair, which was cut short, almost to his skull. Otherwise, the two were eerily alike, down to the slant of their smiles.

As Colin stepped into the light to hug each of his siblings and be introduced to their mates, Dianthe noticed one additional difference that hadn't been there before. He appeared to have a tattoo, the pattern of which ran from the fingers of his right hand, along his arm, to just under his right ear. It must have been paint. A tattoo was impossible for a dragon. Their flesh healed too quickly to hold tattoo ink. Whatever it was, the artwork made his skin look carved into reddened waves.

"Colin, you remember my mate, Dianthe." Sylas gestured in her direction, and she snapped out of her inspection of his arm to give him her full attention.

"Of course I remember her," Colin said, giving her a swift but warm hug. "She was rounding up new members to join the resistance while you were still making sand-castles and deciding if you wanted to be involved."

"Oh Colin, you know just what to say to a girl to make her feel needed." Dianthe couldn't help but notice Sylas frown at that. Colin had once led the rebellion, but Sylas had taken over for him when he went undercover on a secret mission. Although the nature of his work was unknown to her, she'd understood it was important and could take a number of years.

She observed the woman at his side. She was definitely an elf based on her elongated limbs and subtly pointed ears. The tan-colored robe she wore tied at the waist marked her as a scribe. Dianthe didn't know much about the order of elves who saw it as their purpose to chronicle the history of Ouros, but she found the woman completely fascinating. Her dark copper hair was braided down the back of her head, and her eyes were the brightest purple, a color that gave off its own light from within her pale features. Surely Colin's mission must have had something to do with Rogos for the elf to be involved.

Colin turned to the woman at his side and said, "This is Leena. She's a scribe from the Temple of the Sacred Pools. We owe her our allegiance for the aid she has most selflessly provided." He patted the bag under his arm and smiled. "It's big, Sylas. The breakthrough we've been waiting for. Where can we speak?"

Sylas gestured toward the tent behind them. Dianthe hung back while the others, who were blocking the door, filed back inside. But when she started after them, Sylas's hand gripped her upper arm. "You can't."

She stared at his hold on her incredulously. "Why the hell not?"

"You know why." Sylas lowered his voice, his eyes

shifting between her and the tent. "We still don't know the nature of what Aborella might have done to you."

Her protest halted abruptly in her throat as heat climbed to the tips of her ears. "You'd completely cut me out of the rebellion for some... theory you have about a curse? First you can't trust my visions, now you can't trust me?"

"Dianthe, we talked about this."

"About my visions, yes, but—"

"We don't know if Aborella's curse is constrained to your visions. We don't know the nature of what she did to you."

"If anything."

"Everfield didn't burn itself down."

Dianthe flinched as if he'd struck her. The shame that she might be the reason for what happened to the Empyrean Wood made her lungs constrict and her stomach fill with lead. She didn't have the strength to fight him anymore. All her energy had been replaced with guilt and a deep and aching grief.

Turning from him in disgust, she ground her teeth. "Fine. I'll go."

"Dianthe...," he said softly.

Without a single look back, she headed for their tent, the taste of his rejection bitter on her tongue.

CHAPTER SIX

Sylas told himself that Dianthe would get over it. She just needed time to allow everything he'd told her to sink in. Once she realized how dangerous things were for all of them right now, she'd thank him for doing what he had. Out of an abundance of caution, she had to stay out of rebellion business.

He reentered the tent alone and took a seat on one of the benches that surrounded a central table where Colin had set his mysterious bag. His siblings and their mates did the same. Leena, the scribe Colin had brought with him from Rogos, stood silently by his side. Sylas didn't know much about Rogos. No one did, which was why Colin had gone on his mission to begin with. He wondered what her role in all this was.

"Where's Dianthe?" Raven asked, sliding in beside him with Charlie on her hip.

"Headache," he said. "She needed to lie down."

The corner of her eye twitched skeptically.

He quickly looked toward Colin. "What is this breakthrough you speak of, brother?"

"And tell us who did that to your arm?" Gabriel pointed his chin toward the wavelike pattern on Colin's skin.

Sylas was wondering the same thing. It looked a hell of a lot like a burn, but dragons were impervious to fire and impossible to tattoo. Sylas had never seen marks like it before on his kind.

Colin raised an eyebrow. "I did it to myself when I reached into one of the sacred pools of Niven in Rogos."

A collective gasp rose up from his siblings, and Sylas flinched. The substance in the sacred pools was said to be absolutely lethal. It burned dragons like acid burned humans. It burned anything like acid. Any creature that fell into one of the pools never came out again.

"Hurt like a bitch, but it was worth it. Thanks to Leena's help, I was able to retrieve this little beauty."

He reached into the bag and pulled out an orb. Sylas took a step closer to get a better look. Perfectly smooth and round, the thing might have been made of glass or polished crystal. It shone bright royal purple with a swirl of bubbles spiraling in its interior.

"What is that?" Sylas asked. He spied an object at the very center. Metallic and oddly shaped, it had a circular center with projections like a cogwheel.

Raven stood to get a better look, leaning over the table. Charlie reached for the orb and Raven pulled her away. "It's definitely enchanted. I can feel the magic coming off of it from here."

"Strong magic," Nathaniel said, cozying up to her side with Clarissa behind him.

Sylas thought the magical individuals in the room might crawl right into the orb given their heightened interest.

"Not too close." Leena's arm shot out between them and the orb, her body growing tense at Colin's side. Her pointed ears twitched with her annoyance.

"The orb is most definitely enchanted," Colin said, "and as you can see, given that I pulled it from a sacred pool, a scribe has accompanied me here to ensure I treat it and the scroll that led us to it with the respect it deserves."

Leena gave a shallow bow.

"But what is it?" Sylas asked again.

"It's a key," Leena said. She drew a scroll from her pack and unrolled it on the table beside the orb. "Or rather, we believe what is inside the orb is a piece of a key. We believe, based on the writing and illustrations on this scroll, that there are five parts."

A tingle crawled across Sylas's skin and he met Colin's eyes, so much like his own. "A key to what?"

Colin made a noise deep in his throat. "A potential weapon."

"It took Colin and me months to find this." Leena smoothed the scroll.

Sylas glanced down at the parchment and found illustrations of five orbs. Each held a different shape inside, surrounded by strange symbols he recognized as Elvish but could not read. "What does it say?"

"Elvish scribes have been chronicling the history of

Ouros for centuries. I wasn't sure when exactly the book was brought to this world, so we had to search hundreds of scrolls to find one that referenced it. This is that scroll."

Beside him, Raven became agitated. "Book? I thought Colin mentioned a weapon."

"It's a grimoire," Colin explained. "The most powerful magical text to have ever existed. If the rebellion had that book, we'd have a real chance of ending Eleanor's reign."

Raven bristled, her face paling. "You don't mean the *golden* grimoire, as in Hera's golden grimoire?"

"One and the same," Colin said. "How do you know of it?"

Raven's gaze darted to Gabriel. Something unspoken passed between them. "A premonition... It's a long story. Where is the book hidden? How do we get the other parts of the key?"

Leena cleared her throat. "The scroll says that the grimoire was brought to Ouros at the beginning of Eleanor and Brynhoff's reign by Medea, who became the witch queen of Darnuith. Her mate, Tavyss, was the older brother of Brynhoff and challenged him for the throne. When Eleanor and Brynhoff did not comply, Medea attacked Paragon in the fourth century. She and her dragon mate were killed during the uprising despite having the grimoire. Medea was pregnant at the time with their young. The scribe who wrote that noted a common belief at the time that Eleanor or Brynhoff somehow tricked Medea and Tavyss into letting their guard down and took advantage of it."

"If they killed Medea and her mate, why doesn't Eleanor have the grimoire?" Raven asked.

It was a good question. It was unlike Sylas's mother to allow any source of power to slip through her fingers.

"I think I can answer that." Nathaniel held up a finger. "Mother did not start practicing magic until after we were born. It is very possible she didn't recognize the power of the grimoire or else didn't see it for what it was. Perhaps this witch Medea disguised it in some way."

Leena nodded slowly. "The witch had two sisters—"

"The original three sisters." Avery darted a glance toward Raven and Clarissa.

"Likely the source of the prophecy of the three witches that would destroy Paragon," Colin added.

"According to the scroll, although Medea was magically bound to her mate, Tavyss, he was killed first and so, without the benefit of his tooth's magic, she succumbed to her wounds soon after. However, her two powerful sisters raised her from the dead." Leena paused as a murmur rumbled through the group.

Sylas watched Raven and her sisters. Were they powerful enough to raise the dead, he wondered? The tension in the room ratcheted up a notch.

"What happened after they raised Medea from the dead?" Sylas asked.

Leena ran her finger down the scroll. "The witches locked the book away—it does not specify where—and then split the key into five parts and concealed them in each of the kingdoms. Only those destined to bring peace to Ouros and avenge the death of Tavyss will be able to find and access the orbs, reconstruct the key, and—"

"Wield the golden grimoire," Raven finished.

Sylas turned to her. "Raven, how exactly do you know about the golden grimoire?"

Raven kissed Charlie on the forehead before speaking. "The night Charlie was born, I had a... dream that Circe visited me. Her words were strange, mysterious. But she seemed to be telling me that there would never be peace in Ouros or Paragon until Eleanor was defeated and the golden grimoire was returned to Hera."

"Returned to Hera?" Sylas shook his head. "If this grimoire is as powerful as legend says it is, why would we return it to a vengeful goddess?"

Raven licked her lips. "I think Hera is helping Eleanor somehow. I think she's encouraged her to do what she's done. And I think Eleanor has been searching for this book on Hera's behalf for a very long time. Returning the book is the only way to cut off Hera's patronage of Eleanor."

Sylas scratched his jaw as he ruminated on the hypothesis. He had enough to worry about with his mother. Adding a goddess to the equation made his head spin. "Does that scroll say anything about where to find the rest of these orbs? I mean something more specific than the five kingdoms?"

"No." Leena tipped her head. "Unless... I believe this scroll is a palimpsest."

"A what?" Sylas leaned over the scroll.

"New writing over old. If you look carefully, you can see the remains of the original text behind what we can read."

"Is it common for scribes to do that?" Sylas asked.

"Never." Leena leveled an intense stare on him. "I have no explanation for this. Nor can I explain how the old writing continuously moves and scrambles. Look here." She pointed at a symbol like an S behind the message. In the blink of an eye, it moved to the top corner of the scroll. "It's enchanted. There's another message under this one. Only, I cannot read it."

"We think whatever is hidden within this scroll is the answer to finding the other orbs and obtaining the pieces inside." Colin rolled the orb back and forth on the table. "I've tried everything to open this one and get at the key. It's impervious. It spent hundreds of years soaking in a sacred pool. It can't be melted, broken, or crushed."

"Maybe they only open when they are all together," Sylas proposed.

"Maybe they only open using magic." Clarissa left Nathaniel's side to move closer and inspect the orb.

Raven cleared her throat. "Give me permission to touch the orb and the scroll. I might be able to discern the nature of its magic."

Leena speared Colin with a nervous glance.

"I read magic," Raven said. "I can absorb a spell off a page and wield it perfectly the first time. I can also sometimes touch something and understand the magic within it. If we're lucky, I might be able to use the orb's own magic to open it or crack the scroll's magical encryption."

"I'm concerned you'll inadvertently damage the scroll," Leena said.

Raven shook her head. "That's not how my power works. I don't change the magic, just come to understand it."

"You don't know that." Leena's lips flattened into a tight line. "All scrolls are written by elves. Elfin magic is nothing like the magic of witches. It's possible your touch will trigger something none of us are expecting. But—" Her fingers toyed with the edge of her robe. "I know no other way to translate the hidden text. None among my kind are capable of reading it. The hidden message is lost to us like this."

"Leena?" Sylas said, feeling an obligation as their leader to press the issue. "Does Raven have your permission?"

A deep sigh escaped Leena's lips, and she gave a quick nod. "Try it."

Raven handed Charlie to Gabriel and placed her hands on the orb. She closed her eyes. When she opened them again, she reached for the scroll, her mouth twisting into a grimace as her head began to shake. "Strange. I get nothing from the orb. I can feel its power, but the actual magic must be on the inside. I can't get a signature from the surface."

"And the scroll?" Sylas asked.

"Very powerful. I can see the enchantment, but it's the most complicated protective spell I've ever encountered. The magic is strange. Some of it I recognize. Some is foreign to me—I assume it's both witch and elven magic. I can't break it, although we might be able to peek behind it. Avery?"

"No matter what type of magic it is, I should be able to neutralize it." Avery reached for the unreadable scroll.

Colin blocked her from touching it. "Careful.

Nobody touches the scroll without Leena's permission. That was our agreement."

Avery turned toward the elf. "Leena? I won't damage it. Usually when I neutralize a spell, it's temporary. It shouldn't change anything."

Leena met her eyes and gave a reluctant nod. "Yes."

She touched the corner of the scroll. "Hmmm. It's strong. Oh, something is happening."

"It's working!" Raven said.

Sylas watched in amazement as the new writing faded and the old came to the surface.

"The symbols have stopped moving, but I don't know this language," Avery said.

Leena tipped her head and studied the revealed symbols. "I don't either. It's not Elvish. I can't—"

"Oh!" Avery yanked her hand back as if the scroll had burned her fingers.

"Avery?" Clarissa caught her sister as she collapsed, her eyes rolling back in her head.

Xavier rushed in and collected her sagging body in his arms. "Whit in God's name didya do to her?" Xavier ground out, a growl rising in his throat.

Raven cradled her sister's face. "She's drained. It's okay, Xavier. She'll be fine. She just overused her magic."

Avery blinked awake and brought a hand to her head. "Mother of mercy, that kicked my ass."

The others grumbled their relief.

"It's late," Sylas announced, his thoughts going to Dianthe. "Everyone break. We'll give it another go tomorrow. Avery needs to rest, and I need to... think."

The group exchanged good nights and began parting ways for the evening.

Sylas hooked his arm into Raven's. "Would you help me with something? It's about Dianthe."

Raven's gaze darted to the door where Gabriel and Charlie were headed out into the night. "Tonight?" She frowned. "She's the one with the curse, isn't she?"

He nodded. "Please. She's in our tent. We need your help."

Thank the Mountain she agreed.

CHAPTER SEVEN

All Raven wanted to do was sleep for a week. After fighting off the tentacled monster, having her boat destroyed from underneath her, swimming to shore, and enduring a battle between her husband and his wicked mother, all with a baby on her hip, she was bone weary. It felt as though someone had replaced her blood with liquid concrete.

And that wasn't even taking into account the stress of what she had learned tonight. It appeared that the three sisters would play a major role in solving the puzzle that was these orbs. Judging by what happened to Avery, it would not be easy. If she could just have a few moments of quiet to concentrate, she was sure she could come up with a plan to logically address the issue.

But this was important to Sylas. While Raven could put him off, the dragon had once helped her during a dark and difficult time in her life. Clearly, for him to beg for her help, he needed this to happen sooner rather than later. She took a deep, cleansing breath outside Sylas and Dianthe's tent.

"Knock, knock," she called. "Dianthe? Are you in there?"

The flap to the tent opened an inch. "Raven?"

Raven frowned at the broken sound of her name. Dianthe had obviously been crying. Whatever was going on with her, it must be painful, but then if Sylas assumed she was cursed, of course it was. She chided herself for her previously selfish thoughts and stepped inside.

"Sylas sent me. Let's check you out. I'm sure that together we can solve whatever is ailing you." Her heart broke at the sight of the fairy, sitting hunched on the side of the bed.

Dianthe held a wadded handkerchief in one hand and gazed up at her as she entered the room. "Thanks for coming."

"So why do you think you're cursed?"

Dianthe groaned. "I *don't*! Sylas is convinced I am."

"Why would he think you're cursed if you're not having any symptoms?" Raven was more confused than ever.

"Because before Everfield was attacked this morning, I helped heal Aborella."

All the air blew from Raven's lungs, and she gripped her stomach. Had she heard correctly? "Why in the name of the Mountain would you heal Aborella?" Raven couldn't stop her voice from taking on a harsh, judgmental tone. "Do you know what she did to me? To my sisters? She tried to kill us."

Dianthe dabbed under her eyes, her tears increasing

at Raven's obvious anger. Raven hadn't wanted to make her cry, but hell if she could understand why anyone in the rebellion would help that wicked fairy.

"She was close to death. Eleanor had tortured her and then buried her alive. I had a vision that if I healed her, I could turn her to our side. Specifically, I saw her battling Eleanor on our behalf. Up until recently, my visions were always reliable, Raven. There have been times I've misinterpreted a vision, but I can't ever remember being wrong."

"But this time you were." Raven's heart broke for her. She'd gambled her life to take a risk on a horribly evil fairy, and it had gone wrong. "Did Aborella give you anything? Jewelry? An orb of any kind?"

"No." Dianthe shook her head. "She had nothing. We'd dug her out of an unmarked grave. She didn't even have her own limbs."

"What about food... Did she make you anything to eat or drink?"

Dianthe frowned. "We made a batch of cookies together, but I didn't actually eat any."

"Good." Raven sighed. It would be easy to judge her. Aborella had compelled her father using milkwood root and Avery using an enchanted orb necklace. The fairy had also leveled a curse on her sister that had almost crushed her skull. Raven's list of grievances against the fairy was long. But she also had a healthy understanding of magic in all its forms. When practiced regularly, it became a part of you. There had been many times that Raven's magic had guided her in directions that Gabriel hadn't approved of. Could she blame Dianthe for trusting her own second sight about this?

"There's only one thing to do," Raven said. "I need to touch you. If she did curse you, I'll be able to feel it, and if I can discern the nature of the curse, there's a very good chance that my sisters and I can break it."

Dianthe released a held breath. "Thank you. I can't stand another day of this. Sylas looks at me like... like he blames me. Like he doesn't trust *me*. Not just the curse but *me*."

All the magic in the world couldn't cure that kind of hurt, but Raven would do what she could. "If you don't mind lying down on the bed, I'll start with your feet."

"Oh. All right." She leaned back and positioned her head on the pillow.

"Just relax. Close your eyes." Raven lifted the fairy's right foot and concentrated. The chance that Aborella would plant a curse in one of her feet was slim, but considering Dianthe was a seer and a fairy, she wasn't sure if this sort of magical probing would be uncomfortable for her. Raven was diving deep, examining her blood and her bones, sending her magic hunting through her flesh. It didn't seem prudent to start with what was probably the seat of her own magic, her head.

"It feels cold." Dianthe shivered. "Like ribbons braiding themselves inside my leg."

"A curse is cold," Raven explained. "My magic has to look like a curse to find one." She set Dianthe's right leg down and picked up her left. "I've gotten better at this over time. If there's something in you, I'll find it."

"Nothing yet?"

Raven smiled. "Nothing yet." She set down her other foot and slid her hands along her legs to her abdomen. "You have a powerful gut," she said through a smile. She pressed her hand over her belly button. "You have power centered here."

"I've always had strong intuition."

"I can feel it." Raven moved to her lungs and her chest. "Strong heart. You're a good person. I feel light and warmth. No wonder you wanted to help her. You actually believed you could save her."

Dianthe sucked in a sip of air. It took a second, but Raven realized what she'd done. Dianthe *had* thought she could save Aborella. She'd felt it in her bones. And the way Raven had just said those words implied she was stupid for doing so.

"I'm sorry about my tone." Raven moved her hands down her right arm. "You have to understand that Aborella has been a scourge to our family. She's the reason Marius is dead. She used my sister and tried to murder my other sister, took my power, and left me to rot in the dungeon. She's helped Eleanor perform every evil deed. It's hard to believe anyone would actually want to save her. If I had found her buried in a hole, I would have cut off her head and left her there."

Dianthe's eyes met hers, but she didn't flinch at the comment. Raven moved to her left arm and then to her golden gossamer wings, which peeked out from under her shoulders.

"Aborella was abused as a child," Dianthe whispered. "My late aunt told me stories that her mother would withhold food as a punishment, sometimes for days.

Aborella was my aunt's age, and she'd come to school filthy and hungry. Unfortunately, fairies are not always compassionate toward one another. They treated her worse than a rat. All that negative energy, it ignited her magic. She saved herself from the squalor and the bullying, but it did something to her soul. I just thought I could make it right somehow."

The compassion in Dianthe's voice cut to Raven's soul. She'd never thought of Aborella as anything but evil, a nemesis to be destroyed. It was unsettling to know she was something else, something before. Emotions swirled within her. She could not bring herself to feel sorry for Aborella, but she did understand Dianthe's compassion.

"That was kind of you." She moved her hand's to Dianthe's head. This was where her power was strongest. Raven's magic sifted through her mind, her skull, her second sight that glowed like a beacon within her. The soft warm glow of her power couldn't be mistaken for a curse.

"Believe it or not, by the end, after I'd healed her, I thought Aborella was my friend. What happened in Everfield felt like a betrayal. It hurt me. She hurt me. More than just the loss of my homeland. It hurts to be wrong about her."

Raven removed her hands and straightened beside the bed.

"What is it?" Dianthe asked. "What did you see?"

"Absolutely nothing." Cheerfully, Raven held out a hand and helped her sit up. "You are not cursed, Dianthe. Aborella might be the reason Eleanor attacked Everfield, but she did not leave any malignant magic on your person."

A rustle sounded at the mouth of the tent. Sylas stood in the doorway. "Did I hear you say she isn't cursed?"

Raven spread her hands. "To the extent of my knowledge and power—which is extensive—your mate is completely free of curses or ill-intentioned spells."

"What about her visions?" Sylas asked. "If she's not cursed, why did her second sight fail Everfield? She didn't see the attack until it was upon us."

All the joy poured out of Dianthe in a rush. Raven watched her curl in on herself, and Dianthe's words came back to her. *He doesn't trust me.* Raven felt a tide of anger flood her at Sylas's insensitivity. This should be a happy moment. Instead, he was still searching for a way to place blame on his mate.

Raven's hands came to rest on her hips. "I'm sure I don't know, Sylas. I am not a fairy, and I've never had the gift of second sight. But I will tell you as a witch that any spell can fail under the right circumstances. It's really no reason to judge someone's future abilities or to treat them like a bomb ready to go off."

The man gaped at her as if she were insane. *Dragons!* Raven nudged past him and strode toward her own tent, leaving the couple's problems behind her.

CHAPTER EIGHT

"What was that all about?" Sylas asked her, looking completely gobsmacked at the tent door.

"You heard what Raven said, and she's right. You've treated me like I'm a spy for Paragon since the moment Everfield was attacked." Dianthe stood, bolstered by Raven's indignation on her behalf. "You owe me an apology."

Sylas shook his head dismissively. "I'm not going to apologize for a logical assumption that even you must admit was perfectly reasonable given our circumstances."

Emotionally raw, she crossed her arms against his words. Each one was salt in her wound. "Yes, I recognize that your hypothesis could have been true this morning. I wanted someone to blame for what happened in Everfield, and blaming myself seemed easier than blaming anyone else. But now that I think about it, why would you jump to the conclusion that Aborella caused any of this? You are a fugitive from the crown. The guard was clearly talking about you, yet he did not know which cottage was ours. If Aborella was the source of the raid, they would have known."

A growl rumbled from his chest. "No one else knew I was there. I've spent half the time either here or on the road for the rebellion since I escaped the dungeons of Paragon."

"If it was Aborella, why didn't they know our address? Why would you assume she only cursed me? You were with her too, briefly. In fact, you were with her last. Maybe you are the reason Everfield burned. Maybe it wasn't Aborella at all. Maybe someone followed you to Everfield and reported back to the empress." As arguments went, it was a low blow, and Dianthe wasn't surprised when he flinched.

"I guess we know one thing for sure then," he said in a lethally low voice.

She lifted her chin despite a deep exhaustion that tempted her to crumple. "What's that?"

His throat bobbed on a swallow, and his eyes glinted with unshed tears. "We know that one of us brought about the end of the Empyrean Wood. Whether it was you or me or us together, when we chose to keep our home there and still be involved with the rebellion, we invited this, and Everfield paid the price."

Dianthe's spirit shattered. He was right. She couldn't deny it. The truth sliced through her and left her in pieces. There was no getting out from under this guilt. There was no amount of twisting that would make his words untrue. She'd been part of something that led to the probable death of her community.

All at once, her memory filled with the smell of

burning trees. Guilt crashed down, heavy on her shoulders. She had to change the subject or she'd be sick. "What did Colin say? What did he show everyone tonight while I was relegated to my quarters?"

Her mate rubbed the back of his neck and glanced toward the door. "Why can't you just let it go?"

"Let it go? Why would I let it go? I don't even know what there is to let go thanks to you. Tell me what he shared. Maybe I can help."

"You don't need to help." Sylas grabbed the sides of his head. "Can't you see this is your chance to get out? My entire family is here. Even Colin is back. You're safe. Stay safe, Dianthe. You don't need to be involved in this."

Jaw clenched to the point of pain, Dianthe gave a frustrated cry and stormed past him. "The only thing I don't want to be involved with right now is *you*."

She marched toward the end of the row and a tent at she'd noticed was empty earlier in the day.

"Dianthe? Dianthe!" Sylas called from behind her.

"Go to bed, Sylas. Leave me alone." She was relieved to find that the tent remained vacant. She slipped inside and zippered the door closed, then climbed under the covers on the camp bed near the back. For several minutes she waited, wondering if he'd come after her. And then the horrors of the day caught up to her and she cried herself into sweet oblivion.

SYLAS HATED SLEEPING ALONE. AS A MATED DRAGON, his inner beast had longed to go after Dianthe, to throw her down on the nearest bed and show her exactly how he felt about her. His beast, if it had full control, would never allow her to walk away from him. But the long-term consequences of acting like an animal were being treated like one. Dianthe had asked to be left alone. She needed time to process everything that had happened. His beast was part of him. It wasn't all of him. And his logical mind wrestled those base desires until they were under his control.

Still, he hoped she'd come around quickly. He didn't sleep well without her. He kept waking up to feel her side of the bed, his protective instincts driving him to prove she was safe.

Protective instincts. *Fuck.* Why couldn't she just enjoy the island and stay away from the war? Part of him wished Raven had found something. A curse would give him an excuse to keep her separate from all this. Things were heating up, becoming dangerous. Soon someone would have to go in search of the other orbs. Leaving this island carried risks he didn't want to think about. With Aborella working with Eleanor again, she'd likely see them coming.

He still believed Aborella was the cause of the Everfield raid. She had to be the reason Eleanor had known they would come here and had tried to intercept them. Only Aborella could have seen that and shared it with her.

Aeaea was the only place Dianthe would be safe now that her identity was known. If Sylas had his way, his mate would stay here, under the goddess's protection, until the war was over.

He tossed and turned until the wee hours of the night, thinking about her, longing for her, until finally exhaustion overcame him, and he slept.

Late morning, he awoke to the sound of voices. Quickly he dressed and hurried to the central tent. Colin would want to strategize about the orbs over breakfast. Afterward, he hoped Dianthe would be over her anger and he could talk some sense into her.

"Look who finally decided to join us." His twin snarked at him from over a bowl of eggs at the center table.

Leena was by his side, the dark circles under her eyes a telling sign of how she'd slept. Across from her, Dianthe sat with her back to him. His mate slowly turned to face him as he approached.

"What's going on here?" A prickly heat crawled up the back of his neck to his ears.

"Filling your mate in on what she missed last night," Colin said. "Think we've made a breakthrough—"

Sylas grabbed his brother by the collar and lifted him out of his seat, a difficult task considering Colin had a good hundred pounds on him. Fortunately, his twin got the hint that he was upset and came along willingly. He dragged his twin out the door.

"Why would you tell her without speaking to me?" His dragon chuffed and twisted inside him.

"Because she asked and she's an important part of the rebellion." Colin narrowed his eyes. "Why wouldn't you want me to tell her?"

That was a harder question to answer. Why *was* he so angry? Even Sylas didn't know for sure, only that he was. After a moment of consideration, he supplied the first thing that came to mind. "She lost her homeland yesterday. The Obsidian Guard burned the Empyrean Wood to ash. I was trying to give her time to grieve and recover. We're finally safe here. Why does she have to be involved with this mission right now? I think she's earned some time off."

And she'll be safer here, his dragon chimed in.

Colin folded his arms, his biceps popping to a size bigger than Sylas's head. Damn, the guy had turned into a beast during his time in Rogos.

"Have you spoken to Dianthe about this? Because she seemed more than ready to channel her grief into making Eleanor pay for what she did."

"I'm her mate." Sylas growled. "It's my job to care for her."

"Yes." Colin nodded. "But she's a grown fairy. She can make her own decisions."

"Thank you, Colin." Dianthe appeared beside Sylas, her wings flared.

"Dianthe... I—"

"Save it." She tipped her head toward Colin. "Have you told my mate yet about our monumental discovery?"

"No." Colin frowned. "Maybe you two should talk first."

Sylas didn't like the sound of that. Something in his brother's eyes told him he might not like this revelation.

"What's going on?" He focused fully on Dianthe.

"I know where the Everfield orb is," Dianthe said proudly.

A chill traveled the length of his body. *Fuck.* He'd

wanted to keep her out of this. If she knew where an orb was, she was definitely in it. "Where? Are you sure?"

"Positive. When I was a little girl, my aunt used to take me to Solaris Field."

Although Sylas had rarely visited the fields on the outskirts of Everfield near the Nochtbend border, he was familiar with them. Fairies would often visit to collect pollen from the densely growing sunpitcher plants there. The cone-shaped flowers collected the light and glowed like stars, making it an especially entertaining place to bring fairy children. Pollen collected from the flowers had an exceptionally short shelf life, making it too delicate for collecting, packaging, and reselling—another draw for the people of Everfield. Paragon was not interested in the fields. Yet those who had the time and inclination could collect the pollen for free. It was delicious when ingested immediately or baked into a number of dishes.

"What's in Solaris Field? I'm certain if the orb was there, someone would have found it by now," Sylas grumbled.

"Beyond the fields, on the border of the Grimtwist Forest, there is a lake. Solaris Lake. Most fairies never go there because of its proximity to Nochtbend, although it's perfectly safe during the day. My aunt took me because the water is always pleasantly warm. I used to swim with her in the afternoons."

"Your aunt let you swim in strangely warm waters beside the Grimtwist Forest?" Dianthe's Aunt Gemmy had passed away from natural causes several years ago.

She'd always been a little eccentric, but at the moment Sylas had to question her judgment.

"One fall afternoon, Aunt Gemmy took me to the lake to swim because it was too cold for the sea. In the past, I'd only waded into the lake, sometimes playing with the water sprites that lived there. I'd grown into a strong swimmer that year and was feeling exceptionally adventurous. I dove to the bottom of the lake that day, and what I saw there I would never forget. Something bright green glowed from inside a tangle of lake grass. When I touched it, the smooth crystal was hot. I tried to free it to show my aunt, but it wouldn't budge. And when I told her about it, she said that in most cases it was best to leave magical objects where you found them. So I did. But Sylas, it looked exactly like the orb from Rogos, just green instead of purple. It's there."

Sylas brushed a piece of invisible lint from the arm of his tunic and looked toward Colin. "Colin, you and I should go retrieve this orb. I know Everfield. We can be in and out in a day. Between the two of us, I'm sure we can pry it up."

Dianthe gasped. "If you think I'm not going, you need to see a healer. There is something seriously wrong with you. Everfield is my home. I'm the one who found it, and I know exactly where the orb is. You need me."

Sylas opened his mouth to tell her the idea was ludicrous considering Aborella knew her identity. Dianthe couldn't even make herself invisible for the goddess's sake!

But Colin spoke up first. "I agree with Dianthe."

"Excuse me?" Sylas glared at him in righteous indignation. How dare he suggest his mate be sent into a dangerous situation without clearing it with him first? Didn't he understand what it did to a dragon to know his mate might be in peril?

"Leena can't leave the scrolls. She's taken a solemn vow to protect them." Colin gestured toward the tent and the scribe inside. "And I've taken a vow to protect Leena. You can't imagine how brave she was to leave Rogos. Do you know what Eleanor would do to a scribe outside the boundaries protected by elfish magic?"

Sylas frowned. He could imagine. "Gabriel then."

"Gabriel has to stay with Raven, and Raven has to stay with Clarissa and Avery. The three sisters cannot be separated. Their power derives from one another. It's too dangerous. Plus there is Charlie to think about."

"Which means Xavier and Nathaniel are out of the picture. They won't leave their mates." Dianthe crossed her arms and drummed her fingers on her bicep.

Colin tipped his head. "Maiara and Nick are human. Neither of them knows Everfield, and the vampires in Nochtbend will smell them coming a mile away. Plus Rowan's wing is still healing."

"That leaves only Tobias," Sylas said gruffly. Their brother was a talented healer and the smartest among them when it came to history and culture, but as a warrior his skills were lacking, especially now that he hadn't had to fight in a number of years.

Colin leaned back on his heels. "Exactly. You, Dianthe, Tobias, and Sabrina will go. Sabrina is a vampire—"

"From Earth!" All of Sylas's muscles clenched at the idea. It was a recipe for disaster.

"But still a vampire. Vampires notoriously hate dragons and witches and share an uneasy peace with the fairies of Everfield. You've made progress in Nochtbend, but as one of their kind, she's our best bet of convincing them to help us find the orb. When I spoke to her last night, she was pretty confident that vampires, by their nature, are the same everywhere."

"In your own words, vampires have an uneasy peace with fairies. Exactly why Dianthe should not go," Sylas grumbled.

Colin ignored him and continued. "The four of you will go to Everfield to retrieve the green orb Dianthe saw; then you will journey into Nochtbend and search for the one hidden there. Sabrina thinks she'll be able to find it."

"Absolutely not! The very idea!" Sylas wanted to punch his brother in the face for even suggesting such a thing. Had Colin forgotten that Grimtwist Forest was inhabited by carnivorous monsters?

A muscle in Colin's jaw jumped, and he pursed his lips. "I get that you fear for your mate, Sylas, but it's not like we're sending her alone. You'll be with her. This is the perfect team to get this done. Use her second sight. Lean on Tobias and Sabrina. I know you can do this."

He clenched his teeth and stepped closer to his twin until their chests were almost touching. "Over my dead body."

Colin shook his head. "I didn't want to have to do this, but with my return to Aeaea, I officially take over the role I left to you. I'm the leader of the rebellion again, brother. Don't make me pull rank on you. I'll go to the others if I have to."

Sylas shook his head. "You wouldn't dare."

Colin narrowed his eyes as if to say *try me*. "We need you to do this. This is your team. Make the most of it."

CHAPTER NINE

Dianthe wanted to hug Colin for standing up for her. Although Sylas's bright red face warned that he might explode at any moment, she proudly soldiered on, talking detailed plans with Colin beside her seething mate. She'd won this round and it mattered.

In the past, Sylas had always respected her contributions to the Defenders of the Goddess. He'd always had reverence for her gift. But since she'd healed Aborella, he'd treated her like she was a child—inconsequential—or worse, a liability. Not only did it make her feel inferior, it made her question her own abilities. She'd caught herself fighting her intuition and doubting her second sight, that thing that had been with her for as long as she could remember.

If she was going to forgive herself for any role she'd played in what happened in Everfield and regain her confidence, she had to go on this mission. With Sylas there, it would be the perfect opportunity to prove to him she was the same woman he married. She'd earn his trust in her abilities and his respect again. Oh, she knew he loved her. He'd always love her. But love wasn't enough. She wanted him to see her as an equal—like he used to see her.

Her bag was already packed—she'd never had a chance to unpack it—but she moved it to her own tent. Her gut told her that if she gave him the opportunity, Sylas would try to talk her out of this mission or sabotage her involvement. So she did her best to avoid him until it was time to leave.

Mercifully, he wasn't on the boat when she arrived. Neither was Tobias. But she was not alone. A willowy and shockingly pale woman with bright red hair lay in the shade of the sail, a hooded cloak pulled high over her head and a pair of dark sunglasses shading her eyes, which presently appeared closed as if she were napping. Sabrina the vampire. They'd never been formally introduced. Now did not seem like the time.

As quietly as possible, Dianthe stepped on board and stowed her pack in the cargo hold. She took a seat in the sun.

"You must be Dianthe." Sabrina opened her eyes and sat up, adjusting the dark shades. "You'll have to excuse me. I'm usually sleeping at this time of day, and direct sun is quite uncomfortable for my kind."

"Sabrina, right? It's a pleasure to meet you."

The vampire gave a small nod, then leaned her head against the hull and closed her eyes again.

"It's funny about fairies and vampires," Dianthe said cheerfully. "Fairies derive strength from the sun. Really anything celestial. The moon and stars as well. We celebrate many celestial events in our culture, but the sun is the most beneficial to our kind. Our kingdom butts up to Nochtbend, which is the land of the vampires. They live underground and only come out at night when they are the strongest."

Sabrina lifted her head and stared at her over her shades. "So I've heard."

"I've always thought we made perfect neighbors," Dianthe continued. "Everfield sleeps at night and Nochtbend sleeps during the day. If you didn't know the other existed, you might not ever find out."

The vampire blinked at her sleepily.

"Well, it's nice to meet you anyway."

"Likewise." She closed her eyes again.

She sat in silence for a few minutes until Tobias stepped onto the boat wearing a strange pair of shorts with large pockets and a short-sleeved shirt with a collar. He looked very human for a dragon.

"Dianthe." He extended his hand. She grabbed it and he pumped her arm twice. "Nice to meet you. I'm Tobias. Have you met Sabrina?"

"We've met." A hint of annoyance peppered Sabrina's tone. She didn't bother opening her eyes again.

"She's, uh, actually very personable," Tobias said. "It's just that yesterday she was up during the day, facing the sea monster and helping people to shore, in full sun I might add. I helped her heal that sunburn, but then she had trouble sleeping last night because that's when she'd usually be up. Plus she's überworried about her coven because she's left them in the hands of her father, who is, if I may say, way scarier than any vampire you've ever met—"

"Tobias," Sabrina said flatly. "She doesn't need our life story."

The blond dragon smiled down at her, awkwardly nodding his head. "Well... okay."

Sylas arrived then, carrying his bag and looking flustered. He stared at Dianthe and Tobias, then at her bag peeking through the cargo net. "You could have told me you were taking your pack, Dianthe. I was looking all over for it to carry it down for you."

He climbed on board, stowed his luggage, and gestured to Indigo that they were ready to go.

"I carried it myself."

"I see that." His lips pressed into a flat line.

His shadow stretched over her, blocking out the sun, but the aura he was putting off made her far more uncomfortable than the shade. Tension coiled in the pit of her belly, cranked tight by the look of annoyance and disappointment on his face. It made her breath halt in her throat.

"This is happening, Sylas," she said softly. "Accept it."

He scoffed. "I hope we all live long enough for me to have the opportunity." He crossed the deck to take a seat next to Tobias.

It wasn't the conversation she'd hoped for, but at least she could feel the sun on her face again.

Sylas sat beside Tobias, only half listening to his brother's story about how he met Sabrina. There was something about coffee and a hospital. Okay, he wasn't listening at all. His mind was completely preoccupied with not staring at his mate, who was sunning herself on the bench where he'd left her. His eyes kept darting back to her. The light made her skin shimmer like chestnut-colored silk. He looked away, wishing he had a pair of dark glasses like Sabrina's so that he could stare at Dianthe without her knowing.

Grumbling, he leaned forward, resting his elbows on his knees. *Fuck*. He was acting like a schoolboy. If he wanted to stare at his own mate, he should just do it. And for that matter, if he had something to say to her, he should just say it. His eyes drifted to his toes.

"Sylas?" Tobias elbowed him in the side.

"What?"

"I asked you if you thought we should make the boat invisible. We're approaching Serenity Harbor. Do you think Mother will have guards watching Aeaea? She knows we're staying there."

"It's possible." Sylas's stomach filled with lead at the thought of battling Eleanor again with his mate in tow. "But if we make the entire ship invisible, we'll drain ourselves. We're going to need that strength if we run into trouble. Better we use it on ourselves and our mates."

"An oread driving an empty boat into port... that's not suspicious?" Tobias laughed.

"What do you suggest?"

Tobias's blue eyes morphed to green, his platinum hair to dark amber, and his face elongated in shape. Two gossamer wings unraveled from his back. "I think disguise is in order. Eleanor has never met Sabrina. I'm betting by what you've said she has no idea who Dianthe is either."

"She might now, because of Aborella."

"We can put her in a cloak. Cover her face."

Sylas concentrated, changing his appearance to a black-haired native of Everfield with purple wings and a square jaw. "How do I look?"

"Too attractive. You don't want to draw attention."

He added a few pounds around the gut and made his face rounder.

"Perfect. Now, do you want to tell Dianthe the plan or should I?"

"I'll do it. Why wouldn't I do it?"

"Because you two have been in some kind of cold war from minute one. I don't know what is going on, but a cold breeze blows my way every time your eyes meet." Tobias's strange face slanted a quirky smile.

"I'll do it, all right?" Sylas stood and crossed to the other side of the boat again.

Dianthe's eyes were shut, but they opened when his shadow passed over her. At first she looked startled, but then noticed his clothes and realized it was him. "Why do you look like that?"

"You need to put on your cloak. We've got to disguise ourselves before we reach port in case Eleanor has people watching the coast."

"Okay." She didn't move.

"Do you need my help with the bag?"

"No. I'm perfectly capable of getting my own cloak out of my own bag. I'm simply waiting for you to move out of my way." She pointed to the bag in the cargo net directly behind him.

Without another word, he returned to Tobias's side.

His brother shivered. "Cold as ice."

"Shut the fuck up."

Serenity Harbor came into view, and Sylas stood and walked to the front of the boat.

Dressed in her black hooded cloak and a pair of dark gloves, Dianthe sidled up beside him. "Oh my goddess."

That was an understatement. Everfield's largest beach was covered in ramshackle housing. Everything from burnt logs to woven grasses had been stitched together to form the most rudimentary of shelters. As they came closer, they could see fairies, dirty and haggard, huddled together around a fire. Behind them, the Empyrean Wood, once their homeland, stood gray and bare, a skeleton forest of ash and scorched timber.

She reached for his hand, and he did not deny her.

"I'm so sorry Dianthe. I wish I could have saved you from this," he said. "I wish I could have saved them from this."

For a long time they watched the approaching squalor in silence. Until, it seemed, she couldn't stand it anymore. Her hand slipped from his, and she turned so that her back was to the shore.

"Me too," she whispered, her voice raw with emotion. "Promise me you'll make her pay."

He wasn't sure if by "her" she meant Eleanor or Aborella or both. It didn't matter. He intended to make them both pay, along with every member of the Obsidian Guard who'd participated in the burning. "I promise."

CHAPTER TEN

The vision rushed through Aborella like a wave, starting in her stomach and rolling up her body until her lashes fluttered and her eyes rolled back in her head. Five spheres formed in her mind's eye—cobalt, emerald, flame red, royal purple, and gold. The spheres overlapped and the scene changed. They morphed into a key. The key was fed to a dragon. The dragon turned into a book. A golden book.

With a gasp, Aborella snapped out of it, blinking away what remained of the vision. Immediately she regretted it. Her vision was a much happier place than the room she was in. Eleanor had imprisoned her in a hidden stone chamber behind the palace library and adjacent to her ritual room. Although the empress had extolled how virtuous she was for moving Aborella there from the dungeons, the truth was this room was far crueler than the dark death she'd experienced in the bowels of the mountain. Here she did not have the comfort of the sounds of other prisoners. No whispers came through walls in the night. She was alone. Utterly alone. And she was chained, manacled to the wall by the waist with enchanted metal unbreakable by any spell she had tattooed into her skin.

Eleanor was wise to bind her by the waist. If it had been her arm, she would have surely severed it off to escape. Fairies lived to feel the sun on their skin. It strengthened their natural magic and made them feel alive. This room was designed with only one window. A rectangle to let in a shaft of light each day. Compared to the dungeon, which had no windows, it might have been better. Only Aborella's chains were not long enough to allow her to reach the light, and the angle of the window and the direction of the sun meant the light never reached her.

It was torture, to be sure. She could see the light but never feel it on her skin. Every day had become like a small death. Sometimes she'd dream about feeling the sun, only to wake in darkness and then watch as that teasing patch of warmth moved across the stone just out of her reach.

Ironic that Eleanor had claimed this room was her reward for telling the truth that the Treasure of Paragon had fled to Aeaea. The heirs and their mates had passed right through Eleanor and Ransom's fingers, as Aborella had hoped they would. She'd known where Raven and Gabriel had been taking little Charlie for weeks before she'd told Eleanor, and by then it was too late for the empress to organize a proper attempt at reeling in her children. Faced with limited time, she'd gone after them herself and failed.

Aborella smiled. The eight living children were together now and protected by the goddess Circe herself. She'd seen it, and her visions were never wrong.

The heavy wood-and-metal door creaked open on its hinges, sending a wave of anxiety through her. Every day was the same. Tired and hungry, Aborella would withstand Eleanor's aggressive questions about her visions and carefully lie about what she saw. Only the longer she was starved and mistreated, the harder it became to do so convincingly. She just didn't have the energy.

Eleanor strode in, dressed in head-to-toe black. Gone was her usual gown, replaced by formfitting pants and a blouse with large puffy sleeves. The outfit exaggerated her skeletal frame and made her look like the angel of death. She'd lost more weight. And she was alone today.

Aborella wondered what had happened to Ransom. Had he finally realized that everyone who aligned with Eleanor eventually ended up in a box, whether it was a coffin or a prison? Or maybe Eleanor had already grown tired of him and his heart sat on the shelf in her ritual room, next to Marius's and Brynhoff's.

"Good morning, Aborella. Are you prepared to be cooperative today, or am I going to need to find your motivation?"

"I only wish to help you," Aborella said. "Although it is difficult when I am so weak."

"You are strong enough. Tell me, what you have seen?" Eleanor picked at the side of her nail.

"I haven't seen anything, Empress. I'm too weak. Without proper meals and light, I am not strong enough to see."

Eleanor's scowl twisted into something truly horrifying. "Don't play games, Aborella. If I gave you what you wanted, you'd only use your magic to break free. I've known you for decades. I know how you think."

"But—"

"My spies saw a boat land in Serenity Harbor. It might have come from Aeaea. Four strangers disembarked, two males and two females. My man tried to follow them, but he lost them in the stink of that wretched beach colony."

"The people of Everfield had to go somewhere after you burned all their homes." Aborella hugged her knees to her chest and rested her head on them, wrapping herself in her wings.

"They should come to me! Paragon would provide them with lovely homes if they swore their allegiance to the rightful ruler of the five kingdoms." Eleanor bared her teeth in an ugly grin. "It is only a matter of time before they fall—before all the kingdoms fall. Only Chancellor Ciro's bloody ego keeps him from kneeling before me. He will break soon enough."

"Of course," Aborella said dryly. "What was I thinking?"

"I need to know who these people are. Are they my children in disguise? And if so, why are they in Everfield? What have you seen, Aborella? Don't disappoint me, or I will further reduce your meals."

Goddess forbid Eleanor should withhold the barely edible slop she dished out to her each night. Aborella worked to keep her eyes from rolling. But what to tell her? The lie must be close enough to the truth to be believable but far enough a lie as to mislead and misdirect. She must bend the arrow a few millimeters; not enough for the archer to notice but enough that the shot was guaranteed to miss its target.

She forced herself to mimic a vision once again. "I do see something. Yes, I see the arrival of the four you spoke of."

"Well, tell me. I don't have all day."

"First something to eat. I am too hungry and weak to describe what I have seen."

"First the vision!" Eleanor seethed through her teeth.

Aborella leaned back against the stone wall, wondering how she could ever have thought Eleanor was her friend for so many years. She'd helped train her, protected her, even sacrificed her own body for her. What a fool she'd been.

Aborella kept her expression completely impassive as she said, "The four are not your children, but they are members of the rebellion. They arrived in Everfield to meet with sympathizers who survived the fire. Their task is to recover documents from a home that was burned in the Empyrean Wood, one belonging to the leader of the rebellion."

"What is in these documents?" Eleanor asked.

"I couldn't see the contents in my vision, only a metal box. It is buried somewhere, underneath the ash." Aborella blinked slowly and waited. Would she take the bait?

Eleanor paced the length of her cell, arms crossed over the bodice of her black top. "I'll send a team to find this box and intercept the four. If you are right, you will be rewarded." She turned for the door.

"Eleanor, I require food and drink, or my visions will stop."

The empress turned her head in Aborella's direction but didn't meet her eyes. "Will the visions stop, or will you stop sharing them?"

Aborella allowed her silence to permeate the room. "We were friends once. I helped you develop your magic. I could help you again if you freed me. We've been together so long. You wouldn't have given me your tooth if you didn't trust me. Let me go, and let's work together to unite the kingdoms."

For one fleeting moment, Aborella saw softness creep into the edges of Eleanor's expression. The empress took a single step toward her, then stopped. She blinked once, twice. And something happened. Whatever merciful thoughts Aborella had seen twinkle in her eyes dimmed like a snuffed candle. Cruelty sullied her face once more, and darkness bled into her already cold stare.

"If we were friends once, that's over now," she said. "An empress can have no real friends. A goddess does not consort with mortals."

Aborella snorted derisively. "Are you calling yourself a goddess now? Empress is no longer enough?"

"It is the title I've been promised once I banish the goddess of the mountain."

"Banish the goddess? You cannot banish the Mountain herself." Aborella was both confused and distressed by this new motivation. Eleanor must truly have crossed into insanity to think she could murder a goddess.

"I will end the existence of the goddess of the mountain, and when I do, someone will have to take her place as ultimate ruler of the five kingdoms. It will be me, Aborella. And if you help me... become... you will be rewarded."

"I can help you more if—"

"No!" Eleanor snapped. "I will not risk losing you again. You are too important to my cause."

Not too important to *her,* just her cause. Thoughts of Dianthe danced through Aborella's head: the warm smell of cookies that seemed to follow her everywhere, the bright fire she kept burning in the hearth, the kind touch she always had when she was helping her eat or bathe. Dianthe's kindness had been its own curse, making Eleanor's cruelty all the more intense.

"Be careful, Eleanor. A goddess is only as strong as the ones who worship her. If you can't keep a friend, how do you expect to keep the public's adoration?" She'd gone too far. She'd be lucky if Eleanor didn't punish her for that quip.

"I'm not after their adoration or yours," Eleanor said darkly on her way to the door. "They don't need to love me. Neither do you. But they should fear me."

The heavy door slammed shut with enough force to rattle Aborella's bones, and she knew at that moment she would never leave that room.

CHAPTER ELEVEN

"R eady?" Raven squeezed the hands of her two sisters as they huddled around the scroll laid on the table between them. This had to work. It should work. After all, the knowledge hidden in the scroll was meant for them, a message from their common ancestor.

"Try to be gentle," Leena said facetiously from her perch beside them. She poised her quill over the scroll on her lap prepared to document everything that happened. Raven tried not to let the scribe's duties break her concentration.

"I'm ready," Avery said. "I think."

Clarissa nodded. "Let's do this."

The scroll's hidden symbols taunted them from deep within the parchment, under the readable message about the five orbs. Raven released their hands. "Now."

Avery touched the scroll, and the original message faded. The hidden symbols beneath it rose slowly to the surface and darkened. At once Clarissa sang a spell to bolster Avery's magic and hold the enchantment open like a wedge. Which left Raven free to do her part. She drew a symbol in the air above the scroll with her finger. The same translation spell she'd used on the historical texts necessary to resurrect Maiara in Sedona poured out of her. The words ordered themselves before her.

"I've got it," she said excitedly, then began to read. "'With the help of Daluk of Niven, I Medea, Tanglewood witch and queen of Darnuith, bequeath my golden grimoire to the three foretold—'"

The words disappeared as Avery's fingers slipped from the parchment, and she collapsed in a heap.

"Avery!" Raven ran to her and squatted by her side.

Clarissa cradled her head in her hands. "Are you okay?"

"Whatever spell the original Tanglewood witches put on that thing, it's no joke. Neutralizing it is like drinking from a firehose. I can't hold it for more than a few seconds."

"It's not just us then." Leena seemed far less nervous now that the ancient scroll had proven tougher than it looked. She paused her writing to address them. "Everyone in my order tried to translate it before Colin convinced me to bring it here. Our strongest elven magic was useless against its enchantment. Odd, considering an elf was involved in its creation. Daluk of Niven was one of our high scribes in the Temple of the Sacred Pools. He passed into the promised wood several years ago."

Avery plopped down on one of the benches and leaned back against the table as if she were seriously hungover. Raven supposed she needed a break. She walked to the back of the tent and poured the three of them glasses of the cold fruity beverage the island's sprites had made. The stuff looked like lemonade but tasted faintly of coconut. She set the glasses down between her sisters.

"Thanks." Avery selected one and took a sip, then gestured toward Leena. "Are you like a nun or something?"

Raven, who'd just brought her drink to her lips, almost spat it out. Leena didn't give off a warm, ask-me-anything vibe. In fact, she seemed a bit aloof and seriously uncomfortable to be there. She hoped her sister's abrupt question wouldn't be considered rude. Across the table, Clarissa had also stopped drinking and was glancing between Avery and Leena nervously.

"I don't know what a 'none' is," Leena answered, frowning.

"Um, like, are you part of a religious order that protects these scrolls for your gods or something?" Avery pressed.

Leena's previously confused expression cleared. "Yes. The Order of Sacred Pools was established by the goddess of the mountain to record the history of her world. A faction of the elves, my people, have performed this sacred duty for millennia. I am honored to have been called into her service."

Avery swiped a thumb over her lips. "So, you, um, devote your life to recording history? How does that work?"

Leena set her scroll aside and tangled her fingers over her knee. "Normally we never leave the temple. Our magic allows us to see events occurring around Ouros by gazing into the sacred pools. It is said that the deep indentations in the limestone are filled with the goddess's own tears, cried when Zeus exiled her to this island realm. We watch and we write down what we see in ancient Elvish. That is why this scroll is so strange. None of the other scrolls are protected like this. There is no need. No one but our order knows how to read ancient Elvish."

"How did you end up with Colin?" Clarissa asked. Both Raven and Avery turned around to look at her. "What?" she whispered, turning up her palms. "Just making conversation."

A blush stained Leena's cheeks. Raven scratched her forehead to conceal her lifted eyebrow.

"Colin came to Rogos two years ago on a mission to convince the elven high council to support the rebellion. Our leaders have always remained neutral, even during the uprising led by the witch queen. Our kingdom refused to take sides then or now. We've never participated in a war."

"I get it. You're Switzerland," Clarissa said, nodding.

"What is Switzerland?" Leena narrowed her eyes.

"Never mind. Something from Earth. Please... continue." Raven gave Clarissa side-eye.

"Although Lord Niall refused to discuss supporting the rebellion, he allowed Colin his wish to live and work among my people. The truth was, no elf would ever turn down free dragon labor. He'd worked for months, silently speaking his truth while winning over the locals with his tireless efforts. At first no one believed him. The elves were certain that Eleanor only wanted coordination of the kingdoms. But over time, things that Colin predicted came true. The execution of Brynhoff being one, skyrocketing taxes, and then the raids. About a month ago, Eleanor approached our High Lord, Niall, and told him that the future was a united Ouros. She pressured him to relinquish Rogos to her rule. He refused.

"After that, the Lord Niall insisted our archers begin training. Rogos has always had an army, but until recently, we've only practiced defensive maneuvers. Lord Niall ordered our military to increase its efforts and prepare for a potential attack. I am here because I and a small contingent of my kind believe that Eleanor will stop at nothing until she controls all five kingdoms, including Rogos. I received special permission from my Quanling to accompany Colin here. This was the only way that the scroll could be removed from the temple."

"Quanling?" Raven asked. She'd never heard the term.

"Like a mother figure to women who enter the order. Male scribes answer to the Fratern. The Quanling and the Fratern are our leaders and serve on the High Lord's royal court along with leaders of the wood elves and the desert dwellers."

"So when you're done, you'll just go back?" Clarissa asked. "I must have been mistaken. It seemed like you and Colin—"

Raven glared at her. Now she was getting far too personal.

Although Leena's expression didn't change dramatically, Raven caught a hint of sadness in the tilt of her shoulders. "Yes, I'll return when my work here is done. I've sworn an oath to the temple."

Avery glanced at the scroll again, her shoulders sagging. "Which means if you ever want to get home, we need to figure this out."

"Well, what we're doing sure as hell isn't working." Raven rubbed her temples. "I don't suppose one of you two has a better idea?"

Avery shook her head. "A long nap and a few hours on the beach? It won't translate the scroll, but it might make me feel better."

"Ladies, ladies." Clarissa spread her hands and released an exasperated sigh. "Have you forgotten who the fuck we are?"

"We're the three sisters," Avery mumbled with a roll of her eyes.

Raven rubbed her shoulder encouragingly.

"Who the fuck are we?" Clarissa asked again, louder.

"The three sisters," Raven and Avery said in unison.

"That's right, bitches. We are the three fucking kick-ass sisters. We are more magical than unicorns and fairy dust!" Clarissa punched her fists into the air in front of her as if she were boxing a ghost. "One little scroll is not going to defeat us."

Avery's head dropped into her hands. "What do you suggest we do, Clarissa? I don't have much left in me for this."

"Maybe we should take a break," Raven said. "Avery should lie down and maybe have something to eat."

Clarissa gave a beleaguered sigh. "Here's what we are going to do." She picked up a piece of blank parchment beside the scroll that Raven had procured for taking notes. "Avery is going to neutralize the enchantment one more time; then you and I, Raven, are going to copy the symbols we see furiously. You take the first row and I take the second, and so on, alternating. And we are not going to even try to do the translation spell on what we are copying until we reconstruct the entire message."

Raven ran a hand over her face. "That will take days."

Clarissa clapped her hands. "So? Like nothing has been this difficult for us before? We thought we could muscle through it if we worked together. It's proving to be a little bit harder than that. Are we going to give up or give it another try?"

"Give it another try," Avery said, although there wasn't an ounce of excitement in the words. "But I'm seriously drained. I'm not sure how many more times I can do this."

Raven kissed her sister on the side of the head. "We're safe here. All we have is time. Just do what you can."

With one nod, Avery rolled her shoulders back and reached for the scroll again. "On the count of three."

Raven and Clarissa readied their pens.

"One, two, three." She touched the scroll, and they began again.

CHAPTER TWELVE

"Please, miss, do you have any food?"

Dianthe had been trying to walk through the camp on the beach at Serenity Harbor without being noticed when someone grabbed her hand. She kept her gaze down and pulled her hood as far forward as possible. While Sylas and Tobias could change their appearance at will and Sabrina was unknown to anyone on Ouros, if Dianthe was recognized, she could jeopardize their entire mission.

She tried not to look at the person who squeezed her fingers. If she made eye contact, it would be too hard to turn away. These were her people, and they were in an awful state. The young fairies could hunt, but the elderly must truly be struggling. The person whose voice she'd heard sounded old and weak.

She tried to walk on, but her assailant only squeezed tighter, refusing to let go, and Dianthe had no choice but to address her. She turned, peeking from under the hood... and recognized the person behind her immediately. "Wynter?"

The old woman smiled at the sound of her voice. "Di—"

Dianthe cut her off with the press of her finger to the old fairy's lips. She shook her hooded head. Behind her in his disguise, Sylas must have given Wynter a look because her eyes grew wide with understanding.

Wynter lowered her voice to a whisper. "I'm so happy to see you made it out alive. After the fire, we've assumed those we can't find are dead."

"I'm not dead and neither is... my mate. But how are you getting on?" Dianthe thought Wynter looked more frail than usual.

"Hungry, my dear. There is never enough food. The younger ones collect pollen from Solaris Field every day, but I'm too old for that." Wynter's wings sagged over her shoulders.

Dianthe glanced back at Sylas, whose strange face contorted with concern. If people were relying on Solaris Field for food, it might be difficult to do what they came to do without being seen.

"Oh, Wynter..." Dianthe had to force herself not to hug the woman.

"Some are beginning to rebuild. Dead houses of course. All the fairy magic in the world can't grow saplings into proper dwellings. We've started coaxing the forest back to life, but who knows if that beastly woman will attack us again? She wants us to kneel before her and swear our fealty to the kingdom of Paragon and her own overinflated ego, but let me tell you, I'll choose starvation over allegiance to Eleanor any moonrise. And as of now, the residents of the Elder Tree agree with me."

"Chancellor Ciro is standing strong?"

Wynter nodded. "Although there is pressure from the Highborns to give in. Every day it becomes harder to resist. People are hungry." She pointed at a group of children playing in the sea. "Orphans. Their parents died in the fire or at the hands of the Guard. We all try to care for them, but..."

"Keep the faith, Wynter. The goddess knows and sees all," Dianthe said.

"If only the goddess would send us some help." Wynter's voice cracked.

Dianthe reached for the strap of her bag, intending to remove it and dig inside for one of her rations. A hand landed on her shoulder, stopping her. Sylas.

"That's not a good idea," he whispered in her ear. His eyes scanned the surrounding crowd. They were all staring, suddenly quiet, everyone intent on her bag. He was right. This was dangerous. She recognized many faces— all good fairies to be sure—but hunger made people do desperate things. Could she get one ration out without exposing that she had more than one? If these people saw her give anything to Wynter, would they attack her for it? Steal it from the old woman's hands?

Disappointed, she adjusted her bag on her shoulder. "Let us all pray the goddess hears us and sends help." She gave Wynter a slight bow goodbye and then allowed Sylas to lead her from the beach. Together, they entered the scorched woods.

"It stinks of death," she said. "Charred wood.

Charred life. I wonder if this is what hell smells like." Her boots were already covered in ash. Ahead of them, Tobias carried Sabrina, who appeared to be sleeping in his arms. The disguised dragon didn't seem to mind at all. The way he kissed her on the head, Dianthe thought he might walk across Ouros with her in his arms if he needed to.

"You did the right thing back there," Sylas said.

They were deep enough into what remained of the Empyrean Wood that they were alone. There wasn't another soul in sight.

"It doesn't feel like the right thing. I've never seen Wynter look so frail. One of my rations would have meant the world to her."

Sylas laughed. "Wynter may be old, but she's as tough as oak roots. She'll survive. But if you'd given her a ration, she might have been killed for it."

"Seems as though we've made a lot of excuses why we can't help lately." Her eyes filled with tears, and she couldn't tell if it was from the swell of emotion in her chest or the ash that floated in the air like snow around her.

"What we're about to do—hell, what we have been doing—will help these people more than a ration or putting an Obsidian guard in his place. We're going to end this, Dianthe. We are going to make it so that this"—he gestured around him—"never happens again. To anyone. Anywhere in the five kingdoms. We are going to end Eleanor's reign of terror."

"Do you really think it will ever happen?" The

crushing weight of doubt compressed her chest until she could hardly breathe.

"I wouldn't be here if I didn't have hope."

"Yeah." She supposed she wouldn't be there either if she didn't believe they could make a difference. She'd had plenty of opportunity to back out. "Have you finally made your peace then with my participation in this mission? Aren't you afraid I might have an errant vision that brings about our doom? The way you've treated me the past few days, I'm surprised the entire island of Aeaea doesn't think I'm a snapping elderbeast."

"That's not fair. Neither of us knew for sure what Aborella might have done."

Dianthe stopped, her boots kicking up ash between them. "Let's put this to rest right now. You never wanted me to heal Aborella. I had a vision she'd help us and that vision didn't pan out. But you helped me carry her back here. You stayed away so that I could heal her and build trust with her. And as reluctant as you might have been, you yourself invited her to join our cause. So stop this, Sylas. Stop it now. Because I did not inflict Aborella on us or on Everfield alone. We did. We did it together. And you are fully culpable, as much as I am."

"I wasn't the one who had the vision!"

"Raven said that even the strongest witches sometimes make mistakes. Spells fail. Magic isn't infallible." She shook her head. "I made a mistake, Sylas. Frankly, I was overdue. But you know what? People who love each other forgive mistakes. And they *believe* in each other even when it's hard."

Sylas's mouth dropped open as Dianthe stormed off. Was that what she thought? That he didn't believe in her? His jaw started to ache, and he realized he was grinding his teeth. Hardheaded female. By the Mountain, they were walking through a war zone! If she didn't realize that he was trying to protect her from this... this... horror of an existence, he wasn't sure what to say. It was too late anyway. She was here. There was no going back.

Still, for the next two hours, Dianthe walked beside Tobias, leaving him following alone. He was relieved when they finally broke from the Empyrean Wood and arrived at Solaris Field. Ouros's two suns had begun to set, streaking the sky with aqua and lime green, but it was the field itself that was putting on a show. In the mounting twilight, the sunpitcher plants, charged from a day of full light, glowed bright for as far as the eye could see. Sylas emerged from a world of skeletal trees and ash into a field of stars.

Ahead of him, Dianthe reached into one of the conical flowers and plucked the glowing pollen from within. She dropped it into her mouth. The glow shone through the mahogany skin of her cheeks, illuminating the veins there, before disappearing down her throat. Beside her, Tobias set Sabrina on her feet. The vampire seemed to be more alert than before and rubbed the sleep from her eyes. His brother tried to follow Dianthe's example and pluck the glow from the nearest flower but only succeeded at destroying the bloom.

Sylas chuckled as he caught up to the group. "Nice try, brother. Only fairies can harvest the pollen without destroying the flower."

Tobias held up his glowing hand, the remains of the blossom stuck to his fingers like spiderwebs. "I see that now."

Dianthe snatched his hand out of the air and lowered it to his side. "Careful," she whispered. "We're not alone here, and you're supposed to be a fairy."

A giggle reached them from across the field, and Sylas noticed the winged silhouettes of adults and children collecting pollen.

"What should we do?" Tobias asked. "We can't go diving into the lake with an audience."

"That won't be a problem." Dianthe led the way toward the lake. "No fairy would stay here after nightfall, especially not where we're going."

She led the way to the right, carefully navigating the sunpitcher plants like only a fairy could. Somehow she seemed to glide between them no matter how closely they grew together. A fairy's ability to live at one with nature had always seemed paradoxical to Sylas. They ate meat, after all. Fairies would go to great lengths not to kill a tree but would slaughter dozens of narwits to roast over an open fire at a gathering. Dianthe had tried to explain the logic: fast reproduction meant there were too many narwits. It was merciful, she'd said. If left to their own devices, the critters would eat all the vegetation, down to and including the roots, and then starve to death. Killing them was a way to both control the population and make life better for those left alive. Still, Sylas had struggled with the seeming contradictions in their culture.

By the time they reached Solaris Lake, the suns had fully set. The only light was that coming from the plants and the lake itself, which glowed faintly green, just as Dianthe had said it would. It was subtle, the orb probably covered in lake grasses and mud. Had he not known what he was looking at, he might have assumed he was seeing a reflection from something.

"At least we know we're in the right place," Tobias said, staring at the strangely lit surface.

"We should make camp," Sylas said. "We can retrieve it in the morning."

But Sabrina was already stripping out of her cloak. She was fully awake now, her eyes large and bright in the moonlight. "Why wait until morning? In the morning, the pollen gatherers will be back. I'll go now."

"You're not afraid to swim in dark waters?" Dianthe shivered, and Sylas was reminded that fairies feared the dark. It was when they were at their weakest. Her fatigue was evident in the dark bags beneath her eyes.

"I can see in the dark." Sabrina nodded in Tobias's direction. "And if I need backup, so can my mate. Why don't you two set up the tent, and I'll go get us an orb?"

At last Dianthe glanced at Sylas, for the first time since she'd stormed away in the forest. He almost gasped in relief. "Sure. That sounds like a good plan."

Tobias dropped the packs he was carrying and followed Sabrina to the edge of the water. She waded in without hesitation.

"Are you finally speaking to me again?" Sylas asked.

"I never said I wasn't speaking to you." Dianthe unzipped the tent bag and started staking down the base.

"You never said anything. You haven't said a word to me or looked me in the eye in over an hour." He helped her move the supports into place.

"I don't want to talk to you. Every time I do, you make me feel bad about myself. Do you know I haven't had a vision since the fire? I've never gone this long without one."

Sylas growled. "Maybe it's a sign that your abilities have been tampered with as I suspected."

Dianthe kicked the spike deeper into the ground and gave a frustrated grunt. "Raven ruled that out, Sylas!" She shook her head. "I think it's related to us. We've never had problems like this in our relationship before."

"Problems?" He couldn't believe what he was hearing. "What kind of problems?"

"Are you kidding me right now? We haven't had a day of smooth sailing since you escaped the palace. It's been one disagreement after another."

Sylas's jaw clenched. "That was only because of Aborella. We've been... together since then."

"Damn it, Sylas. I'm not talking about sex. I'm talking about getting along. Not fighting every second of the day."

"I don't know where this is coming from. We talk every day."

She stared at him incredulously. "For the first time, you don't believe in me. You don't trust my abilities. And because of that, I feel guilty for what happened. Do you know what I think, Sylas? I think you've gotten into my head. I think you've made me question my abilities. And I think because of that, I'm blocking my talent."

"Well... stop." Sylas finished pitching the tent, wondering how the conversation had gotten away from him. "It wasn't you I was questioning. It was Aborella."

She rolled her eyes toward the night sky. "You still don't get it, do you—"

"Sylas!" Tobias yelled. "Sabrina's not surfacing!"

CHAPTER THIRTEEN

Dianthe ran for the lake, Sylas at her side. Tobias had already stripped and dove in after Sabrina, but he hadn't broken the surface again. Deep within the lake, the water churned, sending up ripples and a few random bubbles. Shadows and silhouettes battled below, blocking out the green glow. What in Hades was going on?

"Oh my goddess!" All at once, Dianthe realized what was happening. Why hadn't she thought of this sooner? "I have to go in."

"What? Why?" Sylas's eyes widened with alarm. He grabbed her arm as she started undressing.

"It's the water sprites." She gestured in the general direction of the lake. "I'd forgotten that I used to play with them all those years ago. They're scared. It's natural they would see a non-fairy as a threat. I'm the only one who speaks ancient fae. I can make them understand what's happening."

"No." Sylas growled. "It's too dangerous. You're not going in there."

"Didn't you hear me? I'm the only one who can help." She fluttered her wings to fly over the water, but he pulled her down to his side.

"Sabrina doesn't have to breathe, and Tobias can hold his breath for ages. You can't." Sylas's expression was pleading.

She got the distinct impression he would have reached down his own mouth and extracted a lung to loan her if he could have. While she could sympathize with his protective instincts, she didn't have time for this shit.

"I've had your tooth. If I die, you can revive me."

"Don't joke. Not about that."

"I can do this, Sylas! I know these sprites. Let. Me. Go." She twisted out of his grip and flew as fast as she could over the deep water.

"Dianthe!" he called.

She dove straight toward the orb and the battle below. The water felt cooler than she remembered, and she tried not to shiver from her fear of what might linger below the dark surface. Fairies in general were stereotypically afraid of the dark, and she was no exception. By sheer will alone, she held her fear at bay as she descended into the murky depths.

As she closed in on the orb, she made out the scene well enough by its green light. The sprites fought Tobias's slashing claws and Sabrina's biting teeth with crude weapons made from sharp shards of stone. Normally the creatures appeared vividly majestic, the lower half of their bodies from the waist down painted with silvery-blue scales and a long fin that ran from their coccyx to the tapered end of their tail. Above the waist, their androgynous torsos—it was impossible to tell the males from the females—were long limbed and graceful. Along with oversized eyes and long, flowing hair, it was easy to understand why they were renowned for their beauty.

But that beauty had taken a dark turn. Tonight their razor-sharp teeth were on display, and they growled wickedly as they jabbed their sharp stones in Tobias's direction. The sprites had captured Sabrina in a tangle of lake weeds, the same type that surrounded the orb. The sheer number of vines holding her proved her capture was intentional and not the accidental work of her own making. Tobias was struggling manically to free her while simultaneously fighting off the sprites. There had to be a half dozen of them or more now.

Dianthe placed herself between the sprites and Tobias and spread her wings. Her fairy glow lit up the lake like a spotlight. The uniting vocabulary of all the natives of Everfield, regardless of species, was the old language, ancient fae. Technically you couldn't merely speak it but must sing the words underwater to be heard. Using every ounce of air she had in her lungs, she told the sprites that the vampire and the dragon were trying to help. As passionately as possible, she described the attack by the Obsidian Guard, the burning of the Empyrean Wood, and the threat the empress of Paragon posed to Everfield. She explained that the orb held magic that could be used to stop her and save the five kingdoms.

Out of air, she rose to the surface for a breath and

then returned again. The sprites acknowledged that they'd smelled the smoke and had wondered about the cause. With most of their lives lived underwater, they rarely heard news of the outside world unless a fairy availed themselves of their lake and was willing to share. As she suspected, once they understood, they halted their attack. Still, they would only agree to help her if she removed the vampire and dragon from their waters. The sprites didn't trust the outsiders.

Dianthe had expected that as well. Living as they did next to Nochtbend, it was perfectly logical the sprites would fear vampires. And considering she'd just told them that Paragon was trying to annex the other four kingdoms, could she ever expect them to trust a dragon? Knowing she'd never have enough breath to convince them otherwise, she quickly agreed to their demands.

Instantly, the sprites freed Sabrina, and at Dianthe's urging, Tobias carried the vampire to the surface. Dianthe met them there, gasping for breath. Tobias adjusted Sabrina in his arms, and she spewed lake water over his shoulder.

"Fucking sprites." She picked a piece of seaweed out of her fangs.

"They'll only give the orb to me," Dianthe explained. "You two have to go to shore. I'll be there soon."

"Sylas isn't going to like you going down there alone," Tobias said.

"Sylas doesn't have a choice. If he tries coming after me, make sure he knows that he might be jeopardizing our mission. I promised the sprites no vampires or dragons in exchange for their help. Don't let him complicate the matter."

Tobias scowled, but Sabrina grabbed him by the jaw. "Get me out of here. This is how it's got to go."

Dianthe was thankful for the backup.

He frowned but seemed resolved. "This isn't going to be pretty. Make it quick, Dianthe. You have no idea what this is going to do to him."

What was that supposed to mean? It wasn't as though she was asking him to hold Sylas's foot to a flame simply to keep his dragon from jeopardizing their mission. Whatever he was implying, it didn't matter—he spread his wings and lifted from the water with Sabrina in his arms.

Dianthe took three deep breaths and dove. The sprites, thank the goddess, made good on their word. Together, they removed the mud and vegetation covering the orb and then pried the sphere from the bottom of the lake. It was hard work and her lungs screamed in protest, hungry for oxygen.

Finally the green crystal was in her hands. She kicked for the surface, even using her wings to help her, but the orb weighed her down and slowed her progress. Dark spots swam in her vision. Her lungs burned. If she didn't reach the surface soon, the need for air would drive her insane. She fought her body's instinct to inhale while she was still underwater. Almost there.

It was too far. She couldn't make it. Until slender hands landed on her waist and pushed.

"She needs help." Sylas lunged toward the water's edge. "Can't you see she's taking too long to surface?"

Tobias grabbed his brother by the shoulders and held him in place. "You can't, brother. She negotiated with the water sprites. They don't trust vampires or dragons. They agreed to give the orb to her and her alone. If you go after her now, you'll ruin everything."

"Can't you see they mean to drown her? They want to keep the orb for themselves. Let me go. I must rescue her."

Tobias wrapped his arms around Sylas's chest from behind, locking down his wings. "No. Give her plan a chance. It hasn't been that long."

"I need to help my mate!" This time the words came from someplace deep and feral within him. His growl echoed over the water, the light from his eyes reflecting red off the lake. His dragon had come to the surface, his deepest self pining for his mate.

"Shhh," Tobias said. "She's going to be okay. Dianthe is a smart woman with good instincts. Give her one more minute. Just one more minute."

Although he had no doubt that his brother had the best of intentions, Sylas could hear a note of concern in the other man's voice. By this point, Tobias had to be wondering how long the average fairy could hold her breath underwater. Truthfully, although he was married to her, he wasn't sure the answer to that question. It wasn't something that came up in regular conversation. All he knew was that she had been under for what felt like an eternity, and waiting, thinking about her without oxygen, was pure torture.

Seconds ticked by. The water taunted him with its smooth surface. Where was she? What was happening? He struggled against his brother's hold, then felt something warm and wet trace down his cheek. Angrily, he wiped the tear away. *Damn it, Dianthe.* He willed her to come to the surface.

All at once, she burst out of the water as if someone had thrown her. From across the lake, he heard her gasp, her wings fluttering, lifting and holding her in the air. Tobias let him go and he burst out of his grip, his wings snapping out. He soared over the lake, swept her into his arms, and carried her and the orb to land. A lungful of water sprayed from her mouth, and he bent her in half and pounded her back with the heel of his hand.

"Hades, tell me you're all right, Dianthe!" At Tobias's prodding, he tossed the orb at his brother. Like he cared about the key right now. Compared to his mate's health, it was entirely inconsequential.

After a long bout of coughing, she leaned back into his arms and blinked up at him. Her hand rose to rest on his cheek where she wiped his tears away with her thumb. "I'm okay, Sylas," she said softly. "Everything is okay."

He stood, lifting her into his embrace, and buried his face in her neck, her wet hair soaking his shirt. "Thank the Mountain." He kissed her neck, her ear, her cheek.

"Sylas..."

Carefully he set her on her feet and cupped her face in

both hands. Her lips were close. Her lavender-and-honey scent invaded his lungs and brought him a modicum of peace. She was here. She was all right. He leaned in a fraction of an inch, captured her mouth with his own.

"Mmmm." Her fingers dug into his hair, her lips parting, welcoming him in.

The kiss was desperate, claiming. He teased her lips, nipped at her throat. All he wanted to do was find a place in the darkness to be inside her. Goddess, he wanted her. Wanted her like he'd never wanted anything. The idea that they were sharing a single tent with Tobias and Sabrina suddenly disappointed him beyond measure.

He brushed her wet hair back from her face. Her hungry gaze raked over him. The magnetic draw between them ratcheted up a notch.

She shivered in his arms.

He paused, pulled back. "You're cold. We need to start a fire."

"I'm fine." Her hand snaked to the back of his head again. "Stay close. You'll keep me warm."

But he could feel she was soaked. Goddess, she'd barely been breathing a moment ago, and he was all over her like an animal. "We need a fire now," he called to his brother. "She's going to catch her death."

"I'm on it," Tobias called from the other side of the tent. "Sabrina's gathering wood."

"I've had your tooth. I *can't* catch my death." Dianthe suddenly sounded perturbed. She lifted onto her tiptoes, pressing into him.

"We should get you out of these wet clothes. Make you something hot to drink."

Dianthe took a step back, her hands fisting. "I said I'm not cold." As she backed away from him, she crossed her arms, huddling in on herself in direct opposition to her words.

"You certainly look cold to me," he said pointedly.

"I'm going to get changed." She shook her head and marched toward the tent.

Totally confused, Sylas massaged the bridge of his nose. Why was she so angry? What the hell had just happened?

CHAPTER FOURTEEN

That obsessive, pigheaded man! Dianthe avoided Sylas for the rest of the evening, eating her ration in relative silence. After all they'd been through: losing their home, Eleanor's attack. After being at each other's throats for days... He'd spoiled a perfect, passionate moment with his overbearing need to protect her. Oh, she'd been mated to a dragon long enough to accept that his instincts were difficult for him to deny. No way did she expect to break him of the instinct to keep her safe, nor would she want to. But lately he wasn't just being protective, he was being demeaning, overlooking her strengths and contributions and demoting her to a damsel in distress over and over again. She couldn't take it anymore.

He'd never even congratulated her for recovering the orb or for saving Tobias and Sabrina from the sprites. He'd been so obsessed with her safety, he'd even interrupted a romantic encounter! He would rather cocoon her in a blanket and feed her tea next to the fire like some ancient and decrepit grandmother than make love to her. If he could, he'd enclose her in a magic bubble and carry her back to Aeaea where she'd float like a balloon at his side for all eternity.

Ugh, it made her furious. She'd more than proved herself a powerful ally to the rebellion, and all she wanted was for him to acknowledge that. She wanted his trust and his respect. She wanted to be treated how she treated him, like an equal.

The moment she'd finished her dinner, she'd excused herself and gone to bed, hoping that sleep would improve her mood. When she woke early the next morning, Sylas was wrapped around her like a blanket, the entire length of his lean, well-muscled body spooning her from behind. The position made it exceedingly difficult to remember why she'd been cross with him. Not that it particularly surprised her. For the sake of efficiency, they were crowded in a tent with a four-person occupancy, their sleeping bag less than a foot away from Tobias's, who was, at the moment, snoring loudly enough to wake the dead. What else did she expect? This wasn't a camping trip. They'd had to travel light. Only the necessities.

Still, if she stayed this close to those hard abs and his delicious smoky anise scent, she'd be tempted to pick up where they left off last night. This wasn't the time or the place. Slowly and carefully she extracted herself from Sylas's arms and tiptoed between the sleeping dragons. Pulling on her cloak, she slipped out the tent flap.

Sabrina had kept watch last night. The orb at her side gave off a strange, mystical glow. She turned to greet Dianthe, and her eyes betrayed her growing fatigue.

Already, light streamed over Solaris Field. She supposed as a vampire, Sabrina would usually be in bed by now.

"I'm up," Dianthe said. "You can sleep if you want. It's barely dawn. Maybe you can get a few hours in before we leave."

"I'll do that." Sabrina moved for the door of the tent but paused and turned to her. "I didn't have a chance to tell you thank you last night. It was a brave thing that you did. If you hadn't addressed the sprites, I fear blood would have been shed. It might have been mine."

"It was the least I could do," Dianthe said automatically.

"No." Sabrina shook her head. "You could have done nothing or sent Sylas in after us. You were brave. You told me you fear the dark."

She looked down at her feet. "Well, I'd forgotten this lake was populated by sprites. I should have warned you."

The tall redhead moved closer to her. Sabrina's gaze was intense, and she carried herself with the long-limbed grace of royalty. Dianthe knew instantly that she never wanted to cross the vampire. One of her pale hands came to rest on Dianthe's shoulder.

"I am thankful that you are the brave, strong woman you are. It's difficult to stand up to one's mate, especially when one is married to a dragon. I know better than anyone. But it's clear Colin was right. We need you on this mission. You've already made a difference. Never forget that." Sabrina slipped inside the tent, leaving Dianthe alone to process the unexpected compliment.

She sat next to the orb by the fire and stared at the

border of Nochtbend. None of them knew what to expect when they crossed into the kingdom of the vampires. What she needed was a vision. She needed to see what was ahead for them.

A seer could not control what she saw or when she saw it, but sometimes they could open a window to their mind in a way that invited a vision in. She thought of it like sprinkling birdseed in a cage and leaving the door open so the bird could fly in. It had been days since she'd had a vision. The trauma of the fire and her deteriorating relationship with Sylas had her tied up in knots.

It was time to loosen those strings. Her family needed her. The mission needed her. She couldn't let Sylas or anyone else get in the way of what she'd promised she'd do. She owed Everfield that much.

Pushing all thoughts from her mind, she closed her eyes and took a deep, cleansing breath. "You can do this," she whispered to herself. Her mind relaxed. The door opened. And she waited.

And waited.

And waited.

The vision started as a cramp low in her abdomen that rolled up through her stomach and stole the breath from her lungs before flooding into her head. Her lashes fluttered against the temporary blindness that accompanied her second sight. She tipped her head back. A rush of color and sound zoomed in—the Obsidian Guard, dressed in their red-and-black uniforms, trudged through the remains of the Empyrean Wood. Goddess no! They were back en masse. Why did they have shovels? Why were they digging in the ash? By Hades, there were hundreds of them.

"What are we looking for?" one soldier asked another.

"We don't know, only that we need to find it before the rebels do."

"That's it? We're just going to dig up the entire forest looking for *something*?"

The man shook his head. "The seer told her it was in a metal box, buried in the ash. Keep digging and keep an eye out for a group of four fairies. Our spies have spotted four known rebels in Everfield. They'll be after the same thing."

Dianthe snapped back into the present, her heart pounding. Frantically she looked around her, then toward the Empyrean Wood. She saw a flash of red moving among the charred tree trunks. A guardsman. Oh dear goddess, they were already here!

"Wake up. Wake up!" she whispered loudly, her head poked inside the tent. She grabbed Sylas's toes and shook.

"Dianthe? What's going on?" he mumbled, rubbing sleep from his eyes.

"We need to go. We need to leave now." She remembered that she'd left the orb unguarded and ducked out of the tent to return to her post, gathering it into her arms. The fire was still smoldering, and she kicked dirt to smother it. She prayed the guards wouldn't see the smoke.

Sylas followed her from the tent. "What's going on?"

"We have to leave. Pack quickly. Tell Tobias and

Sabrina."

"They're already dressing. What's happened? What did you see?"

"The Obsidian Guard is here in Everfield. They're digging in the Empyrean Wood, digging up the ash. They're looking for a metal box that they think holds something four rebels want." She pointed toward the forest.

Sylas narrowed his eyes, clearly spotting the uniforms among the trees. "They're much too close for comfort."

"I know." She frowned. "Let's get out of here."

He hastened into the tent and emerged moments later with their two packs. She took one and slung it onto her back. The faintest green glow shone through the zipper on the side of his bag. Good, he'd packed the orb.

"How do they know?" Tobias broke down the tent at record speed and stuffed it into his pack while Sabrina snored on the ground beside him.

"Mother had spies watching Aeaea. Whoever it was likely saw the four of us arrive in port," Sylas said.

Dianthe frowned. "One of the guards in my vision said that the seer was very specific—a metal box under the ash. They must be talking about Aborella. What other seer has ever helped Eleanor?"

"But it doesn't make any sense." Tobias donned both his and Sabrina's packs and then lifted her into his arms. "There is no metal box, is there?"

Sylas shook his head. "No. No one in the rebellion is looking for anything in the ash. We didn't keep a single thing of importance in our Everfield home."

Dianthe shrugged. "I can't explain it. Nothing in my

vision explains it."

"Maybe Aborella misinterpreted a vision about the orbs. You did retrieve the orb from a type of dark prison. Maybe she envisioned it as a box and the water as ash."

"It's possible. The Empyrean Wood is crawling with guards. I propose we thank the stars that she got it wrong and make for Grimtwist."

"Agreed." They hiked the short distance to the Nochtbend border and paused outside the line of dark, twisting trees that demarcated the edge of the Grimtwist Forest. Mist curled off the forest floor and crept across the ground toward their toes. The dense canopy of leaves blocked out all light, making it impossible to see far into its unwelcoming interior. Dianthe gulped. As if she hadn't had enough chilling darkness the night before.

Dianthe had never been to Nochtbend—it wasn't exactly a vacation destination—but she had heard stories. The vampires lived belowground during the day, only coming topside to hunt at night. It was said that vicious monsters of unimaginable size roamed their lands, put in place by the master vampire himself to protect the kingdom. Master Demidicus had ruled Nochtbend for centuries from an underground palace called Nightfall. She'd heard horrific stories about the things that went on in that palace. It was said that prisoners of all species were kept alive in cold, dark cells, only to be periodically drained of their blood to feed the vampires. She suppressed a shiver.

"Any idea where the second orb might be?" Tobias asked.

They were all still standing at the border, staring into

the woods. No one seemed overly motivated to take the next step. Dianthe knew he meant the question for her.

She shook her head. "I tried. The vision didn't come to me. Sometimes I can't force it."

Sabrina rubbed her face and yawned. "Where does the master of the largest coven in this kingdom live?"

"There is only one coven and only one master. Master Demidicus," Dianthe said. "And he lives in Nightfall. It's a subterranean palace along the northern border."

"Take me there. He'll have the orb," Sabrina said with absolute certainty before snuggling into Tobias's chest and closing her eyes again.

"How do you know?" Dianthe looked at her curiously.

"Because I sat next to that thing all night." Without opening her eyes, she pointed in the general direction of Sylas's pack. "The power coming off of it made my skin tingle. If there is one thing that vampires love, especially powerful ones, it's skin-tingling magic. I'm willing to bet that not only does Demidicus have the orb of Nochtbend, but he also likely keeps it close to his person."

"I don't know the way," Dianthe said. "I've heard where it is in general, but—"

"I do," Sylas said. "I've met with rebels in Nightfall, although I didn't come from this direction. Before, I followed the river halfway to Paragon before cutting through Grimtwist. Still, I'm sure I can get us there." He darted a glance between them.

No words were spoken, but an agreement was made. Together, they crossed into Nochtbend.

CHAPTER FIFTEEN

Dragons could see in the dark. They were born in the heart of the mountain, after all. Designed for cave living. Still, Sylas preferred the light. More importantly, he preferred to see his wife smiling in the sunlight, brought alive by the two suns that daily crossed Ouros's sky.

The darkness in Grimtwist Woods was almost absolute. Just inside the tree line, he reached out to lead Dianthe. Not only could she not see in the dark, she hated it with a passion. But instead of accepting his offered hand, she squeezed and then released it before she spread her wings and glowed. "I know I'm the only one who needs this, but I'd prefer to be able to see where I'm going."

Tobias raised his eyebrows. "That's a neat trick. How long can you keep it up?"

She grinned. "Fairies are naturally phosphorescent when they want to be. As long as we get enough sun during the day, we can glow all night."

"Let's hope it doesn't attract anything... unpleasant." Sylas searched the darkness for the beasts of legend that roamed these woods.

"It isn't practical for me to hold your hand the entire time."

Beside them, Sabrina gave a snort and then resumed her snoring. Tobias shifted her in his arms but kept on walking. A pang of something suspiciously like jealousy shot through Sylas's heart. Would Dianthe ever let him carry her like that? She wouldn't even let him lead her by the hand. Why was it suddenly a sin for him to want to care for his mate?

Sylas took the lead, heading in the general direction of the Palace of Nightfall. Dianthe dropped behind, off to the side of Tobias and Sabrina. He found himself distracted by her distance. If a creature attacked her, would he be able to get to her in time? Why was she so far away from the group?

Goddess, he was a dragon and she was his mate. Nature intended for him to guard her with his life. He would protect her. He would worry for her. He would keep her from harm. Whether she liked it or not. Sometimes a dragon knew what was best for his mate.

He walked closer to her. "Stay near me," he said. "There are deadly creatures in these woods."

"I'm aware." She walked faster, putting more space between them.

"Did you hear me? That's not closer, Dianthe."

"I know."

"What will you do if one of these beasts attacks? You have no claws. Your teeth are barely sharp at all."

She glared at him. "I'll fly away."

Infernal woman! "What if the beast can fly?"

Stopping short, she turned to him, glowing brighter. Her lavender-and-honey scent increased with her light. "I guess it will eat me."

His mouth fell open. "That's not funny, Dianthe."

"Honestly, Sylas, I'd rather be eaten by a Grimtwist beast than act like your helpless pet female, huddling beside you out of fear that some unseen threat will harm me!"

She turned on her heel and strode off again, mumbling something about pigheaded dragons.

He strode faster still, catching up to her. Any faster and one of them would have to break into a jog. "I never treated you like a *pet*. Never."

"No?" Without slowing her stride, she glared at him over her shoulder. "You didn't want to keep me in the gilded cage of Aeaea Island, like your own personal parrot, even though you knew my talents were badly needed on this mission?"

"Only to keep you safe, Dianthe!"

"Don't you get it, Sylas? I don't want to be safe. I want to be—"

Dianthe's attention moved from him to the ground beside him. She missed a step and stopped walking. So did he. The leaves rustled, only there was no wind, nothing to cause their movement. The vibration turned into a full-fledged rumble that filled the forest around them. The earth shook hard enough to rattle his teeth.

"Fly, Dianthe! Fly!" He pushed her out of the trajectory of the vibration heading toward them.

Thankfully, for once she obeyed. She lifted into the air, landing on a twisted, mossy branch above his head. The dirt opened like a sinkhole, and rows and rows of teeth burst forth beneath him. His wings snapped out and he lifted from the earth, barely avoiding its gaping maw.

He'd heard tales of the Grimtwist hornworms, massive carnivorous beasts that were larger than any dragon and lived underground in this part of the world, but seeing one was far more horrific than what he'd produced in his imagination. The thing appeared to have no eyes, only two slits that might have been a nose on a smooth, gray-skinned body. Its defining characteristic was its teeth—rows and rows of teeth as long as he was tall—which spiraled around the tongue and into the throat. The thing was an earth-moving eating machine.

He veered right and it reared, blindly sniffing the air. He was right about it having no eyes; it was clearly following his scent. Only then it stopped and changed direction, reaching for Dianthe in her tree. She lifted off her branch, flying higher, but the thing continued to grow from the earth, ten feet, twenty. How long was the beast?

It was tracking her, locked on Dianthe's delicious scent. He had to do something.

"Over here!" Sylas yelled, flying toward the worm at full speed. Did the creature even have ears? If it did, it didn't turn at his voice until he was almost on top of it. Even when he buzzed by dangerously close to the worm, it ignored him in pursuit of her. Which left him no choice. He flew between the worm and Dianthe.

The beast's mouth snapped closed around him, and everything went dark.

CHAPTER SIXTEEN

Dianthe screamed. Her body trembled with panic. Sylas was gone, swallowed whole and now within the belly of the beast. Worse, said beast was descending back into the earth. What could she do? She didn't have so much as a knife to throw at the infernal creature.

A roar came from the left and a silvery-white dragon swooped in, its teeth sinking into the hornworm's throat. Tobias! Thank the Mountain.

Dianthe landed on a branch and watched her mate's brother dig his dragon claws in and haul the worm backward. Inch by inch, Tobias pulled it from the ground. The slimy gray body kept coming and coming, sliding from a hole in the dirt wider than her entire cottage had been. She gasped when its tail flicked from the dirt.

"Sylas!" she screamed. Could he still be alive in there? Or was he shredded by its enormous teeth? Dragons were tough, naturally immortal, but they could be killed. Beheading was the most certain way, but there were others. She knew nothing of the nature of this beast or its effect on dragons. Panic wrapped around her heart and squeezed. Sylas... Oh Sylas. Why had he flown so close?

Suddenly the worm let forth a strangled cry, its middle bloating like an overfilled balloon. Tobias's dragon dropped the thing's neck. *Pop!* Gray and brown flesh exploded from the worm's center in a spray of blood that left the trees dripping and everything below her covered in goo. Sylas's garnet-red dragon stood at the center of the carnage, wings outstretched, heart glowing bright red within his chest. His dragon sucked in a deep breath and sneezed, sending bits of worm flying across the woods.

Dianthe had always thought Sylas's dragon was exceptionally beautiful. Even in the darkness, his garnet scales reflected hints of sunset orange. He was lankier in this form than his brothers, with a gracefully long body and proportionally long and deadly teeth and talons. The only word she had for him was majestic.

He shook like a dog, clearing blood and guts from his scales before shifting back into his *soma* form. She swooped down from her perch and pulled him into her arms, kissing him ardently. Her hands slid over his naked, slime-covered skin, not caring one bit that the filth was spreading all over her as well.

"Oh Sylas. Goddess, I was so worried."

At first his kiss was as passionate as hers, but then she felt him pulling away. Even before his lips parted from hers, she could feel the mental difference, the subtle shifting of his body, until he grabbed her by the shoulders and forced distance between them. His breath came in ragged pants. He pointed one hand northwest.

"If I remember correctly, there's a lake about a mile in that direction. I need to get cleaned up, as do you. And then we need to talk." He dug through the worm's remains and pulled his pack from a particularly globular mass of flesh. After giving it a good shake, he loaded it onto his back, then strode in the direction of the lake.

"Don't you want to get dressed, brother?" Tobias asked. He was donning the clothes he must have stripped out of before shifting.

"Don't want to get a fresh set dirty. Besides, I doubt that was the only hornworm."

Tobias lifted his packs onto his back and then collected the still-sleeping Sabrina from the base of a nearby tree. Dianthe followed behind them, overwhelmed with warring emotions and wondering if the schism that had appeared between her and her mate had become too deep to mend or cross. For the second time in as many days, a passionate kiss had ended with one of them angry.

It would be easy to presume that all their problems had begun when they'd fled Everfield after the raid by the Obsidian Guard, but she knew their marriage had been on the rocks for far longer than that. He'd been gone a lot the previous year, traveling the five kingdoms leading the rebellion in Colin's absence. And then he was imprisoned in the dungeons of Paragon. When he'd finally escaped and she'd come for him, that was when she'd found Aborella. She'd insisted on bringing the fairy home to heal her even though Sylas was against it. And then he'd refused to sleep in the same cottage as Aborella, and so they'd spent even more time apart. When she thought back to the past year, maybe longer, she saw more loneliness, more separation than togetherness.

Had she allowed this to happen? Was she complicit in their gradual drifting apart? For a dragon, a mating was forever. Sylas would never love anyone but her. And she undeniably loved him. But loving someone and being able to live with them were two different things. Maybe there were just too many hurts for either of them to endure.

They walked in silence until they reached a lake, which thankfully was in full sun. Tobias stopped at the edge of the shadows.

"I'll stay here with Sabrina," he said to her. "Go, talk to him."

Sylas dove in, the blood from the hornworm creating a muddy cloud in the water around him. When he broke the surface, Dianthe's breath caught in her throat. Her mate rose from the water, a tower of tightly corded muscle and golden skin. The water shone like diamonds on the two block-shaped mounds of his chest and carved tempting trails through the shadowy valleys of his deliciously tight abdomen. They disappeared below the surface to where she knew the rest of him was just as inviting.

She raised her eyes to his and was snared by his gray gaze, unable to move. He'd caught her ogling him. He knew she wanted him. A wickedly inviting grin twitched at the corners of his lips.

Dropping her pack next to his on the shore, she waded in and washed the worm stains from the front of her dress. The bottom of the lake was lined with large stones, and she felt off-balance as she leaned forward and splashed her face with the cool, pure water. When she wiped the excess from her eyes, he was there. Sylas was standing right in front of her, his smile gone, replaced by sternly pressed lips.

"We haven't stopped fighting since we left Everfield, Dianthe. We need to work things out between us before it endangers our mission."

She gulped at the intensity in his stare. He was right. This conversation was long overdue. "Thank you for what you did back there with the worm. I know you thought you were protecting me."

"I *was* protecting you."

She tipped her head. "I was out of its reach, almost through the canopy, Sylas. It never would have reached me."

"You didn't know how long it was."

She frowned. "But I did know it couldn't move through trees. I'd moved sideways. It was reaching straight up." She saw a muscle in his jaw jump. "Listen, all I wanted to do was say thank you. I didn't want this to turn into another fight."

"I don't want to fight either," he said. "I just want you to stop taking unnecessary risks."

She blinked twice. "What unnecessary risks have I taken?"

He put his hands on his hips and gave her an incredulous look. "Refusing my hand. Not walking close to me. Planning things with Colin without talking to me first."

A gasp escaped her lips. "I don't need your permission to do my job for the rebellion."

"I didn't mean it like that, and you know it."

"I think you did mean it like that. I think you wish Raven had found a curse so that you'd have an excuse to keep me barefoot in the kitchen while you risked your life saving Ouros."

He scoffed. "It worked out pretty well last year."

Her hands balled into fists and she took a step back, shaking her head. So many thoughts rattled through her brain, she didn't know where to begin. Finally she grasped at what she felt was the root of the issue. "The real problem is that you stopped believing in me the moment I told you about my vision of Aborella helping us. You sat back and waited for me to fail."

He closed his eyes and shook his head. "I didn't want you to fail. I simply knew better what we were dealing with when it came to that wicked, filthy fairy."

"Did you know her better?" She narrowed her eyes. "Are you sure? Were you *so certain* that my vision would be wrong and she would betray us?"

"Someone is behind Eleanor attacking Everfield. Aborella is the most likely culprit. She went straight back to the Obsidian Palace and told Eleanor everything."

The events of the past couple of days had come and gone so fast that Dianthe had barely had a chance to process any of it. But now, thinking back, adrenaline still coursing through her blood, everything became crystal clear.

"If Aborella had told Eleanor everything, those guards would have come straight to our home. They didn't. They were looking for a traitor among our kind, but they didn't know who it was."

He rubbed the back of his neck.

"I think Aborella is telling her something, but she isn't telling her everything."

"What's your point? She told her enough to have the Empyrean Wood destroyed. Not exactly someone we would call a friend."

Memories of Aborella flashed through Dianthe's brain. Nursing her back to health. Conversations they'd had by the fire. Baking together. There was light in her heart, Dianthe was sure of it. "Maybe we can't call her a friend, but I'm not sure we can blame everything on her either."

"Oh?"

"Why are the guards digging in the Empyrean Wood? Why are they looking for four rebels and not the heirs of Paragon? Don't you see, Sylas? She's posing as Eleanor's seer, but I think she's giving her false information."

Sylas shook his head. "It's possible, but you can't be sure."

"What other explanation might you have?"

"Maybe Eleanor wants us to worry about her right hand while she plans something diabolical with her left."

"You think the attack was a distraction."

"Mother did attack my family when they arrived near Aeaea. Aborella must have told her the truth then. Why are you still making excuses for her anyway?"

She'd forgotten about the attack at Aeaea. She bowed her head. "This isn't about Aborella. It's about you *believing* in me."

He scoffed and turned his head away. "I've always believed in you."

"No, you lost respect for me the moment I brought Aborella back with us. You said yes, but you meant no."

"I've always respected you. I still respect you." His voice cracked.

"Do you remember when we met? I was already working for the rebellion. You came in, new, ignorant. I taught you the ropes. We fell in love, and the thing I remember most about those days is how you looked at me. You looked at me like I had all the answers. You were homeless. Cast out by your own mother. We made a home together in Everfield."

"I remember and I'm so grateful, Dianthe."

"So why can't you look at me like that now? Why can't you admit that you need me as much as I need you? You've been treating me like a child."

A muscle in his jaw twitched. "I do need you. I need you as much as the air I breathe. Why in Hades do you think I wanted to spare you this? Why do you think I let that hornworm eat me to distract it from you?"

She shook her head. "This is beyond wanting me safe. You want to control me. You want to lock me up like a jewel and wrap me in wards so tight I won't be able to breathe."

His face was red now, and that muscle in his jaw was doing one hell of a dance. "I never wanted to control you!" His voice was gruff and deep, his dragon rising to the surface. She tried to take a step back, but he grabbed her by the shoulders. "You knew what I was when you mated me. You knew I was a dragon. Dragons protect their mates."

"Of course I knew!" She groaned as he shook her again. He wasn't gripping her hard, but she didn't like how his skin roiled with his anger. His entire body was trembling. "You're scaring me."

"It tears me apart when you're in danger. Do you know what it was like to wait on that beach while you battled those sprites last night? It felt like a million bees buzzing in my head, stinging and crawling until I thought my skull might crack from the pressure. Every cell in my body is charged with one simple command that overrides every rational thought when you're in danger. 'Save her! Protect her.'"

She pulled away from him. "Would it kill you to acknowledge my contributions to our mission? Even Sabrina said thank you. I clung to the words of a vampire I hardly know because you, the person I call my family, did not so much as acknowledge my work. I am the one who accomplished the first phase of our mission. I got the orb." She pointed her thumb at her chest.

"Thank you!" he bit out. "Is that what you want to hear? Thank you for risking your life for a fucking magic ball—"

She pressed her finger into his chest. "You need me on this mission, Sylas. I can do things none of you can do. And yes, I need your protection. But you need me too. And that means you need to trust me. You need to respect me. And you need to stop treating me like a child."

"I never—"

"You're smothering me! Just back off!" Goddess, she wished she could take it back. The words lashed out, and his previously red face blanched. He rubbed his chest as if it hurt. She'd gone too far. She'd broken his heart.

"I understand." His voice was laced with contempt. "I'll do my best not to *smother* you anymore." He passed her to get to the beach and dug in his pack for, she assumed, a change of clothes. For someone whose blood naturally ran hot, the breeze she felt coming from his direction was decidedly cold.

"Sylas..." She didn't know what to say.

When a dragon mated, he mated for life. The bond was both biology and magic. He couldn't break it if he tried. But as her husband dressed and donned his pack without ever looking back in her direction, she wondered if she was about to learn how far a bond could stretch.

CHAPTER SEVENTEEN

The hike toward the Palace of Nightfall was an exercise in tedium. Sylas schooled himself in restraint, refusing to even look at Dianthe. Although it went against every instinct in his dragon body, he realized it was what she needed. It was what she'd asked for. In a roundabout way, it came from a place of love.

Smothered, she'd said. It was a harsh insult to a dragon. There were stories of his kind losing their minds and keeping their loved ones prisoner in their treasure room. Smothered was a way of saying he'd crossed the line into obsession. She'd accused him of killing her with his protective instinct. He scowled. He was still trying to figure out how she was both hiking through a dark forest in the vampire kingdom and being smothered.

But fine, if that's how she felt, he'd give her space. And if that space came with the sharp edge of his anger, well, nobody was perfect.

He was relieved not to have encountered any more

hornworms and to recognize some landmarks from his last visit to Nochtbend. They were close to the Palace of Nightfall, which was a good thing considering the suns were setting. Soon the vampires would awaken, and he would much rather be inside Nightfall's gates, speaking directly to Master Demidicus about their mission, than out here, potentially fighting off the unwanted attention of hungry vampires in a dark wood.

They reached the mouth of the cave entrance just as Sabrina yawned and stretched in her mate's arms. Another pang of jealousy hit Sylas squarely in the heart as the two kissed and exchanged good mornings. Dianthe might be right behind him, but she felt miles away at the moment. Her scent rubbed like sandpaper against his senses. Normally enjoyable, now it simply left his insides raw.

"Nightfall is through here," he said. "There will be guardians at the entrance. Hold very still and allow them to smell you. If you remain calm, we won't have a problem getting inside."

"What kind of guardians?" Sabrina asked. "We use humans in our coven. Tobias told me there are no humans here."

"Hellhounds," Sylas said. "It is said they were a gift from Hades himself to the first of their kind."

Tobias scratched his head. "I've never seen a hellhound. They sound positively unpleasant."

"Think of them like magical wards. They are trained to keep out those with malicious intentions. We don't have any. We simply want their help and cooperation. Keep a positive mindset and they won't hurt you."

"*Can* they hurt us?" Tobias asked.

It was a good question. "I haven't tested the rumor, but the vampires claim the hellhound's bite is poisonous to all but vampires."

Sabrina chuckled. "So if this goes badly, I'm carrying you all out of here. Got it."

"Positive thoughts. Simple enough," Dianthe mumbled.

Funny. After their fight today, thinking positively seemed a particularly difficult task.

As Sylas stepped into the dark mouth of the cave, he thought it was a great metaphor for what was happening in their relationship. Their future was just as dark and uncertain. When he'd stopped to talk to her in the lake, he'd expected they'd exchange apologies and move on. But what she'd said to him was not something an "I'm sorry" could fix.

Smothered. His mind circled back to what she'd said. The word played on repeat in his head; he couldn't seem to move beyond it. She, whom he was leading into a dark, forbidding cave, felt *smothered.*

He still wasn't sure what to do with that information. Nothing about the past few days made him feel he had earned that label. For the Mountain's sake, should he have let her be swallowed by the hornworm?

His reverie was interrupted when the low, menacing growl of a hellhound filled the cave. By the light of Dianthe's glow, he saw the darkness melt into the shape of a dark dog with prominent teeth and long, lean muscles that gave it a sickly and gaunt physique. The things always looked hungry. What they ate, he had no idea, but by the glare in their red eyes, he'd always assumed it must be souls.

"Good doggy," Tobias whispered beside him.

The hellhound sniffed his hand and then the general area of his torso.

Behind him, Dianthe said nothing, but her scent and light shifted. She'd moved from his right to stand between him and Tobias. Clearly she was afraid. He was tempted to take her hand but forced himself to leave it right where it was. Their relationship would never heal if he didn't honor her request to be trusted with her own safety.

"I'm jealous," Sabrina said. He hadn't seen her move ahead of them, but she was already deep inside the cave, scratching a hellhound behind the ears. "They're the perfect guardians. Do you think I could buy one to bring back to Chicago with me?"

Tobias winced. "Absolutely not."

"Oh, but they're so cute." She made a kissy sound, and the hound licked her face. "I think this one is still a baby. He's smaller."

Sylas moved past the hound to the iron portcullis at the back of the cave and pulled a ribbon hanging against the wall. A bell inside rang, and a vampire appeared on the other side of the metal. Ruthgard, thankfully a member of the Defenders of the Goddess.

"Sylas. I never thought we'd see you back here. Last I heard, you were rotting in the dungeons of Paragon."

"Pleasure to see you again, Ruthgard. Lucky break. I was cleared of all charges and freed. My friends and I need to speak with Master Demidicus. It's important."

Ruthgard glanced over his shoulder and then back at Sylas. "I don't believe for a second that Eleanor let you go." He chuckled. "Fugitive or not, you know I want to help you, but no one gets to the master without going through Zaruki."

"Then let us speak to Zaruki." Sylas cracked his neck. Zaruki's loyalties were questionable. Like the master, she wasn't a member of the rebellion but also wasn't enamored with the empress. If she had any loyalty at all, it was to Nochtbend.

"Wait here." Ruthgard left so quickly all Sylas could track was a blur.

"Who's Zaruki?" Tobias asked.

Sabrina picked at something under her nail. "That would be the master's right-hand man. Likely a deadly killer who would just as soon rip us apart as have a little chat. Mine can smell trouble a mile away."

Sylas chuckled. "She's female, but other than that, you are exactly right."

Tobias nudged his arm. "Should we be disguising ourselves?"

Sylas shook his head. "Won't work here. You can't hide the scent of dragon blood in a room full of vampires."

"I can attest to that," Sabrina concurred.

"Being dragons is one thing, but do they have to know we're the heirs?"

"The master will know. He's been around since before we were children. Trust me, Tobias, he'll know, no matter how we look on the outside. Lucky for us, there is no love lost between Nochtbend and Paragon. They have two members on the Highborn Court who are sympathetic with Eleanor, but they do not live here in the palace. Demidicus can't abide their company. With any luck, we won't encounter them."

Tobias ran a hand over his face. "With any luck."

The blur was back. "Zaruki will see you now. Follow me." The portcullis lifted, and Sylas followed Ruthgard inside. The rough-hewn walls gradually gave way to more sophisticated surroundings: warm wood floors, walls covered in art, gold fixtures. Strange music played softly in the background, piped in through camouflaged speakers.

"Here we are." Ruthgard opened a door and gestured into a room with a long gathering table.

At the head of the table, Zaruki waited. She did not smile as they filed into the room, just watched them with an intense, unblinking stare. Zaruki had always reminded Sylas of a cat. Her long crimson nails were filed to sharp points like claws, and her narrow, dark brown eyes had the natural slope of a feline's. If there was one word to describe her, it would be *narrow*. Every part of her was exceptionally long, from her legs that stretched the full height of the table, to her arms that reminded him of tree branches, to her abnormally lengthy neck that supported an oval head with a pointed chin and a ponytail of platinum hair. Under a thick fringe of bangs, her complexion was always pale. He'd never seen it pink from anger, exertion, or embarrassment. He didn't think she was capable of it.

Once the four of them were in the room and had taken positions around the table, Sylas bowed halfway as was the custom among the vampires. He knew better than to extend his hand. "Thank you for seeing us."

"I received word that someone killed a full-grown hornworm overday in Grimtwist. I assume that was you." She scowled her disapproval.

Sylas skirted the issue—after all, she hadn't directly asked a question. "We've come to speak to Master Demidicus about Paragon's recent attack on Everfield. We have reason to believe it was the first but definitely not the last. Your kingdom is likely the next in her crosshairs."

"As much as I am sympathetic to your plight as exiled heir, I think your assessment of the situation is biased by your history with Paragon. Representatives Armand and Viessa claim that Everfield broke the universal law. They were harboring a fugitive from Paragon. Paragon was within its rights to retaliate." Her gaze fell on Sylas. Did she know that he was said fugitive?

Dianthe snapped, "And apprehending this fugitive requires burning the Empyrean Wood to the ground? Killing innocent fairy elders and children? Forcing an entire community into homelessness?"

Sylas wished she hadn't poured so much emotion into her words. The vampires were rarely moved by emotional pleas but loved to use their adversaries' triggers against them.

As expected, Zaruki's face remained impassive. "While I am sure certain fairies found themselves in the wrong place at the wrong time, I am told that the Elder Tree still stands, as does the solarium. Clearly the destruction of Everfield was not as complete as you are suggesting."

Dianthe gritted her teeth. "The homes of Everfield's Highborn Court representatives were untouched. The very citizens who should defend Everfield against Paragon once again find themselves in a position where they've experienced no loss, have no skin in the game, and can easily turn their back on the hundreds of innocent fairies unfairly left in squalor."

Oh fuck. Sylas attempted to smooth things over. "What we are trying to say—"

"Nochtbend cannot become involved in a disagreement between Everfield and Paragon. I will have someone show you out." Zaruki moved dismissively toward the door.

Sabrina blocked her path, her red hair seeming to grow brighter in the intensity of the moment. Her fangs descended with impressive control. "You will take us to your master."

"Who are you, vampire?" Zaruki stared, unblinking, at Sabrina.

The redhead did not smile or bow but raised her chin in order to stare down her nose at the other woman. "I am Sabrina Bishop, master of the Lamia Coven."

"Master? I know nothing of this coven. Where do you hail from?"

"Chicago," she said. "I've come a great distance."

Zaruki arched an eyebrow. "I am not familiar with

Chicago or with your coven. But I'm curious why you would travel a great distance to insert yourself in a minor political skirmish in the five kingdoms?" She sniffed, a clear message in her eyes—*mind your own coven.*

"I will speak with your master now!" Sabrina said firmly.

Zaruki turned her attention back to Sylas. "The vampires of Nochtbend have chosen to remain neutral in this political affair. We've never cared for the empress's vision of uniting the kingdoms, but until the Obsidian Guard sets foot on Nochtbend soil, we will not involve ourselves." Her eyes drifted to Sabrina again. "Now, I will call Ruthgard to show you out."

Sabrina's green eyes shifted to Tobias. He gave her a small nod. "Zaruki, I challenge you for your position in Nochtbend coven."

"What did you say to me?" Zaruki's fangs lengthened.

Sabrina crouched, hissing. Tobias's mate was truly frightening, her green eyes taking on a silvery-blue glow with her anger. Dianthe took a step closer to Sylas, clearly unnerved by the display. Sabrina's voice sounded strange as it filtered through her teeth. "I said, I challenge you. Are things so different among Nochtbend vampires that you don't know what that means?"

Zaruki's eyes narrowed to slits. "Oh, I know what it means, but I fear *you* have no idea." She shoved past Sabrina and threw open the door. "Guards! Take these four to the arena."

"The arena?" Dianthe whispered to Sylas.

He barely glanced back at her. He did not take her hand. She shifted nervously beside him.

"It appears that you will have your wish, Sylas," Zaruki said, glaring directly at him. "You will be in the audience of the master... while I battle your friend to the death."

<h1 style="text-align:center">CHAPTER EIGHTEEN</h1>

Something was very wrong with Sylas. Dianthe followed her mate, Tobias, and Sabrina from the room, led by a group of brutish vampires who seemed dead set on making the experience as uncomfortable as possible. Sylas did not react at all to the guard's firm grip on her arm or move closer to her to protect her. In fact, her mate had barely looked at her since their conversation at the lake. He was angry, that was for certain.

You said he was smothering you, she chided herself. It was a mistake. In her anger, she'd said things she regretted. *Smothered* was perhaps an exaggeration. *Smothered* was perhaps the wrong word choice given that he'd, only minutes before, allowed himself to be eaten alive by a monstrous worm. *Smothered* was likely the reason he wasn't speaking to her.

Damn it all. Why had she chosen that word?

With a shove to the center of her back, Dianthe stumbled forward into a pit of mud and stone. She flapped her wings to right herself, then looked up and up and up. An underground coliseum rose above her, quickly filling with thousands of vamps whose individual mumbles created a cacophony that echoed through the space. Occasionally, Dianthe heard the word *challenge* pop out of the otherwise indistinguishable din of voices.

"By the goddess." Dianthe turned in place, disturbed by the sheer size of the stadium and the fact that she was surrounded by predators. Every one of these vampires would make a meal of her if there wasn't a pact between their people. Here, would anyone even know if one of them decided to indulge? She shivered.

The guards left the four of them alone, the tunnel into the arena closing behind them. That was that. There was no way out of here but for Sabrina to fight. Hopefully just Sabrina. Why were they all in the arena?

"I hope you know what you're doing," Sylas whispered to Tobias and Sabrina.

Sabrina removed her cloak, folded it neatly, and handed it to Tobias. "Do you want the second orb or not?"

"Of course I do, but—"

"Zaruki was not going to give you access to the master. She sympathizes with Eleanor. I could smell her contempt for you the moment you walked into the room."

Sabrina stripped off her shirt until she was left in only a sports bra and leggings. Her fingers danced along her hair, braiding it perfectly with superfast precision. She tied the ends with an elastic she'd had around her wrist.

"We don't know what this challenge entails," Sylas said. "How can you be so sure you can handle it?"

"She can handle it," Tobias said confidently.

"All vampires are fundamentally the same," Sabrina said. "They're violent creatures. They won't respect us unless we demand respect. Trust me on this. I'll be okay."

Dianthe observed Sylas and Tobias. Both dragons. Both mated. Their reactions could not have been more different. Tobias was smiling as his mate prepared for war. Sylas was scrubbing his face with his hands as if this entire situation was making his skin crawl. She had to agree with her mate on this one. All of Dianthe's instincts told her Sabrina was in over her head.

"Tobias, I need you."

"Blood or energy?" Tobias asked.

"A little of both? I expect this will be... challenging."

Dianthe did a double take as Tobias pulled Sabrina into his arms and kissed her like it was her last day on earth. A few whistles came from nearby vamps, but as Dianthe watched, she realized this was more than a kiss. Sabrina's cheeks turned as pink as a fairy's. And when her lips tucked into his neck, she saw her sip blood from his skin. Sabrina and Tobias weren't making out, he was feeding her.

By the time she pulled away, she was positively glowing. "Mmm-mm good. See you later, baby."

"There's more where that came from. Finish this without making me shift, and it's all yours."

She gave him a reassuring nod and then jogged to the center of the arena, waving to the vampires who booed her arrival.

Dianthe tugged at Sylas's arm and gestured toward a box at the front of the arena. A vampire entered, wearing a tailored black suit decorated with red cords. With his jet-black hair and eyes, his very presence was foreboding, even from her spot across the arena. But it was what he carried in his hand that had caught her eye. A scepter in his grip was topped with a glowing red orb.

"By the Mountain," Sylas said. "I guess Sabrina was right about him keeping it close."

"Let's pray Sabrina wins this thing and we have the opportunity to plan how we might pry that thing out of his thousand-year-old grip."

"I don't think he's a thousand years old."

Dianthe scoffed. "At some point I imagine you stop counting."

A portcullis on the other side of the arena rose and Zaruki jogged in, waving to the now cheering crowd. She was dressed in leather with spikes around her neck, waist, and shoulders.

"Interesting fashion choice," Dianthe whispered.

"It looks like this is hand-to-hand combat. I don't see any weapons or shields. That fashion statement is Zaruki's way of wearing her weapons into the ring. If Sabrina tries to grab her, those silver spikes will make her bleed."

"That's an unfair advantage!" Dianthe protested.

"I don't think this competition is meant to be fair." Sylas folded his arms across his chest.

Demidicus stood, and the arena went silent. "What is your name, stranger?"

Dianthe swallowed down a wave of fear-induced nausea for her friend.

"I am Sabrina, master of the Lamia Coven. I came here to request an audience with you, Master Demidicus, to speak about what is happening in the five kingdoms. If you would grant me your ear, I would be happy to explain."

The laugh that left the master's mouth was nothing short of cruel. "Am I to conclude that you challenged Zaruki to circumvent her authority in these matters?"

"Yes," Sabrina said flatly.

Dianthe's hopes rose that the master would now agree to meet with them without requiring Sabrina to fight.

But Demidicus only laughed harder. "Let's leave it to fate then. Battle Zaruki. If you win, I will entertain your request. If you lose..." His eyes drifted to the three of them huddled on the ramp to the arena. "My vampires will enjoy a snack before tonight's banquet. I've never had dragon's blood, but I hear it is one experience a vampire never forgets."

Sabrina lowered her chin. "What are your house rules?"

"We have no rules."

"Do you like Zaruki?" The dark quality of Sabrina's tone sent a chill along Dianthe's spine.

Zaruki looked positively bored.

"What has that got to do with anything?" Demidicus asked.

"If possible, would you like me to let her live?"

The master snarled at her. "Zaruki, finish this quickly. I'm famished."

Zaruki sprang into the air, her boot rounding in a kick

toward Sabrina's head. Avoiding the strike, Sabrina lunged right, snatched her ankle out of the air, and quickly changed direction, sending Zaruki's face plowing into the mud. Splatters of dark brown sprayed across Sabrina's pale face. She smiled.

The blond vampire leaped to her feet and attacked, this time with her fists. The movements became so fast Dianthe could barely follow them—strike, duck, kick, block, hook, dodge, uppercut. For close to a minute, neither vampire appeared to land a punch.

"Apparently the master isn't used to things taking this long." Sylas pointed a chin toward Demidicus. His frown was growing more pronounced.

Sabrina dropped and kicked straight up, catching Zaruki in the pelvis. The blond vampire soared across the arena and landed in a heap on the other side. As she struggled to her feet, now completely covered in mud, the arena grew so quiet Dianthe could hear the *thwuck* of each muddy footstep.

Zaruki scrambled to her feet, and a collective gasp left the audience. All her spikes were gone. Dianthe's mouth dropped open. Her gaze darted back to Sabrina. Red ponytail swinging, she held up a bouquet of sharp silver.

"Looking for these?" With a wicked smile, she tossed them all into the side of the arena, eliciting a gasp from the lowest rung of nearby seats. The spikes sank two inches into the stone.

With a mighty roar, Zaruki hurled herself at Sabrina in a blur of vampiric speed. Sabrina sidestepped so quickly it looked to Dianthe as if she blinked out of existence and reappeared, sinking her knee into Zaruki's gut.

A groan came from the crowd, but the blond vamp wasn't giving up. She grabbed Sabrina and held her close, punching her side, her back, her kidney, the side of her jaw. The blows landed, and Dianthe had to believe they hurt. Sabrina might be the faster vampire, but Zaruki had figured that out and was making the most of it.

"How can he be so calm?" Sylas whispered. He was staring at Tobias, who had his arms crossed and was watching with cool, unflustered pride as his mate got pummeled.

"He knows she can do this," Dianthe said. "He believes in her."

Sylas frowned. "Believing in someone can't save them from everything." The ghost of something dark and evil floated like a cloud through his expression. "I used to think that death was the worst thing that could happen to someone I loved. I know better now."

A murmur rumbled through the crowd. Sabrina successfully caught Zaruki's wrist. With the blonde holding Sabrina close, the two looked like they were ballroom dancing. Both were covered in mud now, with the exception of Sabrina's ponytail, which still swung bright red behind her.

"What happened to you, Sylas?" Dianthe watched the fight, but her mind lingered on her mate and that ghost she'd seen pass behind his eyes. Why hadn't she considered before that there was something more behind his recent change in behavior?

His eyes glazed. He was gone, lost somewhere in his own thoughts.

Sabrina pushed Zaruki with her chest, snaked her arm between them, and twisted. The thrust and snap that followed was too fast for Dianthe to see, and when Sabrina tossed something aside, it took her a second to realize it was Zaruki's arm. Dianthe brought both hands to her mouth and gasped. The bloody scene was grisly, something out of a nightmare. Zaruki fell face-first to the arena floor, her blood flowing and mixing with the mud.

The arena erupted into groans and a din of horrified voices. A young vampire near them gagged and turned her face away.

Zaruki tried to get up, but Sabrina had a knee at the center of her back. She raised her hand and struck, breaking through the blond vampire's rib cage. Dianthe didn't have to have a close-up view to know what Sabrina was doing. With her hand inside Zaruki, it was clear Sabrina had wrapped her fingers around the other vampire's heart. All she had to do was pull her hand back, rip the organ from her body, and this would all be over. Under her, Zaruki made a pathetic attempt to rise, her remaining hand slipping in her own blood.

"Do you wish for me to spare her, Master Demidicus?" Sabrina's voice carried across the arena. It had gone silent again as the vampires accepted the loss of their champion. "I cannot serve as your second. I only wish to meet with you, master to master. If you speak now, I will release her."

"I need her," Demidicus said quickly.

Sabrina slipped her hand out of Zaruki's body.

Dianthe heard an unnerving splat as the blond vampire flopped into the mud and lay still. Sabrina stepped away from her, turned toward Master Demidicus, and bowed.

"I trust that you can provide rooms for my friends and me to get cleaned up. I'd prefer not to meet with you like this." She gestured at her filth-covered body.

Master Demidicus snapped his fingers, and the portcullis behind them rose.

CHAPTER NINETEEN

This time it wasn't guards who escorted them from the arena but three young female vampires dressed entirely in white. Sylas thought they moved like a troop of ballerinas. He followed them into the halls of Nightfall, forcing himself to smile and participate in the mindless chatter they initiated. Dianthe looked exhausted, and Tobias was too busy clinging to Sabrina to bother with diplomacy.

He was relieved when they were shown to a suite of rooms connected by a central seating area. Tobias and Sabrina disappeared into one of the bedrooms immediately, giggling all the way. Which left Sylas and Dianthe staring at each other across a set of wingback chairs.

"I think I'd like to take a bath and a nap," Dianthe said. "The welcome crew said Demidicus invited us to join him at a banquet later tonight, and unlike the three of you, I need to sleep."

He pointed a hand at the open room. "It's all yours."

She took a step closer to him. "You could join me."

His inner dragon perked up inside his torso. There was nothing Sylas would rather do than bathe his mate at that very moment. His body was instantly ready. He wanted her. He always wanted her.

But there was something broken between them. He saw it still in her eyes. A connection that used to be there, a mutual respect, was somehow missing. He wanted to get it back. He was certain he could if given enough time. But it wasn't going to happen in the next five minutes. Something told him that making love now would do more harm than good. It would be empty. She might even end up resenting him for it if she felt the emotional schism between them.

He removed his pack and set it next to the chair. "As much as I'd like to take you up on that offer, I think I should prepare what I'm going to say to Demidicus. It's my responsibility to get this right."

Dianthe dropped her gaze to her toes, her mouth bending into a frown that broke his heart. "Okay." Without another word, she disappeared into the room and closed the door.

Sylas's knees gave out, and he landed in one of the wingbacks, thanking the Mountain it was sturdy enough to handle the abuse. Leaning forward, he rested his head in his hands. Would things ever be right between them? Would they ever have what Tobias and Sabrina had? Would it ever be how it used to be?

He leaned back in the chair, closed his eyes, and prayed to the goddess that one day it would be.

THE SYMBOL ELEANOR HAD FORCED SYLAS INTO ON THE floor of her ritual room radiated heat. Born in the heart of a volcano, dragons were rarely bothered by heat, yet this burn seemed to sink straight through into his bones. This was magic, dark and evil. He tracked her movements as she paced around him.

"You would dare lead a rebellion against me?"

He should remain silent. Admitting his role in the Defenders of the Goddess was a stupid idea. But whatever his mother had in mind, he doubted he'd be making it out of here alive anyway.

"What you're doing to the five kingdoms is wrong. The other species need their independence if they are to have a chance to thrive. The taxes you are imposing are draining them dry and leaving them in squalor."

"It's not like I don't give them a choice, Sylas. If they bow down to me, I will ensure they are taken care of."

"And strip them of their culture and identity."

She scoffed. "Culture and identity?" She waved a hand dismissively toward the ceiling. "How awful that the fairies won't be able to celebrate every blink of light in the sky. The vampires will have to live in dwellings approved by Paragon instead of a hole in the ground. Poor elves, I'm sure they'll weep when we finally fill in those fucking sacred pools in Rogos. Good riddance. They're pests, Sylas! Dragons are the superior species, and once I rule all five kingdoms, everyone will accept that. They will have to after I ascend."

"What do you mean, ascend?" Ice formed in his veins despite the heat.

"I will defeat the goddess of the mountain and take her place."

Sylas jolted at the blasphemy. He looked over both shoulders, sure that a fist would drop from the sky and crush his mother into bloody bits. But nothing happened. If the goddess existed and could hear her, she'd chosen not to act. "What makes you believe you could do such a thing?"

She filled a silver vessel with liquid from a cauldron on her workbench. His gaze fell on a massive diamond there. Was that a dragon heart? Whose? He shivered.

"I have tricks up my sleeve that you've never dreamed of, dear boy, not in your most dizzying nightmares."

Her mouth twisted into a truly wicked grin as she approached him again. She tipped her head in mock concern. "This is going to hurt."

The silver vessel tipped, and blood spilled onto the symbol. Pain flared through his body as purple fire engulfed him. He opened his mouth to scream, but the intensity gripped him in a crushing fist, all his air contained within it. The magic tore through his flesh, tugged at his heart and his internal organs. Sharp, slicing agony followed, and then his hand was yanked toward the edge of the symbol.

He wanted to curl into a ball, anything to ease the suffering the spell had ignited. It rattled his teeth and slithered through his skull. It pounded his bowels, tore through his liver. He could feel it nibbling, ratlike, on his bones.

But the magic held him in place. He watched in horror as his mother slipped his ring from his finger. A dragon's ring was far more than a piece of jewelry. The ring formed around his finger the first time he shifted as a child and held the inherent magic that allowed him to be both dragon and man. All his natural abilities resided in that ring: to ward his treasure, to become invisible, to shift, to fly. It was as much a part of him as his heart.

Now he watched the deep red garnet leave him, clutched in his mother's clawlike fingers. With it went a piece of his soul. Air rushed into his lungs. Finally he could scream, and scream he did. He screamed until his throat was raw. She'd taken his ring. His riiiing.

The fire died and he slumped to the floor, his cheek pressed against the smooth stone. She pushed him with the toe of her boot. He watched her place the ring inside a box and then slide it behind a book, The Saddle of Arythmetes.

"Do you remember being forced to read this drivel as a child?" she asked. "Arythmetes felt much as you did after traveling the five kingdoms. He called for peace, cooperative independence, democracy. He, too, wanted to preserve the cultures he witnessed. He found them beautiful. What an apt place to keep your soul. He died you know, a tragic and lonely death."

He stared up at her as she towered above him, as helpless as a wingless bird, and hated her with every fiber of his being.

"Guards, take him to the dungeon. By decree, no one shall speak of him again."

Hands gripped his shoulders... shaking... shaking him.

Sylas woke with a start to find Dianthe hovering above him, her hands on his upper arms.

"You were screaming in your sleep." The unadulterated concern on his mate's face brought him fully into the moment.

It took him a few breaths to realize where he was. He'd fallen asleep in the chair in their suite in Nightfall. He sat up and glanced toward Tobias's room.

"I don't think they heard you." She placed a hand on her throat. "Your voice was muffled, more breath than scream. I only heard you when I came out of the room."

Thank the Mountain for small favors. All he needed was for Tobias to know he was still having nightmares about his time as a prisoner in Paragon. The dragon would likely want to put on his doctor's hat and try to analyze him.

He sat up straighter. "You look nice." Dianthe practically glowed in a midnight-purple dress with diamond beading. "Where did you get that?"

"Our hosts provided it. You have an outfit too." She pointed toward the room where she'd dressed. "With any luck, we'll actually get to have the conversation we came to have later tonight. I wanted to look presentable. You should maybe get changed as well. There's mud on your boots, and it shouldn't be long now."

He ran a hand through his hair and nodded.

"What were you dreaming about?" She rested her hands on his chest as he stood in front of her.

He sidestepped around her and snagged his bag from the floor. "I don't remember." He didn't sound convincing even to himself.

"I think you do. You said today in the arena that you now understand that there are fates worse than death. I've never heard you talk like that before."

He shrugged. "War changes a person. That's what this is—war. It's the silent part. The unseen bubbles before the pot boils over and we line up troops on the battlefield." He rubbed his chest. "With any luck, we'll find all five orbs and the witches will end this."

"I pray so... if the goddess of the mountain is on our side."

He looked down at his hands. "I'm not sure the goddess of the mountain exists, and if she does, I'm certain she's unwilling to intervene on our behalf. Circe told us as much. The gods can't get involved. If we want change, it's up to us."

Dianthe frowned. "We're here, Sylas. We are doing what needs to be done."

He nodded once and slipped into the room, unable to face her a moment more with the lingering memory of his dream burning like acid in his brain.

CHAPTER TWENTY

Everything Dianthe had experienced with her mate the past couple of days churned in her brain. She narrowed her eyes at the closed door between them, a persistent thought niggling in the back of her mind. How much had they really talked about anything since she'd collected him from the Obsidian Palace? He'd spent weeks in the dungeon and months before that traveling the five kingdoms for the rebellion, yet when he came home, every discussion they'd shared had revolved around Aborella.

They'd made love. They'd participated in things together as part of their community. But had they ever really talked since he'd been back?

No, she decided. He'd never shared what had happened to him in that cell other than to tell him about Raven and his siblings. He'd told her plenty about Raven's suffering, about how Nathaniel had rescued him, but the more she thought about it, she knew absolutely nothing about what had happened to *him* while he was there.

All this time, she'd never even thought to ask. She'd been so wrapped up in her vision, curing Aborella, and defending her choice to do so. And he'd stayed away because of it. Now she wondered what types of horrors he'd experienced at his mother's hand. Could the change she'd noticed in Sylas be more about him than about her?

"Trying to move the door with your mind?" Tobias chuckled beside her. He was dressed in a sleek gray suit with braided detailing that somehow made his eyes seem bluer. Beside him, Sabrina arrived in a stunning mermaid dress that was the blue green of an exotic bird's feathers. It complemented her red hair and green eyes perfectly.

"By the goddess, you look smashing," Dianthe said. "You haven't a single nick or cut from your fight today."

"It's the benefit of being a vampire. I heal quickly." Her gaze roved to Tobias. "Where's Sylas?"

"Still getting ready."

"I hope he hurries. Our hosts should be here to get us in just a few minutes."

"How do you know?" There wasn't a clock in the room, and she wasn't wearing a watch.

"It's four hours until full sunrise. They'll want to eat and socialize before they're asleep for the day. I... Every vampire knows how long they have until sunrise."

Dianthe nodded, suddenly feeling an odd combination of both wired and exhausted. She'd been up most of the night, running on pure adrenaline. And now her mind was reeling with worries about Sylas. The urge to ask Tobias if Sylas had said anything to him about his time as a Paragonian prisoner was hard to deny, but this was between her and her mate. It wasn't as important that she know what happened as it was that he trusted her enough to tell her.

A knock came at the door, and Tobias opened it. The graceful three were back, still in their white dresses, ready to escort them to the banquet.

Dianthe rapped on the bedroom door. "Sylas? They're here. It's time to go."

The door opened, and she thought her knees might give out. Dressed in a velvet jacket that was so dark blue it might have been black, Sylas watched her through slate-gray eyes that seemed to cut to her soul. His chestnut hair was tamed back from his face, and the white shirt he wore looked temptingly soft draped open at the chest. He was stunningly attractive, and for a moment she couldn't find her voice. It was like she was back on Aeaea, seeing him for the first time at the meeting of the Defenders of the Goddess.

"Am I wearing it wrong?" He frowned down at himself. "I don't usually dress like this."

She shook her head. "No. I... You look very handsome."

"You make a striking couple," Sabrina said.

"Everyone ready to go?" one of the graceful three asked from the doorway.

Dianthe slipped her hand through Sylas's elbow. He tensed at her touch, but she held on as they filtered from the room.

The banquet hall might have been one in any grand castle. The walls were lined with timber and decorated with stained glass windows backlit to appear like they were aboveground. Rows of tables filled the interior. A musical group played their stringed instruments in the corner. Dianthe followed their guides to the head table, next to the place clearly reserved for Demidicus. Sylas sat to his right, Sabrina to his left, and Dianthe and Tobias found their places next to them.

Only when the tables were full did the master arrive.

"You have my attention," he said coldly. "Pray tell, what brings you here? Before the food arrives please. I hate to talk with my mouth full."

⁓

OUT OF THE CORNER OF HIS EYE, SYLAS SAW Dianthe grimace. Was she wondering what would be served at this banquet? She couldn't drink blood, after all. And although he and Tobias, as dragons, technically could survive on the stuff, he'd prefer his food dead and cooked.

But first things first. He'd happily go hungry if they got what they'd come for. "You are aware, Demidicus, that my brother Tobias and I are heirs to the kingdom of Paragon. We were raised in the mountain, and we know our mother better than anyone."

"It was a tragedy what happened to your older brother Marius. Everyone in the five kingdoms assumed you were all killed in that skirmish. Although recently I heard a rumor that it was Brynhoff who took you prisoner."

"Lies," Sylas said. "Our mother was responsible for

184

Marius's death and exiled us to another realm to keep the crown for herself. She has always had an unmatched lust for power. Now she plans to force the other four kingdoms to swear allegiance to her crown."

"That's a serious accusation, dragon. I don't need to tell you that Paragon and Nochtbend have a long history of tensions, but our independence has never been a topic of conversation. I might even say that Eleanor wouldn't dare."

"You haven't noticed your taxes increase substantially?"

He tipped his head in acknowledgment. "Our mining operation is quite lucrative. Paragon may be swimming in gemstones, but the gold and platinum used to mount them comes from Nochtbend."

"You're a wealthy kingdom, that's for certain, but surely you must have noticed you are keeping less for yourself."

Another tip of the vampire's head.

"It's only the beginning," Sylas said. "My mother's plan is to become the sole ruler of the five kingdoms. She told me that once she's conquered Nochtbend, she plans to force vampires to sleep aboveground in Paragonian dwellings."

Demidicus hissed.

"She sees herself becoming the new goddess of the mountain. She doesn't just want to rule, she wants to be worshipped."

"We will never bow to Paragon," Demidicus stated unequivocally. "And Eleanor wouldn't dare invade Nochtbend. We would drain her dragons dry."

Sylas felt a tap on his elbow, and Dianthe leaned forward. "Don't you see? It's why she burned Everfield. With the Obsidian Guard now occupying the Empyrean Wood, Nochtbend is surrounded on all sides by her troops."

His eyes narrowed. "The Guard has remained in Everfield?"

"My home forest is crawling with them." Her amber wings fluttered, and her skin glowed softly in the dim light. Demidicus's gaze raked over her as if he were seeing her for the first time. Sylas had a sudden urge to remove the vamp's head from his body.

"It's been centuries since we've had a fairy here." His dark eyes turned hungry, his fangs growing long in his mouth.

"My people prefer the sun." Dianthe leaned forward a little more and her dress puckered, giving Sylas and the master a delicious view of her cleavage. That was it. He indulged in a fantasy of wrapping her in his jacket and carrying her back to their room.

"So I've heard." His nostrils flared. He dragged his eyes from her, turning his attention back to Sylas just in time to calm the jealous fury rising within him.

"Even if I believed you, what do you expect from Nochtbend? We cannot openly support the rebellion, not with the tentative peace between our kingdoms."

Sylas shook his head. "I'm not asking you to. All we need from you is the orb on your scepter." He pointed to the red crystal ball resting beside the master.

Demidicus scoffed. "Now I know this is a joke."

"It contains a piece of a key that can be used to unlock a weapon with the power to bring Eleanor down. The witch queen of Darnuith divided the key and hid one piece in every kingdom. Her descendants have joined the Defenders of the Goddess. The three sisters can leverage the power the witch queen left behind to take back our world from Eleanor, but we need every piece to access it."

A shadow passed behind Demidicus's dark eyes, and he leaned back in his chair. "I knew her, the witch queen. Her name was Medea. So many centuries have passed now that her memory feels like a ghost who haunts my heart."

Sylas glanced at Tobias, who looked just as confused as he was. He'd known Demidicus was ancient, but he hadn't realized that Nochtbend was involved in any way in the witch wars.

"It surprises you that we were once friends? Oh, there were many secrets then. In many ways, Eleanor and Brynhoff got lucky. Had Medea and Tavyss not craved peace, those two would have never gotten close enough to slay them."

He hadn't known the details, but his mother truly was the most manipulative liar he'd ever met. Medea and Tavyss lost to her because they had souls. They had limits. They wanted to preserve lives. Eleanor had no such boundaries. The only thing Eleanor cared about was Eleanor.

"You'd remember Medea if you'd had the chance to meet her. Magic surrounded her, filled her to the point it spilled over to an inch outside her skin. The day she came here, asking for my help, she made my heart beat." Demidicus stared wistfully out across the hall.

Sylas saw something in the vampire's eyes he'd never expected. Demidicus loved Medea, as much as a vampire could love anything. It was all there in the way his face softened as he thought of her.

"What did she ask of you?" Sylas asked.

Demidicus's eyebrow rose, and the corner of his mouth quirked. "She asked me to guard this"—he gestured toward the orb—"with my life. She said one day someone would come for it and know its purpose. I suppose that someone is you."

"Please. I understand that Nochtbend can't risk getting on Eleanor's bad side, but if you give us the orb, I promise you we will do our best to end her reign of terror for good," Sylas said.

The vampire placed his hand on the orb and left it there. "Hmm. Time to eat."

Servants flooded the hall with boxes of piglets. Squeals and screams echoed off the walls as the vampires captured their prey and bit into their dinner. Sylas glanced at Dianthe, who'd paled, her eyes fixating on a spot on the tablecloth. She looked like she might be sick.

A cooked suckling pig landed in front of them. He appreciated the effort, but the thought of eating piglet after watching the bloody display in the hall turned his stomach.

Demidicus waved away the live piglet that was offered to him. "I will give you the orb, but in exchange, I want to taste her blood."

"What? Whose blood?" Sylas narrowed his eyes on the vampire.

The man's dark gaze flicked up to meet his. "Your mate's."

Sylas's growl garnered the attention of the vampires nearest them, who hissed in warning. The din of eating in the room quieted by half.

"Careful, dragon. Mind your manners or it will be more than the orb you leave here without, if you leave here at all."

"Do not threaten a dragon's mate," Sylas warned.

"I did not threaten her. I only asked for a sip of her blood. You could extract it. I don't need it from the vein. It has been three hundred years since I've tasted fairy blood. It tastes of sunlight, you understand. A delicacy for a vampire."

Dianthe tugged at his elbow. "It's okay, Sylas. If it will get us the orb—"

"You'd rather have dragon's blood," Sabrina said from his other side.

"The champion speaks. What was that?" He flashed her a wolfish grin.

"I said dragon's blood is better. Have you ever had dragon's blood?" Sabrina asked, her eyes sparkling as if she had a tightly held secret. She already knew the answer. Sylas vividly remembered Demidicus mentioning he'd never tasted dragon's blood when they were in the arena.

"Have *you* ever tasted dragon's blood?" The master chuckled as if the idea was preposterous. "It is forbidden, an act of war between our species. I have lived a long time, child, but even I have never convinced a dragon to give me his blood, and I have never had the opportunity to take it."

She raised her eyebrow, her red hair falling in a curtain over one of her eyes. "Yes, I have tasted it. After all, I am mated to a dragon. You do know a dragon will do anything for his mate."

Demidicus's gaze darted between them. He licked his lips.

"A taste of dragon's blood for the orb. Only dragon's blood. You will leave the fairy alone," Sabrina offered.

"Done." Demidicus's answer came swiftly, his focus tightening on the couple as if he couldn't quite believe Sabrina could pull it off.

Sylas stiffened. His gaze locked on Tobias. Feeding a vampire their blood had always been strictly forbidden. Sylas hadn't ever asked *why* it was forbidden. He'd never questioned it. Clearly some rules Brynhoff and Eleanor had taught them were simply folklore used to control them. Was this one of those rules, or was there good reason behind the warning?

He'd seen the way Sabrina had changed after drinking Tobias's blood. It definitely gave the vampires energy and strength. Was it wise to imbue the master with that privilege at the moment? Demidicus already enjoyed the upper hand in this negotiation. Why make him stronger?

But Tobias reached for Demidicus's glass, then held his wrist out to Sabrina. She bit into his flesh and nearly filled the goblet. The redhead offered the goblet to Demidicus.

The vampire master snapped the orb off his scepter and excitedly turned it over to her. The exchange was made. Sabrina slipped the red crystal into the velvet cross-body bag that hung at her hip.

Demidicus sniffed the goblet. His eyes sparkled with excitement at the scent. "I never thought..." He shook his head. Raising his glass to salute Sabrina, he drained the cup dry.

Less than a minute later, Demidicus sagged against Sylas as if he were falling-down drunk. Tobias laughed and jiggled the vampire's arm, using the touch to reposition him in his chair. The vampire could barely keep his head lifted.

"Good blood," Demidicus mumbled.

"What's wrong with him?" Sylas asked.

Sabrina smiled. "Nothing. Dragon's blood is intoxicating to vampires. A little is like a snort of cocaine. A lot knocks you on your ass." She wrinkled her nose. "He's had a lot."

Brilliant.

Standing, she turned to the women in white waiting behind them. "We will go back to our room now." They were led from the banquet hall, the master drunkenly murmuring his thanks toward their backs.

CHAPTER TWENTY-ONE

"This is exhausting," Raven muttered. Her wrist ached from copying the symbols frantically while Avery drained the protective enchantment from the scroll.

Across the table from her, Clarissa rubbed her wrist, similarly afflicted. They'd been at this for hours, and it wasn't getting any easier.

"We're more than halfway there. We can't give up now." Clarissa pulled the elastic from her ponytail. The dark roots of her bleached hair had grown out since they'd left London. Between the tropical humidity and the magic she was doling out, her locks were caked in sweat. She ran her fingers through it, forming a messy bun at the top of her head.

"Fuck, I need a break." Avery rubbed her eyes and stretched out onto of one of the tables.

"Go back to your tent," Raven said. "You don't have to sleep here."

But her sister was already snoring.

Xavier pushed off his seat where he'd been observing them from the back of the tent and waved dismissively at Raven. "I'll carry the lass," he said in his heavy Scottish brogue. "She'll sleep better with me beside her anyhow."

Avery snorted as he repositioned her in his arms and carried her from the tent.

"We could try your translation spell on what we have," Clarissa suggested.

Raven shook her head. "We don't know this language or how many symbols equate to a single word or thought. The little I read of it before was from when I'd translated the entire page. We don't even know if it's meant to be read left to right or up and down. Without the entire text, I can't guarantee the translation would be accurate."

Clarissa sighed. "Tomorrow is another day."

Raven gave her a hug before hurrying back to her own tent for a much-needed break. She swept Charlie from Gabriel's arms and planted a firm kiss on her cheek. "How is *my* baby?"

Gabriel grinned. "Wait until you see what *our* baby can do."

Raven's eyes widened, tears pricking the edges. "I missed something else?"

Charlie's development was unlike anything she'd ever witnessed in a human child. When she hatched from her egg, she was already the size of a six-month-old with wings like a cherub's that could almost lift her off the ground. Now she'd grown to the size of a one-year-old who could pull herself up on the furniture with the help of her wings.

Gabriel insisted all that was perfectly normal and

that her development would likely accelerate until she shifted for the first time into her other form. Dragons, he explained, were usually born in their dragon form and then transformed into their *soma* or human-looking forms at some point. It was different for everyone. That's when their rings appeared.

Charlie didn't have a ring and had never looked like a dragon. Her wings were also far different than a typical dragon's. But dragon development, along with what she remembered about human development, was all they had to go on. The only certainty was that Charlie was one of a kind.

"Show me," Raven said.

Gabriel sat down on the rug at the center of the tent and grabbed a coconut from behind him. "Sit, like me."

She did, spreading her legs and seating Charlie on the floor in front of her. The baby waved her hands excitedly.

"Do you want the ball, Charlie? Ball. B-ball."

Raven's heart turned into a puddle in her chest at the sight of her oversized husband making baby talk. But what happened next melted the rest of her. Charlie put her lips together and said, "Ba, ba, ba."

Gabriel rolled her the coconut. She squealed in delight and rolled it back to him.

"My God, Gabriel, she can practically say it. She definitely understands what it is. And look at her push it back to you."

"Our daughter is extremely bright," Gabriel said. "Just like her mother."

Raven turned serious. There was something she'd

been meaning to ask Gabriel, and she'd put it off long enough.

"According to the prophecy, isn't Charlie supposed to be a weapon? Months ago, Tobias warned me that the child of a dragon and a witch could flatten cities."

Gabriel scowled. "Folklore. Brynhoff demonized the witch queen of Darnuith and her dragon mate. He murdered their unborn child along with the queen. It would make sense that he'd spread rumors that their progeny was a monster, otherwise the other four kingdoms might denounce what he'd done."

"But do you think there's any truth to the prophecy? Obviously we three sisters are playing a role in bringing Eleanor down. We hope to bring an end to Paragon as we know it. That part is true. And if that part of the prophecy is true, then maybe..." She stopped short. If Charlie had any deadly power, she would have done something to protect them from the sea monster that almost tore them apart. She was probably worrying over nothing.

"Our daughter is not a monster." Gabriel rolled the ball back to Charlie. "Besides, we won't know what magical talents she might have or not have until after she shifts for the first time."

"Not have? Do you think it's possible she has no power?"

"Her wings are different, Raven. And she was born looking more like you than me. It isn't unheard of for dragons to be born in their *soma* forms, but much more commonly, they look like whelps, er, baby dragons. They look like this after their first shift. Will she have the ability to make herself invisible?" Gabriel shrugged. "We've seen hints that she'll be able to breathe fire. What magic will come naturally to her? We won't know until she's older."

Everything was changing. It was like Raven was standing in the middle of a river, time rushing by her. Already Charlie was growing and changing at an alarming rate. Raven could only speculate what she'd become when she grew up. That was much farther down the river. The hard part was enjoying the temperature of the water right where she was. How could she stay in the moment and enjoy every second of her baby's existence when every day brought her closer to something big, something that could change everything? How did she enjoy where she was when something big and dark was careening toward her at a high rate of speed?

Charlie giggled and patted the ball.

"Can you say *mama*?" Raven cooed at her daughter, kissing the top of her head.

"Ma. Ma," Charlie said with some effort, her huge blue eyes blinking up from a face framed in downy white curls.

"Oh goddess, she said it!" Raven swept her up and kissed her chubby cheek.

Gabriel grinned proudly. "As I said, our daughter is absolutely brilliant."

CHAPTER TWENTY-TWO

Aborella hated Eleanor. The emotion came from a deep well of pain and regret that she sank deeper into every day and night she spent in this infernal cell. Other than her visions, all her magic had been drained from her. The sun hadn't touched her skin since Eleanor had arrested her. Her normally dark purple complexion had faded to lavender. She was sick. Weak. Underfed. And the empress was to blame.

"I am losing my patience, Aborella."

"Unchain me and I'll help you find it." Aborella's head snapped to the side as Eleanor's palm shot out and connected with her cheek.

"My men have sifted through all the ash in the Empyrean Wood. There is no box. There are no documents."

"I must have been mistaken. Visions are open to interpretation. Maybe the buried thing was metaphorical."

Fury rang through Eleanor like a bell and her claws

raged forward. Slashing talons sliced Aborella's wing asunder. Intense pain stabbed through her back into her heart, stealing her breath. Her eyes spread wide. When she finally succeeded in sipping air into her lungs, all she could do was scream. Aborella was no stranger to pain, but this was intolerable. Her back pulsed and bled, her torso burned. Her stomach tried to empty itself, but there was nothing inside her. With the chains shackling her, there was no way to turn for comfort.

"My wing," she sobbed. "You took my wing. How could you?"

Eleanor pressed the bloody wing against the wall across from her, tore a nail from the wooden windowsill, and spiked it through the wing and into the wall. Aborella's sobs intensified at the cruelty. She'd be forced to stare at the missing wing as she suffered from its loss.

"You took my wing," she cried through gritted teeth. "You evil fucking bitch!"

Eleanor whirled, her frame looking bonier and more angular than ever. Her black eyes bore into Aborella, and her red lips pulled back from her teeth. "Tell me what the rebellion is up to, Aborella, or I will take the other wing. And once I've taken your wings, I'll take your limbs, one by one. We already know you can survive it. I will take you apart like an insect."

"Go fuck yourself."

Eleanor's talons shot from her knuckles again, and Aborella cringed against the wall, away from her reach.

"I'll tell you what I know." Aborella squeezed her eyes shut. She was truly the lowest form of life now, no better than a worm plucked from the soil, but she simply could not stand any more pain. She was weak. She admitted it. Eleanor had won. She'd broken her spirit.

"Well? Start talking."

Aborella stared down at a smattering of her blood across the stone as she spoke. "There are five orbs, one hidden in each of the kingdoms. The rebels are trying to find and collect each of them." Aborella leaned her good side against the wall and curled into a ball.

"Why? What do these orbs do?"

"They were created centuries ago by Medea, the witch queen of Darnuith. Each one contains a piece of a key. If all are collected, together they form a way to unlock a hidden vault that contains the most powerful grimoire known to have ever existed."

Eleanor grew suspiciously silent. Aborella peeked at her to find her statuesque, perfectly still, as if in total and complete shock. What had she said? Something had triggered the empress. She'd even stopped breathing.

"Is it the golden grimoire?"

Aborella swallowed. She hated herself for this. "I did see a book bound in gold. My vision did not tell me it had a name."

"I have searched many centuries for this book, Aborella." Eleanor paced to the other side of the room, suddenly jittery and anxious. She rubbed her hands together. "This grimoire could change everything. It is imperative we find it before the rebels do."

"No one can find it without the keys," Aborella explained. "And the rebels already have at least one. The orb that was hidden in Rogos."

The hiss that tore through Eleanor's teeth was

nothing short of deadly. "Why did you not tell me this before?"

"I did." Aborella looked her in the eye so that she could see the truth in her expression. "Back in my ritual room, I told you I saw rebels near the sacred pools of Niven. You didn't believe me. My vision of Everfield was also a misinterpretation but was truthful. The rebels were there, searching for the orb."

The empress started to tremble, her skin bubbling as if she might shift at any moment. "Where are the rebels now, Aborella? If they have not returned to Aeaea, that means there's a chance we can intercept them and take the orbs for Paragon."

Aborella pressed her fingers into her eyes and prayed to the goddess of the mountain that Dianthe, Sylas, Tobias, and Sabrina—the four from her vision—had not lingered in Nochtbend. She'd held off on sharing this vision for as long as she could. She hoped it was long enough that the four had found what they needed and gotten out of there. If not, her next words would be signing their death warrant. *Forgive me, Dianthe.*

"They're in Nochtbend," Aborella said. "The orb is on the scepter of Master Demidicus. The four rebels are attempting to convince him to part with it."

Eleanor growled, likely with the realization that she'd seen that scepter with Master Demidicus for centuries. She could likely picture the orb in her mind. So close and she'd never recognized it for what it was.

"You'd better not be lying about this. I will not be pleased if this is another wild-goose chase."

"I have told you everything, exactly what I've seen,"

Aborella cried softly. "But I am too weak. If you would free me, I could—"

Without a word of comfort or a goodbye, Eleanor strode from her cell and locked the door behind her, leaving Aborella to bleed in the dark room with nothing to look at but her own wing.

CHAPTER TWENTY-THREE

Although Dianthe was tired to her bones, she had to speak to Sylas. The nightmare he'd had, the fear and pain—yes, she was sure it was pain she'd seen in his eyes—rattled her spirit. There was something he hadn't shared with her, something that had changed him. Along with that cryptic comment about fates worse than death, all the clues seemed to point to something bigger under the surface. He'd treated her differently since his escape from Eleanor. The question was, why?

She had to find out what had happened to him. Her marriage was at stake. Their bond was eternal, but their relationship, their intimacy, could be neglected and destroyed. No one ever promised her forever would be easy. If they didn't find a way back to each other soon, she wondered if they'd find themselves loving each other from a distance. It certainly seemed like things were headed that way.

"Let's try to get a few hours of sleep," Sylas said once

the white sisters had returned them to their suite. "We'll head toward Aeaea late morning."

Tobias and Sabrina hastily agreed to that plan and disappeared into their room.

Dianthe met Sylas's gaze and held it. "We need to talk."

"If you don't want to sleep next to me, I can make a bed out here." He nodded his head toward the couch.

"Who said I didn't want to sleep next to you?" Dianthe took a tentative step toward him.

"I want to give you your space. I don't want to *smother* you." The word *smother* came out with an edge, like it tasted bitter on his tongue.

She took a deep breath and blew it out slowly. "I shouldn't have used that word. I'm here. I'm making my own choices. You aren't smothering me or keeping me from anything physically. I'm sorry I grabbed for that word when I was angry. I didn't mean it."

All the light drained from his gray eyes, replaced with frustrated sadness. "Then what did you mean? Because I've been trying my damnedest to figure it out for days."

She thought hard about what she wanted to say. "Before you left... before you were captured, you were my partner. I always felt you valued what I had to offer, both to our marriage and to the resistance. You always said that you and Colin couldn't do what you did without me."

"I value you. I never said I didn't value you—"

She held up a finger. "Something has changed. You had our bags packed and a boat for Aeaea ready, as if you expected the attack from the Obsidian Guard. Did you know Empyrean Wood would burn?"

"No, I didn't know." He made a face like the thought disgusted him. "Do you think I would have kept that to myself when I could have spared so many?"

"It's unlike you, but then why was the bag packed?"

He took a deep breath. "Aborella left. I didn't trust her. I never trusted her."

"You didn't trust me."

He groaned and rubbed his face with his hands. "I'm too tired for this tonight."

"I'm too tired not to do this tonight. I'm exhausted from this tension between us. I want my mate back."

"Then just forgive me for trying to keep you safe. I'm a dragon. It's expected."

"This is more than that. If it weren't for Colin, you never would have let me come on this mission. You allowed yourself to be eaten rather than trust that I could fly faster than a worm could climb. You tried to stop me from saving Tobias and Sabrina from the water sprites. Why don't you admit it—?"

"Admit what?" he snapped.

"Something happened to you. Something terrified you, and the reason you are obsessed with keeping me safe, the reason you wanted Circe herself to underestimate me and keep me under her protection, is because it horrifies you to think the same thing could happen to me!" Her loud whisper floated around Sylas and then dissolved in ripples like a drop in the ocean. As soon as she said it, she knew she was right. This wasn't just being protective. This was fear. This was a terror so strong he'd actually sacrifice their relationship to save her from it.

His throat bobbed on a swallow, and then his lashes fluttered. Suddenly he looked thinner, his skin sallow. "Can we just go to bed?"

She spread her wings, bathing him in a faint glow. Closing the gap between them, she leaned forward and whispered in his ear in her most sultry voice. "I will never turn down going to bed with you."

It was as if she'd waved a red flag in front of a bull. His expression changed, his gaze filling with a deep, hungry need as if he'd been bleeding out and she'd offered him a tourniquet. He grabbed her face roughly, just shy of hurting, and crashed into her. This was no soft request. His lips were demanding, their breaths coming in gasps between long, deep, violent kisses.

He grabbed her dress as if he might tear it from her body. She slithered out of it before he could, not wanting him to ruin the piece of art. Totally naked and glowing brighter with her excitement, she led him into the bedroom and closed the door.

"Goddess, I need you, Dianthe." He dug his fingers in her hair, brought the ends to his nose, and breathed her in.

She'd taken far too long to decipher what was going on with him. She'd torn him down. Built walls. Dug moats. It was time to strip away everything and just be them, together, naked and alone. Only from that could she rebuild.

"You have me," she whispered. She reached for the ties on his pants and pulled them down around his ankles. He was rock-hard. His massive erection reached for her. She took him in her hands, eliciting a deep purr from his inner dragon. His mating trill. Music to her ears.

He kicked his pants aside and removed his jacket and shirt as if the garments were on fire. His breath had quickened, but then so had hers. They'd been together for so long, but something about this moment made her feel like this was their very first time. She felt raw, needy. Her stomach flipped with nerves.

There was a slight tremble to her hand when she pushed him down onto the bed and crawled up his body. Their eyes locked. "You have me," she repeated.

Slowly she lowered her head and slid her lips over his cock, taking him deep into her throat.

His breath caught, and he grabbed the headboard. "Dianthe. Oh goddess."

She swirled her tongue over the blunt head and sucked him deeper again. Her tongue curled around his shaft. As she stared up his body, all she could think was that her husband had definitely been carved by the gods. He was all hard peaks and shadowed valleys, the lean musculature of his arms and shoulders nothing short of intimidating. His size positively dwarfed her. But on his back, with his cock buried in her mouth, he was all hers.

Finding a rhythm, she licked and sucked until his groans of pleasure made her reach between her own legs to ease the hot ache that had started there. Her nipples puckered with her need for him, and she arched her back and worked him faster. The sight of her pleasuring herself put him over the edge. With a howl, he emptied himself down her throat.

She rose above him, still stroking herself as he trembled beneath her from the aftershocks of his orgasm. When his eyes focused on her again, they were glowing red, and the heat his body was putting off made her skin flush.

Hello, dragon.

NOTHING EXISTED IN THAT MOMENT BUT HER. SYLAS watched Dianthe stroke herself, her knees straddling his legs, and felt completely full for the first time in what felt like forever. There had been a giant gaping hole in the general region of his rib cage, an aching that she'd filled with her unwavering attention. When was the last time they'd had this?

His inner dragon coiled tight inside his body, rippling under his skin. He was ready again, and she was the only one who could soothe his inner fire. He grabbed her by the hips, spreading his wings and lifting them both off the bed. In one slick thrust, he entered her. He wasn't gentle, but Dianthe didn't seem to mind. Her mouth came down on his like hot rain. He was drowning in her, wrapped in her dark, lanky limbs. Her embrace, her arms, her legs, her core—it was the only thing holding him together.

Forgetting himself in her was the only thing that mattered.

Her wings fluttered as he landed on his feet at the end of the bed, supporting her with a firm grip on her luscious ass. Her light washed across him, across the bed, her sweet-as-honey scent filling his lungs. Where did he end and she begin? He'd forgotten long ago. His knees bent and his hips matched her thrusts as she started to move. In this position, clinging to him, her legs and arms squeezing tighter to gain purchase, their thrusts became an exercise in deep movements, small but effective. Gravity pulled her closer. Passion brought him to the edge.

He whirled and lowered her onto her back on the bed, rejoining the rhythm. Goddess, she was beautiful beneath him. The most beautiful female who had ever or would ever live. Why did she love him? How had he gotten so lucky as to have her for his mate?

With a cry of ecstasy, she arched beneath him, her head thrown back, her inner muscles milking him. He gave her everything, their mutual pleasure rising to a crescendo that reached through his soul. He was tissue paper and her light had shone through him, driving out the darkness if only for a moment.

Minutes later, once they'd both come back into themselves, conscious of the world again, he fell onto his side and pulled her back against the length of his body. Curled around her, his lips met her ear. "I love you, Dianthe, with everything I am and everything I will ever be."

She glanced over her shoulder at him. "I love you too. Always. No matter what this secret is..." She shook her head. "Whatever you see when you close your eyes, it's never going to change how I feel about you. We can move beyond it. We can face it together when you're ready."

He kissed the side of her jaw and closed his eyes. He most certainly wasn't ready. There was so much shame wrapped up in the memory, layered with pain, weakness, vulnerability. Some of it he understood. Some of it he was only now coming to understand.

He gripped her tighter, his hand forming a fist between her breasts. The garnet ring that held his magic winked at him in the dim light. All the darkness she'd banished from his soul snapped back like an over-stretched rubber band and he trembled.

"It's okay. I'm here," she said sleepily.

He waited for the dark, crawling feeling to pass, but it didn't, and when her breath came evenly in his arms, he decided he had to tell the story. She was likely asleep and wouldn't hear him anyway. He'd speak the words. Maybe it would lighten this weight burdening his soul.

"Our mission started years ago with one and only one goal—recruit enough members to the Defenders of the Goddess that the rebellion would have a fighting chance against the Obsidian Guard."

CHAPTER TWENTY-FOUR

Dianthe used all her faculties to remain absolutely still. She did not respond when Sylas began to speak. Like a skittish animal, Sylas, she sensed, needed her to remain calm. If she kept her eyes closed and her breath even, with any luck he'd keep talking.

"Colin and I agreed that he'd go to Rogos and live among the elves with the goal of finding rebels among the populace there. We already had representatives from all the other kingdoms, but Rogos has always maintained its neutrality. Their scribes had chronicled the history of the five kingdoms for centuries. Colin wanted to convince them—well, any he could find that admitted disloyalty to Paragon—we needed to act."

Dianthe remembered that. She didn't know the details of their plan, but she'd played a part in the general idea of it. She'd also okayed Sylas's rise to power within the Defenders of the Goddess during Colin's absence.

"While Colin was in Rogos, I assumed his responsibilities as ARO—Aeaea Red Zone One, the ultimate leader of the resistance. After firming up our support in Everfield over the following months, I traveled here to Nochtbend. That's why people here know me. Vampires have never had an affinity for dragons. Our peace has been tentative at best. Although Demidicus would deny it publicly, he was loyal to Medea during the witch wars and hates Eleanor. Over the course of the following months, I brought more vampires than ever onboard. Only when my presence started garnering the attention of the Highborn representatives, loyalists to Paragon, did I leave and travel to Darnuith to meet with the witches."

This part Dianthe was less aware of. Oh, she'd known he'd have to go to Darnuith, but the witches there were notoriously secretive. They had to be, considering their history with Paragon. Aside from dragons, witches were the most powerful beings in the five kingdoms. To say they were dangerous would be putting it mildly.

"It took me months of living with a local innkeeper named Zander to gain the trust of their citizens. He was serving as DBO, Darnuith Blue Zone One, an officer in the resistance, and helped me get a foothold. Together, we grew the resistance in Darnuith to unprecedented levels. Once I revealed my true identity, I felt like the entire kingdom was on our side.

"After so much success, I was on top of the world. By my estimation, the Defenders of the Goddess had a following almost large enough to coordinate a true challenge to Eleanor. I even succeeded in creating a black market for goods moved between Everfield, Nochtbend, and Darnuith to avoid detection by Paragon and the

Highborns. The Obsidian Guard couldn't raid or tax what they didn't know existed."

Dianthe could hear the pride in his voice. She remembered those days. He'd stopped home regularly to let her know he was safe. Meanwhile, she'd kept appearances up, participating in the community and passing correspondence to fairy rebels right under their Highborn representatives' noses.

"By the time I journeyed to Hobble Glen in Paragon, I was overconfident. I'd been recruiting for almost two years. I had a list of people Colin had worked with in the past and took up residence at the Silver Sunset, disguised as a barkeep. At first everything was fine. We were growing. Many of the older dragons are concerned that Eleanor is recruiting younger and younger dragons for the Guard, some of whom have disappeared without a trace. Fighting in the pits has become more deadly as well. When I lived in the palace, I never heard of any dragons dying during a fight. Now it is almost commonplace, especially among the young ones."

He paused and Dianthe worried he might not go on. It was all she could do not to say something. But she was afraid if she did, she'd scare him from sharing any more anyway. She forced herself to wait and listen.

"There was a rumor," he whispered finally, "that Eleanor was collecting the blood of the dragons who died in the pits and using it in her dark magic."

A chill spider-walked up her spine and curled at the base of her neck despite the heat radiating from his body. She couldn't suppress the tightening of her muscles as her stomach churned at the thought, but thank the goddess, Sylas kept talking.

"Initially, I thought the rumors were inventions born of hate and a passion for freedom. Then one day, Aborella walked in the front door of the Silver Sunset. I was disguised, but she looked right at me and ordered a drink. I should have known something was amiss. I should have aborted my mission that very minute. But when she left without any indication of recognizing me, I pushed my luck. The Obsidian Guard arrested me that night. They raided the Silver Sunset and dragged me from my bed."

This time she couldn't resist running her hand up the arm he still had wrapped around her and threading her fingers into his. She kissed his knuckles.

"I wondered if you were awake."

Turning in his arms, she snuggled into his chest. "Please don't stop talking. I need to hear it all."

His heart beat fast against her ear. This was hard for him. How painful must a memory be to cause a dragon's pulse to race at the mere thought of it?

"They tortured me, Dianthe. Eleanor and her fucking new sidekick, that bastard Ransom who took over for Scoria. They starved me. Shocked me over and over with their batons. Cut off chunks of my flesh. I wouldn't tell her a thing about the rebellion."

She swallowed down a need to vomit. If he knew how much this upset her, he might stop. She needed him to keep going.

"After—I don't know how long it went on, it felt like forever—she took me into her ritual room." He'd started to tremble, and she held him tighter. "Eleanor performed a spell using blood magic, the blood of dragon children I would come to find out, to remove my ring. I lost all my power, even my ability to spread my wings. She stole my inner dragon."

Dianthe's thoughts stuttered, the idea a crushing pain in her chest. "H-how is that possible? It would kill you! It would be like stopping your heart."

"Dark magic. Painful magic. Goddess, Dianthe, it hurt, hurt like you wouldn't believe. It felt like my soul was torn in two. And then she threw me in the dungeon and forgot about me. I'd still be there if Nathaniel hadn't come along and used his magic to free me and restore my ring."

"Oh my goddess." Dianthe circled his neck with her arms. "I should have done more to try to rescue you. I should have formed a task force from the DOGs."

"Did you even know?"

She frowned and pressed her forehead into his chest. "Not initially. Not until word reached me through the underground, and that was only days before you called me to you. But I should have known. I should have seen it. It had been so long since you'd been home. I had a feeling something was wrong. What good is being a seer when you can't always see the futures of the ones you love?" It had always been thus after her first visions of her mother's death. Her talent seemed to avoid her closest personal connections. The unfairness of it burned behind her breastbone.

"You didn't know." He kissed her forehead. "And there was nothing you could have done. She's too strong.

But Dianthe, that's why when we learned it was Aborella in that grave, Aborella you were healing, I couldn't be part of it. Not after what she helped do to me."

"I thought you just didn't believe in my vision. I mean, I understood you hated her. We all hated her. But I didn't know it was personal." Her heart grew heavy and her stomach twisted under the weight of emotion that flowed into her. She thought at first it was guilt, but she didn't feel guilty for trusting her vision and healing Aborella. She felt guilty for not paying closer attention to the mental health of her mate. She hadn't stopped to think how what she was doing was affecting him. What she thought was guilt carried the heaviness of grief, of lost opportunities, missed conversations. In retrospect, she should have handled it differently, should have listened to him and guarded against the possibility that Aborella would turn on her.

"She is as evil as they come. And now she's back in Paragon, healed, working for the empress, and with a hell of a lot more information on the rebellion." The tone of frustration and what she now recognized as fear that lined his voice made her heart ache.

Dianthe swallowed her pride. "I see it now. I shouldn't have trusted her, vision or no vision. I'm not sorry I trusted myself or my vision, but we could have done it in a different way. I could have disguised myself or healed her in another location. I shared too much. I trusted her too fully. I should have listened to you, Sylas, if for no other reason than you are my mate. You have a say in what goes on in our home. Please forgive me for that. My visions have never been wrong before. I still can't believe it. I was so sure."

"I forgave you a long time ago."

"But you still don't trust me. You still question my abilities and my visions."

"No." He released a heavy sigh. "Dianthe, I just framed it that way because I wanted you to stay in Aeaea. I didn't care about the mission. I didn't care that you were the right person to retrieve the Everfield orb. All I cared about—all I still care about—is keeping you out of my mother's clutches. For the first time since we started with the Defenders of the Goddess, Aborella knows who you are, and she's most certainly told Eleanor. They know I was the leader of the rebellion. They know that I would do anything for you. For the first time, you have a bull's-eye on your back that's never been there before. That's why I wanted you to stay in Aeaea, not because I don't believe in you or your abilities."

"The bull's-eye has always been there. Since before I knew you. I was a seer for the rebellion, and at any time I might have shown up in Aborella's visions or been found out by Paragonian spies. Yes, she knows my name now and where we used to live, but knowing me makes it harder for her to see me. Just as it makes it harder for me to see her. This political game we're playing, there's nothing safe about it. I've always known what I was getting myself into. If I die doing this, it will be for a worthy cause."

"Don't say that. No cause is worthy enough, and I will not survive it. You're my very soul, Dianthe. The only thing left that matters."

"Then I guess you must continue to save me when I get into trouble." She smiled and kissed him under his jaw.

"Do you forgive me for the things I said?" He stroked the hair over her ear. "I embarrassed you in front of Circe. I'm a total ass."

She wrapped an arm and leg around him and squeezed him to her. "I forgive you. I don't want to fight anymore. Let's just agree that whatever we do from now on, we do it together. We take care of each other."

He reached over her and dragged the edge of the blanket over her shoulder and his, wrapping her in a cocoon against him. With a kiss to her forehead, he said, "Agreed. We'll save each other. Now sleep. Once we're back in Aeaea, I plan to keep you awake late into the night making up for lost time."

She curled into him, positioning her cheek on his chest. "Sounds like heaven."

Sleep came for her quickly, wiping out all thoughts of Paragon, the rebellion, and even Aborella.

CHAPTER TWENTY-FIVE

Heaven. Sylas was in warm, sleepy heaven, wrapped around his mate and back in her good graces. She still carried his scent from their lovemaking. Like a brand, it perfumed her skin. *Mine.* His inner dragon stretched sleepily inside him, completely at ease with the current situation.

He had no idea what time it was, but he guessed late morning. He'd awoken on his own, feeling refreshed and ready for the day, but dragons needed far less sleep than other creatures. His fairy mate, for instance, was still far off in dreamland.

Dianthe released a cute, high-pitched snore, and he pulled the blanket tighter around her before scooting out from under her and dressing quickly. He'd let her sleep a little longer. It would give him a chance to discuss plans for the trip home with Tobias. Sylas pulled on his boots and slipped out the door of the bedroom.

The sounds of dogs barking reached him. He held his ear to the door. The barking came from a distance and through earth and stone, but he could make it out if he focused his dragon senses. It had to be the hellhounds at the gate. Their baying was as good as any security alarm.

"Do you hear that?" Tobias charged into the sitting room, closing the door behind him. "Is that the hellhounds?"

"It must be daylight by now," Sylas said.

Tobias nodded. "Sabrina has been out like a light for several hours already. It's late morning. I'd guess around noon. What do you think is going on topside?"

A knock came on the door. Sylas opened it to find Ruthgard, unsteady on his feet, in the hallway. "Help."

"What has happened?" Sylas asked.

Ruthgard blinked like he was struggling to keep his eyes open. "Raid. The Obsidian Guard is here."

Tobias caught the vampire as he toppled over. He looked back at Sylas. "Let's go see what's going on."

Sylas carried Ruthgard to the front entrance. The hounds were deafening there, along with the screams of their victims. Ruthgard woke up long enough to unlock a command center full of scopes. "These will allow you to see around the palace." He flopped face-first onto a cot near the back of the room. "Must sleep."

"*Fuck,*" Sylas said.

Tobias groaned. "It's noon. Even for Sabrina it's hard to stay awake at full sun. For these full-blooded vamps, it's next to impossible. They're at their most vulnerable. They can force themselves awake for a few minutes but nothing more right now. If Ruthgard isn't mistaken and the Obsidian Guard is here, it's no accident. Mother is attacking at Nochtbend's weakest."

Sylas swung a leg over one of the chairs and brought his eyes to a scope labeled FOREST. "Ruthgard isn't mistaken. Mountain have mercy, Grimtwist is crawling with guards."

"That's not even half our problem." Tobias motioned to Sylas to look into the scope marked GATE.

"Fuck." Sylas watched his mother stride into the cave, surrounded by guards who were beating back hellhounds with silver prods. Uniformed bodies lay motionless under growling canines, but the soldiers had the dogs outnumbered. Eleanor had reached the gate, and her fingers sparked with magic. "They're raiding Nochtbend? At high light? It's an act of war!"

Tobias frowned. "Someone ratted us out. One of the vampires from last night or, fuck, maybe Zaruki. Eleanor must suspect we're here. If she finds us, she has cause for the raid. If she doesn't, she'll say she had reason to believe we were here. It's exactly what she wants. A chance to intimidate Nochtbend and possibly catch us in the process, all while the vampires can't fight back."

"Warded by a witch," Ruthgard murmured sleepily. "Can't get in."

Sylas exchanged glances with Tobias. Their mother's power was far stronger now than any of them understood. She would make it through that door, and the vampires would be helpless against her and the guardsmen until nightfall.

The sound of an explosion came from the front gate. Tobias checked the scope. "She's not through yet, but that's not going to hold."

Tobias gripped the neck of Ruthgard's shirt and

shook. The vampire's lashes fluttered. "Is there any other way out of here other than the front gate?"

His brows arched sleepily. "Worm tunnels." He yawned.

"Where?" Sylas demanded.

"Behind the arena." They released the vampire, and he curled onto his side. "Avoid the hornworms."

Sylas met his brother's eyes. "*Fuck*," they said in unison. Nothing else was spoken. They ran for the room and their mates.

"What's going on?" Dianthe asked as soon as they opened the door. She was dressed and packed. Sabrina was too, although the vampire appeared to be sleeping in one of the chairs.

Sylas threw his pack onto his back. "We've got to go. Now. The Guard is here. They're raiding Nochtbend."

"What?" Dianthe gasped in disbelief, but there was no time to waste. He took her hand and led her toward the arena, Tobias following with Sabrina in his arms. They passed behind the stadium and under the seats. He breathed a sigh of relief when he found a crude tunnel carved into the mud off the west end of the palace.

"What is that smell?" Dianthe raised her hand to her nose and mouth.

"Worm shit," Sylas said.

She gaped at him in unmasked disgust.

"Believe me, it's worse from the inside." He tried to flash her a slanted grin to lighten the mood, but she wasn't having it.

"Are you saying we need to go through the worm's lair to get out of here?"

"This is the only way," he said, "other than the main gates, and those are teeming with guards. Oh, and my mother... who came herself."

"Eleanor is here?" Now Dianthe's expression filled with fear. "Aborella must have tipped her off!"

"It's the only explanation. This is tantamount to declaring war. She wouldn't risk it if she didn't think we were here."

Dianthe's face twisted, but she moved forward, her boots making a suction sound with every step. "Brave face and onward. I'd rather face the worm than your mother."

Sylas smiled. The fairy expression "brave face and onward" was something teachers in Everfield usually said to fairy children who didn't want to practice their numbers. He found his wife's use of it incredibly endearing.

"If we weren't knee-deep in shit, I'd take you in my arms right now," Sylas said.

She passed him a pitying glance. "If we weren't knee-deep in shit, that would be romantic."

Tobias groaned. "Wonderful to hear that you two have made amends, but we have a decision to make." He paused at a branch in the tunnel. "Right or left?"

But Sylas never got to answer because at that moment, Dianthe toppled.

⚬

DIANTHE WELCOMED THE VISION LIKE AN OLD friend. She hadn't realized until then how much her soured relationship with Sylas had been affecting her sight. The energy flowed into her unfettered. It flooded her with awareness until her skin prickled with energy. She knew how far they were under the earth. She knew exactly where the hornworms were. She could feel the Obsidian Guard like a dozen pinpricks of light, populating the woods above their heads.

Sylas caught her before she hit the floor of the tube. Thank the goddess. The last thing she wanted was to fall face-first into festering worm shit. The vision was so strong all her muscles had seized, even her lungs.

When she came out of it, she gasped, pulling the foul air deep into her. "I know the way."

Sylas positioned her back on her feet. "You had a vision?"

"A strong one, Sylas. My sight is back, stronger than ever. I can lead us out of here."

He kissed her thoroughly until Tobias cleared his throat. "Again, congratulations on your reconciliation, but a little help here."

"Left," Dianthe said.

After they'd walked for some time, Tobias broke the silence. "I thought you couldn't have visions about yourself. How is it you had this one?"

She could hear the worms moving past them in alternate tunnels above and beside theirs. It gave her the creeps, but she kept going, navigating the way she'd seen in her vision. "It's not that I can't see a future with myself in it, it's that the closer something is to me personally, the harder it is to see. I don't have an emotional connection to these tunnels, so it really isn't that surprising I can see the way through them, but it would be rare for any seer to see herself fall in love, have an accident, or even die. Which means even though I can see which way to go, it's very possible I wouldn't see myself being eaten by the worm. Visions of a personal nature are extremely rare."

"Hmm." Tobias adjusted Sabrina in his arms. "That's inconvenient."

"Agreed."

The entire tunnel rumbled, and a piece of mud fell from the ceiling between them—a worm passing over them. Dianthe shivered. Screams followed the rumbling sounds.

"I think the worms have developed a taste for dragon," Sylas said, looking up toward the surface. "I hope the poor thing doesn't get a black-and-red uniform caught in its teeth."

Dianthe grunted. "Am I imagining it, or can you hear the crunch of bones?"

"You're not imagining it. I fear those men didn't think to shift as I did. How much longer?"

"This way." Dianthe hung a sharp right and climbed a ramp of rising earth into a dense clump of trees. She looked both ways. "We're alone. I don't see any guards."

Sylas took her hand. "You did it," he whispered, then planted a kiss on her cheek.

There it was. The way he used to look at her was back, but she didn't think it was because of the worm tunnels. The way he looked at her, it was like somehow, last night, they'd healed each other. The doubt was gone, but then it hadn't actually been doubt at all. It was fear. And last night they'd made a pact to protect each other.

He was her partner again. Whether through their physical connection or their emotional one, after Sylas had shared his secret, all the walls between them had crumbled into dust. How could she have ever believed they were insurmountable?

"I suppose I owe both of you another note of thanks for saving my life yet again," Tobias whispered.

"Both of us?" Sylas shook his head. "I can't take the credit for this. Dianthe showed us the way out. If it had been me leading the way, we'd likely be worm fodder. And she was the one who saved you from the sprites as well. I can't take credit for that one either."

Tobias's low chuckle came over Sabrina's sleeping body. "No, I mean from before, how you warned the rest of us that Eleanor was coming to London with the shadow-mail candle."

Dianthe exchanged a glance with Sylas, who shook his head. "I don't know what you're talking about. How would I know Eleanor was in London? It's true Nathaniel gave me a candle, but I have never used it."

Tobias looked utterly confused. He adjusted Sabrina in his arms, and she released a broken snore. "The shadow-mail candle that Nathaniel gave you *was* used. Someone sent Nathaniel a message that said, 'She's coming. Run.' That's why we all left for Aeaea together when we did. Nathaniel assumed the message came from you. He said you told him you'd be there."

Dianthe watched the exchange between the brothers, trying to remember what the shadow-mail candle even looked like. "It wasn't me," she finally said, shaking her head. "I don't even know what a shadow-mail candle is."

"The silver candle I brought home after Nathaniel rescued me. I kept it on the bookshelf." Sylas tipped his head in her direction. Everything about that emotional time was a blur. They'd spent so little time together with Aborella in the house.

"Our bookshelf? I hardly remember it." She tried to picture it in her mind and couldn't.

"What are you saying? If neither of you sent it, who did?" Tobias squinted. "That message likely saved our lives. Nathaniel received word from his oreads that Eleanor had all but destroyed Mistwood Manor looking for Charlie. They missed us by a matter of hours."

Dianthe could not imagine who had sent the message or how they'd accessed the candle until a thought wrapped around her heart and squeezed. All the blood seemed to drain from her face, her cheeks growing cold, and she felt like she might be sick. "It was her."

Sylas shook his head. "Her who?"

"Aborella."

Tobias made a noise like a snort. "That would be the day. Why would Aborella warn us Eleanor was coming? She's helping Eleanor."

A strange tingle started at the back of Dianthe's skull. "No, she's not. She's pretending to help Eleanor, but she's really helping us."

Dianthe's vision had shown Aborella helping the rebellion. How she would help was open to interpretation. "It was her. I know it was," Dianthe said. "My vision wasn't wrong, Sylas. She went back to Eleanor, but she hasn't been helping her; she's been thwarting her."

Tobias shook his head. "No way. That fairy is evil to her core."

"No one else had access to the candle. She must have taken it. She must have sent the warning." Dianthe was sure now. She'd been right about Aborella. She'd just misinterpreted the details.

Sylas gave a slow and reluctant nod. "It would explain why the Obsidian Guard raided the Empyrean Wood instead of coming directly to our cottage. Eleanor probably knew a fairy had helped Aborella but didn't know who. Perhaps her spies saw her leave the kingdom."

"Eleanor must have sent the Guard to search the Empyrean Wood rather than Solaris Field based on a false tip from Aborella," Dianthe said. "She's telling Eleanor half-truths, bringing her close to her goal but not close enough to be successful. Even her attack on Aeaea was late. Eleanor came herself. If she'd had time to plan, she would have brought the Obsidian Guard with her."

Sylas winced. "The night Aborella left and I confronted her about possibly joining the rebellion, she said something that has always confused me. When she was about to leave, she said, *A seer is never wrong, but a picture only shows part of the story.*" A low growl rumbled in Sylas's throat. "I hate being wrong about this, but I have to admit it's possible. It makes sense. She is the only one who could have used the candle."

"But the Obsidian Guard is here now," Tobias pointed out. "If your theory is true, how does Eleanor know we're here?"

"When I saw Mother at the gate, Aborella wasn't with her," Sylas said. "When was the last time you saw

Eleanor do anything without her? She used to bring her everywhere."

Understanding dawned as if the light was shining directly on Dianthe's face. "Aborella is a powerful seer. Her visions are usually of the future," Dianthe said. "She would have seen us collecting the orb from Demidicus last night. The fact that Eleanor is here today and not yesterday means Aborella is delaying information. Maybe she thought we'd be gone by now. Maybe..." Dianthe closed her eyes as if she were in pain. "I have a terrible feeling about this. If Aborella isn't here with Eleanor—"

Dianthe's eyes rolled back in her head and her body went stiff. She felt Sylas steady her.

"She's having another vision."

Images flooded her mind, and she rattled them off as they came to her. "Silver wings nailed to a wall. Blood. Aborella in chains." Tears cut trails down Dianthe's cheeks. "Oh goddess. I see her. I see her, Sylas. Eleanor is torturing her. Aborella is trying to help us, but she can't hold out much longer. It's too painful. She's a prisoner in the palace."

Dianthe snapped out of it. Sylas's face had gone pallid and slack, horrified. All at once, she sensed he was back in Eleanor's ritual room. His mother knew how to cause pain. If she was torturing Aborella the way she'd tortured him, the fairy would eventually crack or she'd die. Dianthe cradled his face. "Come back to me. I'm here. You're okay."

He blinked rapidly at her. Some of his color returned.

Tobias cringed. "I can't bring myself to feel sorry for Aborella, but even I know we can't leave her in the palace if this is true. Aborella is a strategic weapon. She may be trying to help us, but her visions are still deadly in Mother's hands. Eleanor will use her magic to wring every last drop of information out of the fairy. The resistance needs to either abduct her or kill her."

Kill her! Dianthe couldn't believe what she was hearing. "My vision *was* accurate. Aborella is on our side. We can't leave her in Eleanor's clutches. We have to try to rescue her!"

CHAPTER TWENTY-SIX

Dianthe understood that what she was asking of Sylas was too much. After what he'd told her the night before, intentionally journeying to the Obsidian Palace to try to rescue the fairy who'd enabled his torture wasn't likely to suit his fancy. But everything inside her told her it was the right thing to do. Tobias was right—Eleanor could and would use Aborella like a weapon. How long could the fairy be expected to withstand that kind of torture?

As expected, Sylas shook his head. "I agree that leaving Aborella in Eleanor's hands is risky. She *is* a weapon, and Mother has a way of forcing others to do her will. But we don't have the firepower to get her out. We're not ready to face Eleanor."

Dianthe's eyes narrowed as her brain turned over a new idea. "There is one way." He wasn't going to like this, but she had to say it. "We know exactly where Eleanor is at the moment, as well as the majority of the Obsidian Guard. She's here, herself, and she's going to search every corner of the Palace of Nightfall trying to find us."

Tobias grunted, then turned deadly serious. "She's right, Sylas. This is possibly the only time you'll ever have a chance of getting in and out alive. If Eleanor is here, she would have left only a skeleton crew behind. I can't believe I'm suggesting this, but maybe we should send Dianthe and Sabrina to Aeaea with the orbs and try to rescue Aborella while we can."

Sylas remained silent for a long moment, his face impassive. Dianthe waited for him to decide. Would he risk entering the Obsidian Palace again? If they waited, it would be too late. The opportunity was now.

"No," he said.

Dianthe's heart sank into her stomach. That was that. They'd all be going back to Aeaea.

"I think you and Sabrina should take back the orbs. Dianthe and I will get Aborella."

What? Dianthe couldn't have heard him correctly. Did he say he wanted to go with her?

"Dianthe can see what's coming, and Aborella trusts her. Our chances of success are better together. Return to Aeaea and tell the others what has happened. If we're not back in twenty-four hours, we're either dead or imprisoned. Do what's best for the rebellion." Sylas adjusted his pack on his shoulders as if it had just grown a tad heavier.

Tobias scowled. "What's your plan for getting through the wards?"

Dianthe thought for a moment—she didn't need a vision to guess what might work. "We can steal one of the mountain horses while the guards are distracted inside.

They all have the seal of the palace on their bridles. If we disguise ourselves, I bet we can pass through the gate undetected."

The way Sylas looked at her was a cocktail of fear and admiration. "It's possible."

"All we need is possible," Dianthe said softly. With any luck, it would be enough.

Sylas took his pack off his back and dug out the Everfield orb. He added it to Tobias's pack for him, alongside the red orb from Nochtbend. "Will you be okay?" He tipped his head toward Sabrina, still sleeping in his arms.

"I'll use my invisibility and fly her out of here, as far as I can go. We should be fine once I put a few miles between us and the Palace of Nightfall. We'll travel all night. Should be back on the island by daybreak tomorrow."

Sylas slapped Tobias's shoulder. "Good luck, brother."

The blond dragon shook his head. "You too. You're going to need it. I don't need to tell you what you are about to try is certifiable."

Dianthe waited for Sylas to deny it or at least respond with a snappy retort, but he simply nodded in agreement. Tobias turned invisible, and a rush of air brushed over her as he took to the skies. Sylas took her hand.

"Are you sure about this? He could be right, you know," Dianthe said.

He gazed down at her, his face unreadable. "He could be. But I trust my mate. She's a powerful seer, and her instincts are rarely, if ever, wrong."

Warmth bloomed behind her breastbone, and she

threaded her fingers into his. "I can't tell if you truly believe that or if you're simply trying your best to, but either way, I love you for it." She pressed her lips to his.

"I love you too. More than you could ever know."

Getting into the palace proved easier than Sylas had expected. Eleanor had left her home poorly guarded. Sylas wasn't sure what to think of that. Either she was so haughty as to believe no one in the five kingdoms would dare invade Paragon, or she'd used her magic to set a trap for anyone who dared. As he rode past the checkpoint at the gate, he couldn't help but think they were mice heading for the cheese, unaware of where or when the deadly snap would come.

He waved to the boy in the guardhouse. *Boy* was the only word for the youngster who barely filled out his uniform. Disguised as a random guardsman he'd seen near the mountain horse they'd stole, Sylas was relieved when the youth didn't stop him or ask any questions. With one hand on Dianthe's waist, he kept her invisible, but it meant holding the reins at an odd, uncomfortable angle.

An experienced guardsman might have noticed. Dragons lived in a world of magic and illusion, and Paragon's soldiers had once been trained to question anything out of the ordinary. But that was when Scoria was doing the training. The now deceased captain of the Guard had been a force to be reckoned with. It appeared Ransom was far less regimented with his men. Perhaps he didn't need to be, considering Eleanor's significant gains in power.

"We need to go on foot, through the gardens," Dianthe whispered. "I saw her imprisoned in the back tower."

Sylas dismounted outside the stables and helped Dianthe to the shelter of a nearby hedge. "I can't leave the horse. It would be a dead giveaway that something was amiss. Wait here. I'll be right back."

"Be careful, Sylas."

He almost laughed at that. If anyone was in danger, it was her, who would be without invisibility until he returned to her. He kissed her lightly and then walked the horse into the stable and found an empty stall. With a bit of effort, he pried the seal of the palace off the horse's bridle and tucked it into his pocket. He couldn't pass up a chance to steal a free pass into the palace for the resistance.

He removed the bridle and saddle as a guardsman would, but just as he was leaving the stall, a young girl dressed in red and black appeared in front of him. *Stable girl.*

"You're back early. Has Nochtbend fallen so quickly?" The girl stared at him with far more suspicion than the boy at the gate.

"No. I came back to perform a task for the captain."

"What task is that?" she asked brazenly.

He narrowed his eyes. Clearly the girl was smart. What would a guardsman say to such an inquiry? "Mind your own business," he said gruffly, "and do your job." He thrust the saddle into her hands and tossed the bridle on top.

He heard her grumble as he exited the building, but she bothered him no more. He found Dianthe where he'd left her. Relief filled him as he took her hand in his and they both blinked out of sight.

"Everything go okay?"

"For now," he whispered. He gestured toward the stable. "The stable girl is going to ask questions the minute she has someone to ask them of. Let's get this over with before we have more company."

She led him through the gardens and around the back of the palace, a substantial hike considering the place was built into the side of a mountain. But he followed her without comment. He trusted her. Was proud of her and her abilities. As much as the silent wraith of fear threatened to take control from the dark recesses of his mind, he held it at bay. They'd made a choice together to come here, and he planned to see it through.

"Here." Dianthe pointed up to a small window in the side of a tower near the back of the palace.

He scanned their surroundings, then did some quick logistics in his head. "That's the back of my mother's ritual room."

Dianthe closed her eyes. "I'm sorry. I know this is hard for you, but I saw her there. I saw her chained."

The temptation to ask her if she was sure was almost unbearable, but he knew she wouldn't say it if she wasn't. Now he *was* afraid. This was the one place he'd hoped to avoid.

"That's where she did it." His voice caught, and he

held up his ring by way of explanation. "Her ritual room."

Dianthe cupped his face in her hands. "You can wait for me here. My vision showed her alone. I can try to get her myself."

He shook his head. "No. We said whatever we did, we'd do together. I won't let her do that to me. I won't let her win. I'm facing this."

"There are no winners or losers here, Sylas. It's natural you wouldn't want to go back there."

He met her gaze and held it. "I'm going." Even as he said it, it felt like he was standing on a cliff and leaning over the edge. His stomach waited for the drop.

She nodded. "Our packs aren't going to fit through that window."

He shrugged out of his, then helped with hers. He stacked them between the shrubbery along the side of the palace.

"Ready?"

He gave her a nod. Hand in hand, they flew straight up to the narrow window. As they closed in, he wondered if he'd fit through the opening, but it was wider than it looked from the ground. With one firm kick, he knocked in the glass, then slipped inside, into the dim interior.

Dianthe landed behind him, still clutching his hand. He looked around to see if it was safe to drop their invisibility. The room was empty except for a heap of gray leather in the corner. No, that wasn't leather. His eyes adjusted to the dim light, and what he saw chilled him to the bone. He wished he could save Dianthe from this, but she'd already seen it in her vision.

Still, her face, once she'd taken in the room as he had, showed a range of emotions. He supposed the smell hadn't come through in her mind's eye. This prison smelled of death, and its contents reeked of things worse than that fate. It stank of blood and dark magic. He very badly wished to leave immediately. But that was Aborella, chained and skeletal in a heap near the wall, and those were her wings, rotting across from her. Was she even alive?

He dropped their invisibility, and his mate released his hand. Dianthe strode around him and crouched next to the fairy's body.

Hesitantly, she laid a hand on her shoulder. "Aborella?"

CHAPTER TWENTY-SEVEN

Aborella squeezed her eyes shut and tried to ignore the scent of fresh air, lavender, and honey that had reached her nostrils. At first she thought she must be dreaming. She prayed that she wouldn't wake up. Once she was sure she was awake, she thought the scent had been brought about by Eleanor's dark magic. It reminded her of Dianthe, and she feared if she opened her eyes, Ransom would be standing there with her friend's head dangling from his fingers. What a cruel trick to play on her. Remind her of a happy memory, then wake her and let her find she was still in hell with her wings rotting, hanging from a nail in the wall.

"Aborella?" a soft voice whispered to her.

Now she was *hearing* Dianthe. The smoky scent of dragon mixed with the lavender. Strange. She sniffed for Eleanor, but there was no new tang of blood and dark magic. Unable to resist any longer, she opened her eyes.

Dianthe and Sylas stood in front of her. Goddess, the

illusion was good. Tears ran down her cheeks at the sight. Was this magic, or was she hallucinating? She couldn't tell anymore what was real. Not for sure.

"I'm going to get you out of these chains," the hallucination of Dianthe said. "Sylas, I need your help. Her waist is raw and her back..." Dianthe's breath hitched. That's exactly how the fairy would sound if she saw the raw meat that was her back.

"Are you real?" Aborella asked her. Dianthe looked real. Sweat beaded on her lip, and her eyes were terribly sad. Aborella wasn't sure even the best magic could produce such a sophisticated likeness.

"Yes, Aborella. I'm here. We're going to help you. We're going to get you out of here." Dianthe reached out and touched her face as Sylas broke the chain that held her to the wall, then went to work on the manacle welded around her middle.

They were real! She had to tell them—before Eleanor came back—she had to make sure Sylas and Dianthe knew how sorry she was.

"I tried to warn you," Aborella rasped through parched lips. "I sent my bird, my familiar Abacus, with a note warning you that Eleanor's spies had seen me in Everfield. But that snake Ransom shot her down. My message didn't make it to you. He found it and then she suspected me."

"It's okay, Aborella." Dianthe stroked the side of her face, her voice as soft as a feather. "There will be plenty of time for you to tell us more once we're somewhere safe."

"She knew I'd been in Everfield," Aborella said again. "I didn't know about the raid until after it happened. I didn't see it coming. I think I was too close. I never told her your identity. She tortured me, but I didn't tell."

Sylas's gray eyes met hers, and she thought she saw pity there. She didn't deserve his pity. She'd done horrible things to the dragon. To all his siblings.

"I saw the orbs. I saw your mission. I tried to keep it from her, but..." She closed her eyes and shook her head. "My wings. She took my wings." She saw Dianthe's gaze dart to the wings shriveled and hanging on the wall across from her, and the horror she saw reflected in her eyes brought the trauma back in full. More tears slipped down her face. She was too weak to wipe them away.

"You had to tell her something." Dianthe swept her tears away for her. It broke Aborella's heart. So much undeserved kindness.

"I tried to lie. I tried to delay. Somehow she always knew. There was so much pain."

"I understand," Dianthe said.

This time Sylas spoke. "Your plan worked. She didn't catch us, and we have the orbs." The band around her waist finally broke, and Sylas tossed it to the side.

"Can you stand?" Dianthe asked. "Sylas will fly you out of here. We'll go out the window."

Aborella gave her best effort to get to her feet. In comparison to Dianthe's, her arms and legs looked skeletal, and her normally purple skin had turned gray. She dismissed a swell of embarrassment at her appearance as she swayed on her feet. Overuse of magic, underfeeding, lack of light—they would have been a fatal combination for any fairy who didn't have the benefit of a dragon's tooth.

Sylas reached for her, but she held up a hand.

"Wait. There is something I must tell you. I know where the Paragonian orb is." Aborella wanted to escape. She wanted to leave immediately, more than anything. But this was the only chance for the Defenders of the Goddess to get that orb, and she owed it to Sylas and his siblings to help them.

"Where?" Sylas asked.

She raised her eyebrows. "All this time, it was right under our feet. We had no idea. No one remembered the history. No one cared."

Dianthe held her shoulders, steadying her. "What did you see?"

"The location wasn't in my vision, but when I saw what it looked like, I remembered. It made me laugh actually. All that power... the key to the thing Eleanor wants the most... right under her feet."

Sylas's brow furrowed in agitation. "Where exactly is it, Aborella?"

Aborella laughed until she coughed from the effort. "It's in the mosaic."

"The mosaic in the veranda? Here in the palace?" Sylas exchanged glances with Dianthe at the revelation.

"The witch queen had quite a sense of humor. She bribed the artist commissioned to create the crest: a dragon wrapped around a fruit tree. If Eleanor had known the queen at all, she would have suspected she was behind the artwork. Medea, the witch queen of

Darnuith, had met Tavyss, Eleanor's brother and the true heir to the kingdom of Paragon, in the Garden of the Hesperides. The garden is known for its golden apples. All those years I stepped over her legacy, her last jab at Eleanor. The empress passes over it every day, never knowing that a piece of the key to what she seeks, what she has sought for hundreds of years, is right there for all to see."

Now Sylas's eyes widened, and Aborella felt the intensity of his stare. She trembled in his presence. Truly, she was so weak, and she deserved to die at his hand.

"Sylas, you're scaring her," Dianthe whispered. "Aborella, we won't hurt you. We're going to get you out of here. We just... this is a lot to take in."

"You say the orb is in the mosaic? Like, it's part of the picture of the dragon wrapped around the fruit tree?" Sylas clarified.

Aborella nodded. "It's gold. One of the apples hanging from the tree. They all look identical at first glance. But one is the orb."

"By the Mountain." Sylas swore. "And you say Eleanor is looking for the orbs as well?"

Aborella sighed. She was so tired. So weak. How she wished she could just fall asleep. "She's looking for the book. The golden grimoire. She's been searching for it for Hera for centuries. Those orbs hold the key to reaching the book. It's here on Ouros, and if Eleanor finds it, she will use it to kill the goddess of the mountain."

"I heard her say that before, when I was her prisoner."

"I couldn't believe the depth of wickedness to her

plan. Hera has been helping her. The goddess of the mountain is currently in a deep sleep thanks to their blood magic. Hera promised that if Eleanor finds the book and uses it to kill the goddess of the mountain, Hera will raise Eleanor to take her place. Eleanor will become a goddess."

Dianthe covered her mouth with one hand. "She's insane."

Aborella sighed. "You might think so, but there are forces at play here even I don't understand. I know her, Dianthe, probably better than anyone. Eleanor has dabbled in magic that is slowly killing her. Evil magic. Blood magic. It's the type of magic one might learn from a god. Don't dismiss her as crazy. She is mad, but her madness is fueled by a dark and terrible truth."

"Should we try to get the orb while Eleanor's gone?" Sylas asked Dianthe.

His mate closed her eyes but shook her head. "I can't see it."

"I can," Aborella stated. "You must retrieve the orb now or it will fall to Eleanor."

Sylas stared at her and stroked his chin. She knew what he must be thinking.

"I hurt you. Worse, I helped Eleanor hurt you in unimaginable ways. I am sorry, Sylas. I am not the same fairy I once was, thanks to your mate." Her eyes shifted to Dianthe. "I'm telling you the truth."

"It will be faster if we fly around the outside of the palace. I'll have to carry you."

As soon as she agreed, Sylas swept her into his arms. Aborella winced as the stubs of her wings brushed against his arms. But then Sylas stepped into the sunlight and the heat of the afternoon baked her skin. She closed her eyes and moaned.

"Am I hurting you?" he asked.

"No," she said. "Go now. We're running out of time."

CHAPTER TWENTY-EIGHT

They had to move fast. There was no other choice but for Sylas to carry Aborella. She had no wings to fly, and he wasn't about to let her out of his sight. Even as weak as she was, she was too powerful to allow to fall into enemy hands. He stopped short of actually trusting her. Not yet anyway. Oh, he believed she'd changed as much as a person could, but he wasn't ready to put his or Dianthe's life in her hands.

He wasn't sure he could ever forgive her for what she'd done to him and his family, not entirely. Her wicked magic was behind Marius's murder, and she'd tried to kill Raven and her sisters, along with other serious crimes. Her actions were beyond overlooking no matter how much she repented. But he could and would treat her humanely, and he'd trust Dianthe's judgment about her visions.

He slipped out the window and around the palace to the grand veranda. Keeping three people invisible required concentration and a drain of power and magic.

He was relieved there was no one there when he landed on the mosaic of the dragon and the fruit tree. The jeweled floor twinkled up at him. Funny how things came back to you. He remembered playing here as a child, the stones smooth and colorful under his bare feet.

A configuration of black diamonds formed the body of the dragon, its topaz eyes staring out of the floor for all eternity. The artist had created a curled red tongue from red rubies. Brown agate and emeralds formed the tree the beast wrapped around, and in the tree was perfectly round golden fruit. They might have been apples or some otherworldly variety he'd never tasted. But they were all large, round, and gold. Why had he never noticed how strange they were, perfect round crystals rather than constructed of pieces of jewels like the rest of the mosaic? Now that he knew what was hidden there, they stood out as laughably obvious.

"Which one?" he asked Aborella.

At her prompting, he set her on her feet, and she lowered herself to the floor, crawling across the picture and resting her hand on each golden fruit. "I need to feel it," she murmured and closed her eyes. "This one." She pointed to the bubble of gold crystal closest to the dragon's head.

Sylas focused on the one she'd selected. There it was —the inner light, the swirl of bubbles within. If you weren't paying attention, it would look like a trick of the light, simply an unusual sparkle in a faceted gemstone. And who really paid attention to the floor they walked over every day? "It's like a universe trapped in glass."

"Sylas?" Dianthe pointed over his shoulder.

From their high vantage point, he could see over Hobble Glen, all the way to the river that divided Paragon from Nochtbend. There was definitely a formation of black and red crossing the river. The Obsidian Guard was coming home.

"The suns are descending. She's retreating from Nochtbend before the vampires wake." Dianthe gripped his arm.

"If she's in Nochtbend at sundown, Demidicus will hand her her ass. She'll have thousands of vampires draining her troops dry." He sprouted talons from his right hand. "Stand back." These orbs were supposed to be indestructible, right? Sylas was about to test that theory.

Dianthe helped Aborella clear out of the way. Sylas jumped and brought the full weight of his fist down on the mosaic. The floor shattered into pieces, coming apart at the masonry that held it to the obsidian. He used his talons to pry up the orb. "Got it. Let's get the packs and go."

"I'm not sure we should bother with those packs," Dianthe said. The guard had picked up speed and was riding hard toward Paragon.

Sylas shoved the orb into Aborella's hands and swept her into his arms. "Hold on tight to me, Dianthe. I'm going to move fast. I can only keep the three of us invisible for so long, and we need to get through that gate before the troops arrive." He showed her the seal of the palace he'd stolen off the horse's bridle. As long as he could keep them invisible, they should have no problem slipping through the wards.

She gripped his hand. "I'm with you."

They took off together, soaring over the grounds and slipping past the guardhouse, then veering behind Hobble Glen. By force of instinct, he headed toward the hills on the edge of Everfield.

"No, Sylas. We can't go to Everfield. She's stationed troops there," Dianthe said.

Exhausted, Sylas dropped his invisibility and swerved in the only direction left to take. He flew east, toward Darnuith, into the black mountains.

The moment they crossed the border, snow and wind howled into them. There was a reason Sylas had avoided coming here until he had no choice. The borders of Darnuith were protected with magic that made it always winter. A magic spell intentionally rendered the environment unbearably cold to strangers. It wasn't long before he felt Dianthe struggling to fly.

"My wings are freezing," she yelled over the gale-force winds. Her wings were icing over. Much longer and they would freeze entirely, and then she'd come crashing down.

"We have to land." He dropped to the snowy mountainside and gathered her into his arms. They didn't have the gear for this weather. Aborella rested, helpless, in one arm, and Dianthe pressed herself against him, desperate for his warmth. He wrapped his wings around both of them.

"We need to find shelter," Dianthe yelled. "Someplace to warm up until we can figure out what to do."

He searched the mountainside. The suns oozed lower behind the mountains. Aborella didn't even have shoes.

"It's been a long time since I was here. We've got no warm clothing or gear, I'm too tired to fly us out of here undetected, and the nearest rebel safe house is in Mistcraven, which is at least a ten-mile hike at altitude through icy terrain."

Aborella's eyes loomed large inside the shelter of his wings, her grip firm on the orb. He regretted laying things out as grimly as he had. She looked like she hadn't eaten a proper meal in days and was a filthy, bloody mess. Although there was nothing but terror in her expression, she didn't say a word, just hugged the orb to her chest as if she trusted he would not abandon her as long as it was in her grip.

Sylas had long hated Aborella, and his empathy was far thinner than his mate's even now. But he had to admit to some sympathy for her. What Eleanor had done to her was dark indeed. He knew better than anyone that it would be a punishment she'd carry with her for the rest of her life.

"I don't suppose you could fly us to Mistcraven without invisibility?" Dianthe leaned into his side, looking drawn.

"You'd freeze to death before we got there. I can't keep my wings wrapped around you and fly at the same time." Dragons were impervious to cold, but fairies were not.

She groaned. "Our choices are a ten-mile hike huddled together like narwits in mating season or a potentially suicidal jaunt over the mountain into Everfield where the Guard might be waiting for us?"

"I'd prefer door number three if there is one. Fire up

that second sight." Sylas looked at her expectantly.

Dianthe took a deep breath. "I'll do my best."

A VISION WAS NOT SOMETHING SHE COULD DEMAND from the universe. It wasn't owed to her. For Dianthe, seeing the future was like a biological function. It happened regularly, like a heartbeat, and just the same, happened in its own time.

Still, there were ways she'd found to welcome or hinder her sight. As she had at Solaris Lake, she closed her eyes and relaxed her shoulders. Breathing deeply, she visualized a light branching outward with a million bright and welcoming hands. *I am here and I am ready.* She opened the cage of her mind, sprinkled the birdseed, and waited.

It worked. A vision rammed into her, sending her eyes rolling back in her head. She watched the images unfold one after the other. By the time she came back into herself, she had what they needed.

"There's a cabin." She pointed east. "An old hunting cabin, less than a mile from here. There's a woodburning stove, and I saw us eating."

He landed a kiss on her forehead, lifted her, and broke into a jog in the direction she'd pointed. They reached the small log cabin in minutes, just as the suns set and a fierce snowstorm moved in.

Dianthe pulled open the door and saw the room exactly as she'd pictured it. While Sylas placed a barely conscious Aborella on the sofa and covered her with a dusty blanket, Dianthe did her best to start a fire in the stove. There was dry wood, thank the goddess, and a tin of matches. In no time, the small space began to warm.

Sylas came up behind her and wrapped a fur blanket around her shoulders.

"Where did you find this?"

"At the end of the bed." He placed a kiss on her cheek. "You've saved us again."

The wind and snow picked up outside the window, howling against the walls. She started opening cupboards. "Don't thank me so quickly. I don't see the food or drink my vision promised."

Sylas frowned. "Aborella is resting. She's very weak. Any other fairy—"

"She's survived worse."

"With the help of a zum zum tree and an apothecary of healing herbs."

A dark, cold feeling overcame Dianthe, and she pressed her hand into her chest. Grief and loss seized her as if they'd been waiting in the wings for a sliver of an opportunity to take over. A soft mewl escaped her lips.

"I don't think the loss will ever get easier." She wiped away a stray tear. "It could take hundreds of years to regrow that forest. Even if the fairies sprout new oaks, maples, and redwoods, do you think there are any zum zums left? They were already so rare."

Sylas frowned. "I'm sorry. I didn't mean to reopen the wound."

What could she say? The wound had never closed to begin with.

Three hard knocks interrupted their conversation.

Sylas flashed her a worried look and crept toward the door. He peeked out the window, squinting into the storm.

At once his eyebrows shot up and his mouth widened into a grin. "The rest of your vision has arrived."

"Excuse me?"

He threw open the door, and Nathaniel, Clarissa, Avery, and Xavier entered, laden with supplies.

"Bloody hell, it's a blizzard out there," Nathaniel said. "If I'd had any common sense before coming here, I'd have lost it to frostbite while waiting at the door."

"Aye, pure Baltic. 'Tis cold enough to scare yer skin right off yer body." Xavier gave Dianthe a friendly nod. "Gud thin' for Avery I've fire in my blood or she might not 'ave made it."

"What are you doing here?" Dianthe asked happily.

Avery shook the snow from her hair and walked to the fire. "Nathaniel, Clarissa, and I used magic to teleport us here once Sabrina and Tobias told us what happened. We thought you'd probably need our help."

"How did you know where we were?" Sylas asked.

"Nathaniel's cards," Clarissa said. "His tarot cards were screaming not to leave you to your own devices."

"Mum isn't the only one with a bit of magic," Nathaniel said.

Clarissa spread her hands. "It takes three witches for this type of portal, so we all had to come."

"And I go where Avery goes." Xavier pointed his chin at his beloved.

"Raven sends her love. It was too risky for her and Gabriel to leave with Charlie," Avery said.

"Colin was in a sweat over splitting up the three sisters, but given the possible scenarios, this one was the least unfavorable," Nathaniel said. "The resistance needs both of you. Be prepared for a proper chewing out upon your return. It was very stupid doing what you did."

Dianthe looked around the room, which had quickly filled to the brim with dragons. She could cry from the relief. She'd had no idea what she and Sylas would have done tomorrow if they were on their own.

"Speaking of what you did, were you successful?" Clarissa asked.

Without even thinking about it, Dianthe had moved in front of Aborella when the others came in. The injured fairy was curled beneath a blanket in the corner of the sofa, and up until that point, no one had seemed to notice her. Dianthe moved aside now to reveal the fairy whose skin was an awful shade of gray, her silver eyes looming too large in her starved frame.

"By the Mountain, you've got her," Nathaniel said, the same way you might comment on the successful trapping of a rat. His mouth twisted in disgust. Avery reached for the hilt of the sword on her back. Dianthe held up a hand, stepping between Aborella and the others.

"It's not what you think. She's helping us. Sylas, show them."

Sylas retrieved the orb from the place he must have put it after setting Aborella down and held it up between them. In the candlelight, a cogwheel, a piece of the key, floated in a milky wave of twinkling stars.

"Good God," Nathaniel said. "You've found the fourth orb."

CHAPTER TWENTY-NINE

In her vision, Dianthe hadn't seen the others arrive, only a bright light, a feeling of warmth, and a table laden with food. Now the vision made sense. The others had brought provisions, including a cauldron of beef stew that they warmed over the stove, along with several bottles of strong wine. Before long, the cabin filled with laughter and merriment. She ate and drank late into the night, detailing her adventures with Sylas in Everfield and Nochtbend. They also told the others everything they'd learned from Aborella, who said very little but ate well.

After dinner, each of them found a place on the bed or the floor to take their rest. They'd polished off a fair amount of wine, and it wasn't long before Dianthe slipped into happy oblivion. She wasn't sure exactly what woke her—she'd been having a wonderful dream about flying through the Empyrean Wood in the heart of summer—but she opened her eyes to see Aborella staring out the window. Dianthe took a moment to come back to reality, pushing aside the grief and disappointment that her forest home was indeed still gone, then slipped out of Sylas's arms and approached her.

"Can't you sleep?" Dianthe whispered, trying not to wake the others.

Aborella blinked at her. "Seeing your friends, I am reminded of my greatest regrets. I've done some horrible things, Dianthe. Things for which I can never make amends."

Dianthe rubbed the sleep from her eyes. "No one can take back what is done, but you can do the right thing going forward. You've already started. You're helping us."

Wistfully, Aborella stared out the window. "The suns are rising. Can you feel it?"

"In my blood, yes." All fairies did. Even though the black mountains still blocked their rising light, she could feel the sunrise in her veins, anticipation of the day zinging through her.

"It's pure joy to be free. I can't wait to feel their warmth on my skin. Thank you, Dianthe. Thank you for coming for me. Thank you for being my one true friend."

"There's still time for you to make other friends." Dianthe tried to be positive. She didn't like the look on Aborella's face. "Once people get to know you, how you've changed, some may forgive you. Some may become friends with time."

"I've had another vision."

The way she said it, almost absently, gave Dianthe a hollow feeling. Not exactly sad, but empty, resolved. Whatever Aborella had seen weighed heavily on her soul.

"What of?" Dianthe asked.

Drawing in a deep breath, Aborella turned to her again, her face brightening. "It has to do with the three sisters. I wonder if you might wake Avery. I have a message for her."

Dianthe balked. "Clarissa too? She's also one of the three."

Aborella shook her head adamantly. "No. This is just for Avery. You'll understand once I share it. Tell her to bring her sword."

"Okay."

Ice seemed to form in Dianthe's stomach at Aborella's tone, but she did as the fairy asked. Tiptoeing around sleeping bodies, she crouched beside Avery and shook the woman's wrist, careful not to wake her mate. She held her finger to her lips. Avery carefully extricated herself from Xavier's arms. The dragon gave a few warning snorts but then fell back into a rhythm of rumbling snores.

At least she didn't have to ask her to bring her sword. It appeared Avery had slept with it on her back. Dianthe motioned for her to follow to Aborella. Light shone on her face now through the window. The suns must have broken past the mountains.

"What's this all about?" Avery whispered once they were all huddled together.

"Aborella had a vision. It has to do with you," Dianthe explained.

"With me?" Avery's eyebrows lifted in surprise and she crossed her arms, seeming suddenly uncomfortable.

Aborella pulled the blanket she was wearing tighter

around her shoulders and gestured toward the door. "Come outside so that we don't wake the others."

"Are you sure? It's freezing out there." Dianthe didn't wish to go outside, but visions were a tricky thing. The expression on Aborella's face told her this was necessary. There was a secret, one she could only share with Dianthe and Avery. She'd been there before. Seen things she couldn't share widely.

Avery leaned to whisper in Dianthe's ear. "Should we trust her?"

She nodded. "Absolutely."

Aborella opened the door and slipped out into the snow. Dianthe followed and so did Avery, albeit reluctantly. She closed the door behind her.

"So what's this vision?" Avery asked.

Aborella took a few steps into the bright sunlight. "I've seen where the last orb is hidden. It's not far from here, but if you are to retrieve it, you must go soon. If you wait too long, you will miss the opportunity."

Dianthe's heart leaped. "Where, Aborella? You have no idea how important this is to the cause—"

"It is in the Ice Forest in the belly of Skelna, the frost demon. You will have to kill her to extract it. It won't be easy."

"Where do we find her?" Dianthe asked.

Aborella folded her hands. "If you go to the Ice Forest, *she'll* find you. She is its protector."

"I thought you said your vision was about me." Avery hugged herself against the cold.

Aborella gave her a slow nod. "The reason you and your sisters are having such trouble translating the scroll is that you don't have the tools your ancestors thought you would have."

"Tools... What? How do you know about the scroll?" Avery shifted uneasily.

Dianthe gripped her hand in support. It wasn't always easy to be in the presence of a seer, especially when their vision was about you.

"Your ancestors left you the tanglewood tree. They assumed you would have it. You need it to focus your power or you won't be able to do what you need to do to stop Eleanor. You will need what remains of the tree to do that." Aborella's expression was gravely serious.

There was more to this vision. Dianthe's stomach sank as she waited for the other shoe to drop.

"The tanglewood tree?" Avery shook her head. "It was chopped down and used to burn one of my ancestors at the stake. It no longer exists."

Aborella stared at Avery as if she were looking into her soul. "Parts of it *do* exist. They've been carefully passed down from generation to generation. Think, Avery. What have your ancestors ensured would come to you in this time?"

The witch's eyes grew wide. "Oh my God. Not my mother's bar! Are you telling me that part of the tangle-wood tree is there?"

"I have seen it. In my visions, it grows there at the heart of the building. I don't think this is to be interpreted literally. I see it hazy and glowing, a representation of something rather than a living tree. I suspect the original three left you a piece or pieces. Maybe a seed."

Avery shifted as if the news agitated her.

Dianthe desperately wanted to ask for more of an explanation about what the tanglewood tree was and what bar Avery was talking about, but the revelation seemed to have struck Avery mute. She rubbed her head as if it hurt.

Aborella spoke again. "There is one more thing, Avery. Now that you know, you must kill me."

"No!" Dianthe's voice came out high and sharp. She shivered against the cold, but it was nothing compared to the ice that had formed in her stomach. "Aborella, what are you saying?"

The fairy turned her face to the sun, her skin already growing darker from the healing light. "I asked Avery to bring her sword for a reason. She must kill me, and then you all must leave this place as soon as possible. Eleanor knows where we are. The only thing delaying her is the vampires. They surrounded Paragon last night, threatening revenge for Eleanor's raid on Nochtbend yesterday, but now that the sun has risen, she will be selecting her troops and coming for you. It will take her longer, of course. Darnuith has stronger protections than the other realms."

"How?" Dianthe yelled. "How does she know?"

Aborella frowned. "The same way she knew someone in Everfield helped me." Aborella's hand pressed into her abdomen. "She fed me her tooth; bound me against my will. It was meant as a punishment. Meant to keep me alive while I festered in that shallow grave you found me in. I've felt her calling me down the bond since yesterday. Anywhere I go, she knows. She can compel me, make it very uncomfortable for me not to obey. My blood burns with the desire to go to her even now. Please forgive me for not revealing this sooner. I needed time to tell you what you needed to know."

Dianthe's breath caught, and Avery appeared equally appalled. It was a grave sin to force a bond. Once in place, it could not be undone, not even with the strongest magic. The tooth was a part of Aborella now. There was no way to remove it without killing her. Her bond to Eleanor was complete and irreversible.

Aborella reached out and wiped a tear from Dianthe's cheek. "My friend, I don't want your tears. We both know what needs to be done. This isn't a sad day. I am free because of you. And what Avery will do for me will free me from this bond. It is my only means of escape, you understand. It must be done."

Dianthe only cried harder. She knew that Aborella had done atrocious things in her life, even to Sylas, but there had been times, times when she was healing the fairy, when she saw the child within. Aborella's life had never been easy. In many ways it had never even been her own.

"Avery," Aborella said. "Please. It's time. If you wait any longer, you'll place everyone in danger." She extended her neck and looked toward the suns.

Avery drew her sword. Fairy Killer, Dianthe had heard it called. The broadsword scared her, but then it was crafted of iron and poisonous to fairies. She took a step back. Aborella was right. It had to be done.

But she didn't have to rejoin the universe alone. There was one simple thing Dianthe could do. She opened her mouth and sang. She sang the song fairies everywhere sing to the dying. It was said that the song opened the way to the next world.

Aborella's silver eyes met hers. "Thank you."

Avery's sword whistled through the air, slicing cleanly through Aborella's neck in one swoop. There was no blood. Her head never even hit the ground. Her body broke apart into confetti, the sparks peppering the snow, melting holes into its icy surface. And then she was gone.

"Holy shit!" Avery yelled. "Where the hell did she go?"

Dianthe wiped the tears streaming from her eyes and swallowed the lump in her throat. "It happens to some fairies. It's normal, although rare. She t-turned into light. It usually... it happens to fairies when it's their time, when they've accepted their fate."

Avery sheathed her sword, wiping her own cheeks. "I didn't want to do it, Dianthe. You know I didn't want to, right?"

Dianthe pulled her into her arms. "I know. You had to. You did the right thing."

Behind them, the door opened and Sylas squinted into the sun. "What happened? I heard singing. Where's Aborella?"

Dianthe threw her arms around him and cried into his shoulder. "She's gone. She's g-gone."

It was a few minutes more until she was able to explain to the others what had happened and why they had to leave immediately. She also told them about Aborella's vision concerning the orb of Darnuith.

"I didn't see this turn of events. We told Colin we'd retrieve you two and be back on Aeaea by early morning,"

Nathaniel said. "It's dangerous keeping the three sisters apart. If we do this, it could be a disaster."

Clarissa shook him by the arm. "If we don't do this, we may lose our chance to retrieve the fifth and final orb. Think about what this means for the resistance."

"I've ne'er been one to back down from a fight," Xavier said. "If ma Avery goes, I go too."

Avery looked like she'd eaten nails for breakfast. "I don't think I can walk away from this one. Aborella sacrificed herself to give us a chance at this. I'm the first to say that I thought the fairy was pure evil, but it appears that even she believed Eleanor needed to be stopped and was willing to pay for it with her life. I believe she was trying to help us. I can't walk away. If we have a chance at the orb, we have to take it."

Sylas stared at Dianthe, looking as exhausted as she'd ever seen him. "One more for the road?"

She bumped his fist with her own. "If we're going to do it, we do it together."

"We'll need gear," Sylas said.

"We have it." Nathaniel gestured to a pile of cold-weather clothing beside him. "Clarissa and I conjured enough for everyone."

Dianthe sifted through and found a set in her size. "Then, in honor of Aborella's sacrifice, let's go find the orb of Darnuith."

CHAPTER THIRTY

With impressive speed and efficiency, the rebels dressed, packed, and exited the hunting cabin, leaving everything exactly as they'd found it. Sylas thought it would do no one any good to give the rightful owner a reason to be upset. One could never be too careful when dealing with witches.

It took little coaxing to convince his brothers that the best course of action was to fly their mates to the Ice Forest. Traversing the mountainous terrain of the kingdom of Darnuith on foot was a task none of them wished to take on.

"Ice Forest isn't a misnomer," Dianthe said.

Sylas landed on a slippery patch of ground between white-coated trees. He was profoundly thankful for the rows of metal teeth on the bottom of the boots Nathaniel had given him to wear. Without them, he was sure he'd fall on his ass. Everything was white and slick, from the ground to the trees whose leafless branches were encased in ice. Even the occasional evergreen wore a coat of snow and ice that turned its needles white.

"You have to admit it's kinda beautiful," Clarissa said from inside the fur-lined hood of her parka. "Like a winter wonderland."

Avery flexed the fingers of her gloves. "Fuck that. If I want a personal experience with ice, I'll order a margarita."

Dianthe snorted. "I'm with Avery on this one. Fairies were definitely not built for winter."

"Why is it so cold here?" Clarissa asked. "The rest of the island is warm all year, right? It's volcanic."

"Magic." Nathaniel brought his pipe to his lips and lit up. "The witches intentionally make their kingdom uninhabitable to non-witches. If you ever actually visit one of their communities, you'll find the environment there as warm and comfortable as the rest of Ouros, but to get there, you have to go through this."

"It wasna always thus," Xavier said. "Only after the war with Paragon did they take this step. Dragon's canna freeze, ye ken, but our mountain horses donna fare well on the ice."

"If the Obsidian Guard ever did attack, they'd be slowed significantly, giving the witches time to wage a full-on magical battle. Even dragons fear witch magic. I suppose it worked to our advantage today though, considering Eleanor didn't reach us in time." Sylas scanned the trees around them, feeling oddly nervous. "Aborella didn't happen to tell you what Skelna looks like, did she?"

"No," Dianthe said. "Only that she'd find us if we came here."

Sylas cast a questioning glance in the direction of his brothers. "Any suggestions?"

Nathaniel blew purple smoke toward the trees. He watched his spell freeze a few feet from his mouth and fall like dust to the ice. He frowned. "Hmm. Well, I'm out of ideas."

Xavier made a grunting sound. "Move yer dragon arses. I wager she'll find us faster if we make ourselves a bit easier to notice."

He waddled forward, slipping and sliding among the trees even with spiked boots. Sylas and the others followed. They hadn't gone far before three hoofed beasts galloped toward them, their shaggy heads white with frozen breath. The creatures passed them without even looking in their direction.

"Now what do you suppose they're running from?" Nathaniel puffed nervously on his pipe.

"Sylas, do you see that tree?" Dianthe tugged on his elbow.

"I see lots of trees."

"It has a face," she whispered. She pointed toward one tree in particular.

Sylas watched its branches sway in a wind that didn't exist, its extremities long and crooked, the tips frozen to sharp points. As they watched in wide-eyed horror, the tree pulled its roots from the ice and took a monstrous step.

"You know how we said we would save each other?" Dianthe squeezed tight to his side. "Your turn."

"Xavier!" Sylas called to his brother, but it was too late. Skelna's hand, which was no more than a collection of five frozen branches, swung through the air and stabbed him straight through his shoulder.

Clarissa screamed. Power exploded from her voice, throwing Skelna back at least one hundred feet.

"What's happening to him?" Sylas rushed forward as Xavier started seizing, white foam coming from his mouth. He didn't like how much the wound was bleeding.

Avery rushed to Xavier's side and pressed her hand against his wound. "He's not healing!"

"Goddess, Sylas, what is that thing?" Dianthe asked from behind him. He didn't blame her for standing back. None of them were equipped for this.

"An animated tree," he said to her. "A demon possessed, organic organism. I need to shift."

"Wait!" Nathaniel grabbed his arm. "This is witch magic. It's going to be resistant to dragon fire. Xavier's lost consciousness and is still bleeding. Whatever that thing is, it's poisonous to dragons."

Avery drew her sword and stood over her mate. Her hood had knocked back from her head, and the mounting wind whipped her dark hair around her face. Skelna had closed the gap between them, her razor-sharp branches whistling through the air, her multihinged limbs reaching for Avery, stabbing and slicing. Avery circled Fairy Killer, lopping off a wooden hand, which tumbled into the snow. The trunk of the tree roared, revealing a mouth of jagged, icy teeth.

"Bloody hell, I think she's royally pissed it off now," Nathaniel said.

Skelna's roots crept forward. The creature's branches

were over twice as long as Avery's sword. Without help, she'd never get a blow in before Skelna stabbed her. Sylas took charge. "Clarissa, you were able to shove it with your voice. Can you do it again? Perhaps use the other trees to hold it?"

Clarissa nodded. She opened her mouth and sang. The trees around Skelna reached for her, animated by Clarissa's magic. Branch tangled with branch, freezing together as a wall of wind caged the demon in. Skelna fought. Branches flew past their heads. Avery dodged and thrust, trying to get a clear shot at the trunk of the tree. The demon wailed like a banshee.

"Nathaniel," Sylas yelled. "Can you use your magic to transport dragon fire into its mouth?"

"I can try," he said with a tip of his head. He puffed on his pipe and blew a perfect bubble of smoke.

Sylas took a deep breath and sent a spray of dragon fire toward the smoke. The flame was captured inside the hazy purple bubble.

"Let's see if she burns from the inside," Sylas said.

Nathaniel drew a symbol in the air with his hands and pushed. The bubble sailed into Skelna's gaping maw. This time the demon shrieked in pain, flames flickering within its throat.

"Her branches are melting!" Dianthe yelled. "It's working."

Clarissa's song couldn't last forever. Sylas sprang forward and tore off the thickest of Skelna's arms, casting it aside. Nathaniel followed suit, dodging the stabs and slices of her branches. Avery, not to be outdone, sank her sword into Skelna's wooden belly. Piece by frozen piece, they dismantled the demon until she was nothing but a wailing trunk, smoking from the mouth.

Avery glanced back at Xavier. "He's too quiet, Sylas!"

Dianthe rushed forward and pressed her hand to Xavier's wound. "I have him, Avery. He's breathing. Get the orb and we'll take him home."

Avery sliced down the center of the trunk. Sylas held his breath. Was Aborella's vision accurate? It was possible this whole thing was a trap. She might have hoped Skelna would wipe them out. He wouldn't put it past the fairy.

But as Avery pried the log apart, they all gagged.

"Stomach. Intestines," Nathaniel said. "What was this creature?"

Avery sliced open the stomach to the mutual groans of the others. There, inside the gory pit of the thing, was the blue orb, twinkling up at them like a hidden treasure.

"By the Mountain, that is nasty business," Nathaniel said.

Sylas gave him a slanted look and snorted before reaching in and pulling the crystal from the thing's bowels.

"You mess with my mate, you mess with me." Avery twisted her blade before removing it from Skelna's remains.

"Avery, you're bleeding!" Dianthe exclaimed.

Avery glanced down at her arm and blinked. "Oh. It must have gotten me."

Sylas saw it now too. Skelna had torn through her parka at her forearm and blood had soaked through the inner fluff.

Clarissa pressed her hand to Avery's wound. "We need to find a healer. You've had Xavier's tooth, right? It's just a cut. It will heal soon."

But Sylas wasn't so sure. Xavier's wound was oozing a strange, poisonous green, and he was still unconscious although breathing evenly.

"Actually, no." Avery cracked her neck. "I'm immune to magic. He tried to give me his tooth, but every time I put it into my mouth, it turned back into an actual dragon's tooth. No way to swallow that sucker."

"Oh Avery..." Clarissa frowned.

Sylas winced. For all intents and purposes, that meant Avery was human. "It may have saved your life," he said. "The poison affected Xavier immediately. Aside from the bleeding, you look fine."

"I feel fine. I just need a few stitches, I'm guessing." Avery shrugged off her sister's grip and dropped to Xavier's side. "But what about Xavier? He needs help."

"Nathaniel, can you get us back to Aeaea?" Sylas asked.

"Possibly," he said through his teeth. "I can't simply tear a portal between realms. Clarissa, Avery, and I need to teleport everyone. It's heavy magical work, and we're all exhausted. Xavier isn't even conscious. Avery is hurt. I'm not sure we have enough juice to get us there."

"Sylas, Xavier's lips are turning blue," Avery yelled. "We need to find help."

Sylas wanted to punch something. He was their leader. He needed to do something, but what? A frustrated growl tore through his chest, making the frozen branches around them tinkle like wind chimes.

The sound of barking dogs called Sylas's attention to the mountain ridge that bordered the Ice Forest. A sled rushed toward them, pulled by a team of tall and lanky canines with long, shaggy hair, eyes that glowed red, and wolfish teeth. The person guiding the sled was too swaddled in furs for Sylas to tell if it was a man or a woman.

Avery stood from her mate and drew her sword, blood dripping from her wound and sizzling on the ice. Sylas, Nathaniel, and Clarissa stepped to her side, protectively blocking Dianthe and Xavier. The sled came to a stop in front of them.

"Tell the girl to put her sword away, Sylas. I prefer not to be threatened when I'm offering aid." The hood swept back from a round, red-cheeked face with a bulbous nose.

Sylas rushed forward and embraced the innkeeper, his chest flooding with relief. "Zander Wraithwing! Mountain, am I glad to see you!"

CHAPTER THIRTY-ONE

Eleanor, empress of Paragon, was not used to losing. Since she'd advanced to practicing dark magic, she rarely had to compromise and almost always got her way. Everfield, for example, had finally fallen. Just yesterday, Chancellor Ciro, unable to rebuild after the loss of the Empyrean Wood, had finally steered Everfield's Highborn representatives to vote to become Paragonian citizens. Of course, everyone expected that the population of Everfield might resist this decision once they heard the news, but it didn't really matter. The fairies had no power and thus no choices.

Power was important.

Power was what allowed her to tear through the Palace of Nightfall while the citizens of Nochtbend slept. Although they'd made threats of retaliation, Master Demidicus knew as well as she did that a society of vampires could never best an army of dragons. Dragons didn't sleep during the day. Didn't have to sleep much at all, to be sure. A few hours a week would suffice. And a dragon's ability to breathe fire was surely a bane to vampires, who could die of burning. Immortal vampires might be, but they were remarkably fragile during the day.

No, Eleanor was not used to losing, which was why she'd screamed when she'd found Aborella gone, taken from her cage in the tower. She'd smelled Sylas in that room and someone else, a fairy. She should have killed her son when she'd had the chance. Should have bathed in his blood. Not only had he taken her seer, but he'd also destroyed the mosaic in the floor of the veranda. Why, she wasn't sure yet, but it gave her a terrible feeling that her son was one step ahead of her.

Still, she'd had the bond. She'd tugged on her connection to Aborella, tracking it to somewhere in the mountains of Darnuith. Ransom had prepared a small task force to track the fairy down. He'd sent a falcon to the witch queen, asking for permission to retrieve her seer. She knew better than to pick a fight with the witches now. It was too early in the game for such a brazen move.

But before she received a response, the bond went slack. Eleanor cried out at the emptiness left behind. Perched on her throne, she gripped her chest and howled at the pain. Aborella was dead. Nothing short of death could break a dragon's bond, and theirs was most definitely broken. She was dead. Eleanor knew it as if she'd been there to see it herself. The worst part? She'd felt a surge of joy come down the bond seconds before it was severed. Aborella, she suspected, had found a way to kill herself.

Eleanor writhed in torment at the thought. How dare the fairy remove herself from serving Eleanor's needs? The seer was hers. HERS. And now she was gone.

"Empress?" Ransom stood near the back of the throne room, the coward clearly too afraid to come any closer.

"What's the matter, Ransom? Haven't you ever seen a grown woman cry?"

He swallowed. "The witch queen has given her permission for up to four guardsmen to accompany you on your search of Darnuith. We have twenty-four hours."

"Write her back. Tell her we won't need to enter her territory after all. Aborella is dead."

Ransom's brow furrowed. "You found her?"

Eleanor squinted at the man... boy, really. He truly was a pretty idiot. "She is dead."

He cleared his throat. "Is there anything I can do?"

"Come to my chambers tonight, at nightfall. I'll think of a way you can comfort me."

His throat bobbed. He bowed low before backing out of the room. So he knew enough not to turn his back to her. Maybe he was smarter than he looked.

Eleanor strode out of the throne room, through the great hall, and onto the destroyed floor of the veranda. She slipped out of her dress and shifted into her dragon form, her gold scales gleaming in the sun. She offered no explanation to her guards as she took to the skies and flew north, leaving Ouros and crossing into the realm of the gods. She landed on the island of Kryptos. This was Hera's island and the closest the goddess could get to

Paragon as long as Aitna, the goddess of the mountain, lived.

Eleanor touched the peacock feather that waited in the temple at the center of the island. There was a flash of blinding light and the goddess appeared, her golden hair shining like a star.

"Do you have the book, Eleanor?"

Eleanor shifted back to her *soma* form to speak, standing naked and vulnerable before the goddess. "Not yet, but I will soon. The rebels are assembling a key that will access the place where the book is hidden."

"The rebels." Hera's lips pressed into a flat line. "And how do you plan to get my grimoire from the rebels? If they have the key, won't they have the book?"

Eleanor crossed her arms. "Hardly. I need the three sisters to risk their lives to build the key and find the book; then I will use my considerable magic to take it from them. This is good news. After all this time, I have reason to believe that they are the only ones capable of retrieving your grimoire. The only ones capable of undoing Medea's protections on it. The fact they are collecting the orbs proves the book is on Paragon. I have spies everywhere. Once they have your book, I will know and I will retrieve it. Soon you will be free to roam Paragon at will."

The light that flared from Hera's body was blinding. Eleanor's skin burned with Hera's anger to the point she was sure had she not been a dragon, she would have been incinerated. "I do not want to roam Paragon! I want my book!"

"And you shall have it." Eleanor placed a finger in the

crook of her chin. "Only, my seer is now dead. It would be easier for me to take back the book if I had more power. Perhaps if I ascended now—"

"Quiet," Hera seethed. "You have plenty of power. I've given you the darkest of magic and all you've done is waste it on trivial matters. I am a patient goddess, Eleanor, but what has been given can be taken away. Bring me that book, or there will be no ascension. On the contrary, I will introduce you to Hades myself." Hera sneered. "He's not the charmer you might expect."

Eleanor was proud but she wasn't stupid. She bowed her head. "I will get you the book."

"Wise, dragon." With a wave of her hand, a bottle appeared in Hera's clutches. Its blue contents bubbled inside its round belly. "More sleeping elixir for Aitna. We wouldn't want the goddess of the mountain to wake before you have a chance to kill her."

With a grin she hoped would hide her annoyance, Eleanor accepted the bottle. She wasn't looking forward to flying back to Paragon in her *soma* form in order to safely carry the load. "I'll take care of it."

"Excellent. I love when we click, Eleanor. From the bottom of my heart. So often you remind me of me." She pressed a hand over the center of her chest and smiled wickedly.

"Only someone who's been in your grandiose presence could truly understand what a magnanimous compliment you offer me. I fear I am unworthy of it." Eleanor refrained from rolling her eyes although she physically hurt from the effort.

Hera gave a haughty laugh and shrugged. "I'm a

giver. What can I say? Zeus has never appreciated it. But because you do, Eleanor, I have a gift for you, something to replace your seer."

"Oh?"

"Grigori, come."

A peacock strode from the forest, spreading its feathers in a gorgeous fan of green and blue.

"I-isn't he a bit conspicuous?" Eleanor mumbled.

Hera made a sound like a growl and snapped her fingers. The bird transformed into a peregrine falcon.

"I believe peregrines are used to send messages in your world, yes?"

The dark gray bird blinked knowingly and stretched its formidable talons.

"Yes, my goddess." Eleanor gave her a bow.

"Grigori will show you what he sees with the command *vlépo*. Try it now."

"*Vlépo*," Eleanor repeated, and suddenly she was looking at herself from the bird's perspective. She closed her eyes and gave her head a firm shake. When she opened them again, her sight had returned to normal.

"Very good. Close your eyes for three seconds to regain your own sight. And Eleanor..."

"Yes, my goddess?"

"This bird can go anywhere, even Aeaea."

Eleanor's mouth split into a wide grin. "You are too generous." She bowed low and then spread her wings and turned to leave.

"One more thing," Hera sang out from behind her.

What now? Eleanor turned back to the goddess. "Yes?"

"Do not return to this island without the golden grimoire. If you do, I will feed you to Grigori."

With a diagonal tip of her head, Eleanor pursed her lips and flew for home, Grigori following behind her.

CHAPTER THIRTY-TWO

At times like these, Dianthe did not want to see the future. Xavier was badly injured, foaming at the mouth as if he'd been poisoned, and bleeding. On top of it all, a man had arrived on a sled pulled by a team of dogs that would give Nochtbend's hellhounds a run for their money as the scariest beasts imaginable. She feared they'd all meet their end soon.

But then Sylas embraced the man, exchanged a few words, and a flicker of hope warmed her chest.

"This is Zander, leader of the resistance in Darnuith and owner of the Black Mountain Inn. He's a friend. He's here to help."

Zander nodded his hello. "Your friend needs antivenom quickly. Load him onto the sled. I'll haul him back. Can the rest of you follow along?"

"This is Xavier's mate. She was wounded too." Sylas gestured toward Avery, who sheathed her sword.

Zander narrowed his eyes. "Interesting. Very interesting. Okay, come along, Miss Avery. Perhaps you can tell me on the way how you happen to be immune to Skelna's curse." He kicked the remains of the demon's trunk and shook his head. "The coven is not going to be happy about this, Sylas."

"We can talk about it once we find help for my brother."

Zander nodded in agreement. Dianthe helped her mate load Xavier onto the sled. Avery tucked into his side and they were off, the dogs barking in excitement as they climbed the mountain.

Sylas swept her into his arms. A moment later they were in the air, chasing the sled with Nathaniel and Clarissa.

"Wasn't Zander the man you lived with when you were in Darnuith?" Dianthe asked.

"Yes. We are very lucky he found us. I'm not sure what we would have done if he hadn't."

"Why didn't you simply fly to his inn and request his help before?"

Sylas shook his head. "The magic doesn't work that way. You don't find the Black Mountain Inn. It finds you. The place moves constantly to meet weary travelers in need. I guess we got lucky that we needed it most tonight."

They arrived at a large log cabin with a wooden sign that read BLACK MOUNTAIN INN. The place didn't look mobile. It was as large as the solarium in Everfield. A team of witches emerged and ushered Xavier and Avery inside. Dianthe almost cried from relief as she stepped into the place to find a roaring fire and a sitting area with plush, brightly colored furniture.

A friendly face appeared before her and offered to take her coat, then handed her a cup of something she'd never tried before but was hot, delicious, and clearly alcoholic. She felt guilty accepting the drink considering what was happening with Xavier, but Zander appeared and assured all of them that he had a dose of antivenom for Skelna's poison on hand and his people were administering it to Xavier immediately. They were also bandaging Avery's arm.

Only moments later, Avery emerged from the back room wearing a white bandage and propped herself in a chair next to the bar. Xavier hobbled out after her, looking better although still a little green. The bartender served them drinks as large as Dianthe's head. Nathaniel and Clarissa joined them. But when Dianthe started toward what looked like a wonderful celebratory drink, Zander gestured to her and Sylas.

"Come, sit," he said. "I have questions, and as fellow DOG officers I suspect you have answers."

Dianthe reluctantly followed him to a table near the fire. She sipped her drink, feeling languid and sleepy in the warm room, and absently wondered if either the drink or the fire was enchanted.

"Thank you again for helping us," Sylas said. "You are a true asset to the resistance."

"Be that as it may, Queen Penelope is going to want to know why you killed Skelna. That demon has guarded the Ice Forest for centuries. She will be missed."

"She almost killed us first," Dianthe said.

"Only because you weren't where you were supposed

to be," Zander said. "Outsiders are forbidden in the Ice Forest."

"We had no choice," Sylas said. "She had something we needed, something essential for the Defenders of the Goddess to move forward."

The warlock gave them a pitying look. "I heard about your latest situation in Everfield. I can understand why you'd be uniquely motivated to end Eleanor's reign, but you must be careful here. You know as well as I do, the people of Darnuith do not welcome strangers, especially when those strangers damage their heritage. You should have sent a falcon. I could have escorted you."

"There wasn't time!" Dianthe started, then forced herself to take a deep breath. "It's true, I am motivated. Eleanor burned down my home. She left my people in squalor—"

"That too," Zander said. "But I was speaking about yesterday... the news that Chancellor Ciro handed Everfield to Paragon."

The room started to spin. "Excuse me?" Dianthe gave him a quizzical look.

"You haven't heard?" Zander glanced between her and Sylas, clearly bewildered.

"Did you say Everfield fell?"

Zander nodded. "It's been annexed by Paragon. We are now the four kingdoms."

Dianthe's mug slipped from her hand and landed on the table with a wobble. Zander steadied it. She was shaking, trembling so hard that her teeth were chattering. Sylas wrapped an arm around her shoulders.

"We're going to make this right," he said softly. "We will stop Eleanor and we will take back Everfield."

Zander cleared his throat. "I hate to be rude. I realize this is a sensitive time for your mate, but you need to tell me why you're here, Sylas. I can't help you if you don't. As I mentioned, Skelna was a part of our heritage. Children leave her offerings once a year to thank her for guarding the forest. As scary as you two found her, she is going to be missed. She may have been a monster, but she was *our* monster."

"I understand," Sylas said, "And I'm sorry."

Dianthe couldn't speak, couldn't move. Everfield had fallen. Somewhere in the back of her mind, she heard Sylas drag his pack in front of his knees and saw, out of the corner of her eye, him pull the blue orb from it.

"We had to kill Skelna for this. It was in her stomach." Sylas held out the blue orb.

"Fates above," Zander said. "No... Is that? It can't be." He took the orb and rotated it, holding it up to the light to spy the piece of the key within.

"Do you know what this is?" Sylas asked.

He shrugged. "Only from legend. It looks like one of Medea's lost orbs. If I remember correctly from my reading, there are supposed to be five?"

Sylas's eyes sparked. "We have the other four, Zander. We have the key."

Zander's gaze met his. "Do you know what the key unlocks?"

"A vault somewhere with a weapon." Sylas rubbed his palms together. "We will get that weapon, and we will overthrow Eleanor."

"The folk tales say it's her grimoire," Zander said, his face suddenly serious. "And if it is Medea's grimoire, it belongs to Darnuith. Medea was our queen. Her lost magic belongs to us."

Sylas lifted the orb from his hand and returned it to his bag. "I don't know what type of weapon it is, but I'll keep what you've said here in mind."

"Do that, Sylas," Zander said firmly, suddenly sounding much less friendly. "Our kingdom grieved the loss of Queen Medea and her unborn child for centuries. She is revered here. Anything you find ultimately belongs to us, her people. You don't want Darnuith as an enemy."

An enemy? Dianthe suddenly found her voice. "Enemy? We're trying to help you. You know what happened to Everfield and Nochtbend. Darnuith could be next. Are you threatening to side with Eleanor against us?"

"Of course not. We will never support Eleanor." Zander shook his head dismissively.

"Well then, think twice about what you are saying, because Eleanor will use our division against us. Medea didn't leave these orbs or the weapon to Darnuith. She left them to her descendants."

Zander sniffed. "She didn't have any descendants. Her baby died with her. We are her people."

Dianthe shook her head. "She and her sisters lived on, and those two witches"—she pointed at the bar where Clarissa and Avery were laughing and drinking something black and bubbly—"they are two of three descendants of Circe. They are the three sisters foretold to end Paragon's reign, and this weapon belongs to them."

Zander looked again at Clarissa and Avery as if seeing them for the first time. "By the fates, you have the three sisters, here and ready to fight for the Defenders of the Goddess."

Sylas nodded. "We do. You've healed one of them."

"Couldn't heal her. She's completely immune to magic. Simply bandaged her," he said absently.

"We have to get back," Dianthe said. "Colin doesn't know what's happened. If we don't return soon, he'll consider sending out a search party and put more of us at risk. We've already tempted fate by keeping the three sisters separated."

"Again, thank you, Zander, for your help," Sylas said. "You are and always have been a key member of the Defenders of the Goddess. If Queen Penelope gives you hell about who killed Skelna, I won't blame you for whatever you have to say, but right now we have to go. We have a war to plan."

"Very well. Enough for now." Zander stood. "Go then. I'll clean up this mess with Skelna. But we *will* discuss the ultimate ownership of the grimoire should you find it."

"Fair enough." Sylas shook the warlock's hand.

A short conversation later, Dianthe circled up with the others, hand in hand with her mate. Nathaniel, Avery, and Clarissa opened the way home.

Arriving on Aeaea with Dianthe in his arms was a relief to Sylas in more ways than one. Yes, she was safe. They all were. But more importantly, she was his again. They'd reached a crossroads in their marriage where they were both challenged to either dive into the dark recesses of each other's souls or take the sunny path away from each other. He was glad he'd dove.

"Oh, this feels heavenly." Dianthe spun from him and raised her arms to the sun. "As much as I am passionate about our mission, I could do without spending another day in Darnuith."

He grinned at her and cocked an eyebrow. "All it takes to break you is a little snow and ice?"

"And perpetually gray skies. And the wind. Don't forget the cruel, biting wind."

He pulled her back into his arms. "I'll keep you warm."

She fluttered her lashes up at him. "Always."

While Avery sought out Tobias to assess her wound, Sylas led Dianthe to their tent to change into something more comfortable for island weather. He would have enjoyed celebrating their successful mission with some time in bed, but she held back when he pressed his mouth to hers.

"You promised to keep me warm, but will you keep me fed? I'm starving."

"It smells like dinner in the main tent, and I'm guessing a debrief is in order. Everyone is going to want to know about Aborella." He slung the bag with the orbs over his shoulder and allowed her to lead him toward the food.

As soon as they walked into the tent, cheers went up from the others who had gathered there, Alexander whistling and clapping his hands while Rowan and Nick whooped and punched the air.

"Welcome back," Colin yelled, jostling through the crowd to draw both him and Dianthe into firm hugs. "I send you out for two orbs and you return with four. You two always were overachievers."

Sylas kissed the side of Dianthe's head. "This experience has definitely taught me that there's nothing we can't achieve together."

Dianthe cradled his jaw, her eyes misting.

"Well, let's see them!" Colin said.

Sylas dug in his bag and tossed him both the blue and the gold orb. Colin carried them to the center table where he added them to the collection in front of Leena and the scroll. Sylas led Dianthe to the buffet where they loaded their plates. They found a seat at a side table next to Gabriel and Raven. Charlie was sitting on her lap, eating something raw and meaty.

"You look like you're going to gag," Sylas said to Raven.

"She can't get used to the baby eating meat," Gabriel said.

"Why can't it be cooked?" Raven stuck out her tongue.

Sylas and Gabriel laughed.

"I'll hold her if it bothers you," Dianthe offered, making gimme hands toward Charlie.

Raven handed her over, and Dianthe bounced her on her lap. All Sylas could do was smile. Dianthe was a natural. Dragons and fairies could not produce young together, but he'd always thought she'd make a perfect mother.

Colin and Leena dropped their plates on the table across from them. "Start talking. I want to know everything that happened from the time you left for Everfield until now."

"Didn't Tobias and Sabrina fill you in?"

"As well as they could. I want to hear your version of events." Colin folded his arms and waited.

Beside him, Leena pulled out a blank scroll and a quill, readying herself for Sylas's story.

Sylas gave Colin a rundown of everything, from the sprites in Solaris Lake to the raid of Nochtbend to how they'd found Aborella and she'd told them where the Paragonian orb was. He told him about Darnuith too. And when it came to Aborella's death, he turned it over to Dianthe, who handed baby Charlie back to Raven and gave a heart-wrenching account of the fairy's last moments.

"Aborella is dead," Colin repeated, shaking his head. Beside him, Leena transcribed furiously. "I never thought I'd see the day. But she was right. Had she not sacrificed herself, Eleanor would have come for you."

Dianthe wiped a tear away. "She told us how to find the Darnuith orb before she died."

"Did she tell you anything else before Avery did what she had to?" Colin asked.

Dianthe glanced at Avery, and Sylas saw the witch shake her head. "That's all she told *me*... Avery?"

Sylas wondered what had truly transpired between the three women, but then it couldn't have been easy for

Avery to kill Aborella under any circumstances. He supposed the witch had mixed feelings about it.

Colin shot Avery a quizzical look.

Avery cracked her neck. "Aborella told me she had a vision about us, the three sisters." Raven's and Clarissa's heads snapped around. "She said that the reason we can't translate the scroll is that when Medea laid the enchantment on it, she assumed we'd have access to the tanglewood tree."

Raven shook her head. "But we don't. Circe was burned at the stake over the remains of the tree in the early 1700s in New Orleans."

Avery chewed her lip. "Yeah. I hate to be the bearer of bad news."

Sylas suspected she was hiding something, but when he opened his mouth to ask, Dianthe shook her head. He leaned back. His mate would explain in time. Around him, the group shifted uneasily in their seats. Was this the end? Did their success depend completely on a properly translated scroll? Sylas refused to believe it.

Colin abandoned his plate and walked over to the center table. "I had hoped that putting them together would have a beneficial effect. Emerald from Everfield, crimson from Nochtbend, royal purple of Rogos, sapphire from Darnuith, gold from Paragon. Medea wanted us to find them. What are we missing?"

His twin's frustration was palpable. Sylas threaded his fingers into Dianthe's and snorted. "She didn't want us to find them. She wanted her descendants to. You heard Avery. Medea intended this message for them."

CHAPTER THIRTY-THREE

Raven's stomach clenched. Sylas was right. He and Dianthe had risked their life for these orbs. Figuring out how to open and use them was up to her and her sisters. But so far the three of them had failed to contribute much to the cause. Despite their best efforts, they hadn't even succeeded in translating the hidden message in the scroll.

She stood with Charlie on her hip and crossed to the orbs. Without so much as a glance in their direction, Avery and Clarissa joined her. They felt it too, the unspoken pressure to solve this riddle. They were supposed to be the most powerful witches that ever lived. Somehow they needed to figure this out.

"What do you think she was trying to tell us?" Raven asked her sisters.

"Obviously that all the kingdoms have to work together to defeat Eleanor. She wouldn't have hidden them the way she did if she didn't believe that," Clarissa said.

Avery picked at the sides of her bandage. "She didn't make it easy. Every step has been a test. Medea wanted to make sure that only her descendants could get this book."

Raven sat at the table beside the orbs for a closer look. Magic swirled at the center around those oddly shaped metal pieces that winked at her in the light. They were supposed to form a key, but she didn't see how.

Charlie slapped the table with her chubby palm, breaking Raven's concentration. She reached for the golden orb. "Ba, ba, ba."

"No, Charlie, that's not your ball." Raven grabbed her little hand and held it.

Colin, arms crossed in concentration, did a double take. "Really, Raven? The things are indestructible. I fished one out of a pool of acid in Rogos. I doubt a bit of chicken juice or a few teeth marks are going to hurt it." He rolled the gold orb to Charlie with a chuckle.

Charlie squealed, reached out her little hands, and caught the ball. Only she didn't. Her hands passed right through the crystal to the cog-shaped piece of key within. The crystal rolled back toward Colin.

"Holy God in heaven," Raven murmured. Her gaze darted between Avery and Clarissa as if they could explain what just happened. They just stared, disbelieving.

Colin gaped like a beached fish. He held the empty orb in his hands, shaking his head.

Raven blinked as Charlie put the metal cog in her mouth and chewed. "Can Mommy have that?" The words came out as a whisper. She honestly didn't believe she could speak any louder.

The entire tent had gone conspicuously silent, although Gabriel and the others had stood and approached, forming a circle around the table.

Raven turned the piece in her hand as everyone around her leaned in. Metal, maybe iron, it was shaped like an octopus with six irregular shaped extensions protruding from the inner portion. The metal was entirely covered with magical symbols.

"Give her another." Gabriel motioned to Colin to roll another orb to Charlie.

Colin pushed the green and then the yellow, the blue, and finally the purple. The same thing happened over and over again.

"Ba! Ba! Ba!" Charlie screamed in delight. She handed her prizes to her mother one by one.

Once she was done, Gabriel approached with Charlie's coconut ball and lifted her from Raven's lap. "Let's play with this one, sweetheart. Those others are broken."

With her hands freed, Raven began to fit the pieces together like a puzzle.

"I see it," Clarissa said, helping to arrange the pieces.

"No, like this." Avery changed the position of one gear, and suddenly everything fit.

"This is supposed to be a key?" Raven tilted her head and inspected the contraption in front of her. It looked like the inside of a clock, five cogwheels that clicked together in an oddly shaped S formation.

Avery picked it up and turned it over. It didn't come apart. The pieces had locked together once they had them in the correct order.

Colin rubbed his chin and took it in. "It has to be a

metaphorical key. Do you think it could be a magical object? Perhaps a piece needed for a spell?"

Leena looked up from her scroll and frowned at the object. "It's a crypt key."

Raven and everyone else stared at the elf. She adjusted her robe. Her gaze jumped between them. "Don't you have crypt keys where you come from?"

Everyone shook their heads in unison.

She cleared her throat, looking uncomfortable at being in the spotlight. "In Rogos, when an elf dies, the family buries him or her with riches to help them in the afterlife. It could be jewelry or artwork, weapons, or even expensive pottery. They lock it in a tomb using a crypt key." She pointed to the metalwork in front of Raven. "After one year has passed, it is generally believed that the dead elf has made use of the items and has successfully passed to the other side. The family returns, places the key in the lock, and turns it to spell the code word."

Raven rotated the bottom cogwheel and watched the interlinked gears above turn, moving the symbols. "These are letters that spell a word?"

Leena nodded. "It's Elvish, and that is definitely elfmade metalwork." She squinted at the symbols on the gears. "You'll need to know the keyword and where the tomb is, but once you position the gears to spell the crypt key, the tomb will open."

Colin stood and leaned over the table to get a better look at the gears and the individual symbols on the cogwheels. He ran a hand over his face. "I think it's safe to say this fits a grave in Rogos."

"Without question." Leena gave a heavy sigh. "It

would be unheard of for an elf to allow their craft to be used in another kingdom. This key fits a tomb in Rogos."

"I was afraid you'd say that." Colin winced and rubbed the back of his neck.

"Why do I gather by your tone that's problematic?" Clarissa asked dryly. She suddenly looked exhausted. Raven could relate.

"Elves are very protective of their culture. Aside from Colin, no outsiders have successfully lived among us for long," Leena said. "And even Colin was not allowed near our dead." She laughed. "Our graves are sacred. It's not as if you could go grave to grave, trying the key. You'd have an arrow through your heart before you could fit it to the lock."

Heat rose in Raven's blood. She could no longer hold back the anger building inside her. "This is beginning to feel like the quest that will never end," she ground out through her teeth. "Every time we find one clue, another five pop up. And we don't even know what this book can do. Why is it even necessary? Oh, aside from a dream I had that Circe won't own up to that suggests that Hera wants it. What if Hera planted the dream? What if this is all some wild plan to get us to retrieve this grimoire so that she can steal it from us? What if it doesn't even help the rebellion?"

Gabriel placed a hand on her back. "Raven..."

She buried her face in her hands.

"That's not what I've seen," Dianthe said, her voice loud and clear in the nearly silent room.

Raven lowered her hands and stared at the fairy whose toasted-cinnamon skin seemed to sparkle with gold, or maybe that was glitter from her wings. They fluttered behind her, the same color as her eyes, and Raven wondered how she hadn't noticed before how ethereal she looked. The fairy could never be mistaken for human.

"What have you seen?" Raven asked.

"I've seen Charlie, older, maybe six, playing with you in the gardens of the Obsidian Palace. Both of you are smiling. Red petals blow from the trees, filling the air with a heady perfume. They sprinkle you as you spin her around. You are dressed in the traditional Paragonian garb of a queen."

Raven waited for her to say more. What about Gabriel? What about everyone else here? But Dianthe had stopped speaking.

"That's it? That's all you've seen."

Sylas glared at her. "She can't control what she sees, Raven. But as visions go, I'd think that one would give you a small measure of comfort."

He was right. She was being a complete bitch. No one promised her this would be easy. She'd faced Eleanor before. She'd seen the wickedness in the woman. Ever since she'd mated Gabriel, she'd known what she was signing up for. This relationship would never be a house in the suburbs with a fenced yard. Being married to the heir of Paragon meant taking risks and doing what was right. It meant trusting that she'd figure things out, whatever might come.

Charlie though had made all the difference. When she'd mated Gabriel, she hadn't thought children were possible. And now she was trying to mother a dragon/witch hybrid. They didn't write a "What to Expect" book on her situation. It was all too much. When Charlie's hands had passed through the orbs, she'd realized that her baby girl was part of all this. She couldn't hope to leave her safely on the sidelines of this war.

"I need some air." Raven rushed from the tent and ran. She didn't stop until her feet met sand and the ocean lapped toward her toes. She found a shady place next to the beach where she leaned against a palm tree and braced herself on her knees.

"I know you want to be alone, but I need to tell you more about what Aborella told me." Avery's tone left no room for delaying the conversation, and when Raven turned around, she was surprised to find Clarissa had come as well.

"Don't look at me for answers," Clarissa said. "Avery practically dragged me out here with her."

"I thought there might be more to Aborella's vision," Raven said. "But I couldn't figure out why you'd hesitate to tell the others."

Avery dug the toe of her sandal into the sand. "Because it was about us. It was about the three sisters. It's the type of thing I think we should decide how to handle before we tip our hand to the boys in charge."

Clarissa crossed her arms. "Colin isn't the boss of me."

"Exactly." Avery cracked her neck.

Raven exhaled and readied herself for whatever news was about to come out of Avery's mouth. "Go ahead. Don't keep me in suspense."

Avery licked her lips. "Aborella didn't just say that Medea assumed we'd have pieces of the tanglewood tree.

She specifically said we can't translate the scroll without it. We need pieces of the tree for the enchantment to recognize us as the three sisters."

Raven groaned. "The tree is gone. Believe me, I know. I saw it burn under my feet when Crimson pulled me into the past."

Avery shook her head. "I thought so too, but Aborella told me that the sisters saved some of it and left it behind for us. She confirmed that what we need has been carefully preserved and passed down from generation to generation."

"Oh no." Raven's head bent back, and she looked up at the sky, wishing she didn't know exactly what Avery was about to say.

Clarissa cleared her throat. "Do you mind filling in the most recent Tanglewood sister on why you both look like you are going to die?"

Raven rubbed her face. "There is one thing that has been painstakingly preserved and passed down for generations in the Tanglewood family. One weirdly enforced thing that has been a constant in my life and Avery's life since the day we were born and now is part of your life too. It is the one thing that existed when the original three sisters lived in New Orleans, and it is still there to this day."

Clarissa's eyes widened. "The Three Sisters Bar and Grill!"

Both Raven and Avery nodded their heads. "All the female descendants have had to keep the Tanglewood name, and the property has passed from matriarch to matriarch."

"Which means..." Avery shook her head like she couldn't quite believe it. "Somewhere in that bar, a part of the tanglewood tree remains, and it is exactly what we need to translate the scroll and open the tomb."

A burst of laughter came from Clarissa's mouth. She stopped, her lips straining, and then gave in to the urge and let it all out. She doubled over with body-shaking guffaws.

"What is so funny?" Raven asked.

Clarissa composed herself. "After all that mess with Avery basically telling your mother that she never wanted to work at the Three Sisters, you two have to come up with an excuse to go back to New Orleans and see our *mom*." She laughed some more. "And let's face it, you are going to have to ask for her help because she's your best bet at determining what part of the bar might hold said tree parts. And..." Clarissa gave Raven a pitying look. "She's going to want to see the baby."

"*Fuck, fuck, fuck!*" Raven fell on her ass and beat the ground with her fists. "How am I going to disguise Charlie? She looks too old. She has wings for heaven's sake!"

Avery groaned. "Mom is going to assume I'm considering coming back." She plopped down beside Raven shaking her head. "You know she isn't happy with how things went down."

Still chuckling behind them, Clarissa said, "Oh, come on. It won't be that bad. Sarah seemed completely reasonable when I met her."

Raven gave her a withering stare. "You know you have to come too, right? We have to stay together."

Clarissa stopped laughing. "Right. Sure."

"And our mom is going to want to introduce you to our dad," Avery added.

That sobered Clarissa directly. She sat down in the sand next to them, suddenly contemplative. She'd never met her real father. This would be quite a visit for all of them.

"Hey, look at that," Raven said. She gestured toward a palm tree only a few yards from them.

"Look at what? It's a palm tree. They're all over the island," Avery said.

"The falcon in the branches. Black head, gray feathers. I haven't seen one of those on the island before, have you?" Raven squinted against the sun. The bird was definitely watching them.

Avery shook her head. "Isn't that called a peregrine? I've never even seen one in real life. Just in the movies."

Clarissa agreed. "It's my first time too. It's beautiful, but I think you're right, Raven—it's completely out of place. He belongs in the mountains, not the tropics. What are you doing here, sweet bird?" Clarissa made a kissing sound toward the branches.

"Hmm. I'll have to ask Gabriel about it when we get back." Raven leaned on her elbows and stared out over the water.

"Can we just stay here for a while?" Avery asked. "I am not looking forward to the conversations with our mates about how we have to go back to the realm we literally just escaped from."

Clarissa shook her head. "No rush. Plenty of time to break the news, perhaps after a few drinks and a little soothing magic."

Raven leaned her head on Avery's shoulder. "I wish just one thing about all of this could be easy."

Avery took her hand and joined it with Clarissa's. "It may not be easy, but we can do this."

"How are you so sure?" Clarissa asked with a laugh.

"Because we're the three sisters," Avery said. "We can do anything so long as we're together."

CHAPTER THIRTY-FOUR

Stretched out beside her husband, Dianthe admired his naked body in the sliver of moonlight that shone through the tent flaps. He lay on his stomach, barely conscious after a marathon session of lovemaking. She ran a nail along the golden skin of his shoulder, under his wing, along his spine to the top of his buttocks.

"You're insatiable," he murmured against the pillow.

She sighed. "I'm just relieved to have you back. It's good to be home."

His eyes opened wider. "Our home burned down. We're in a tent on a benevolent goddess's island."

A lazy smile split her face. "It's home if I'm with you."

He kissed her forehead. "You're right. We're home."

"Besides, Aeaea is where we met and fell in love. If anyplace could be called home for us, it's here, don't you think?"

He ran his fingers over her hair as he pondered that question. "I'd lived here a long time before you and the other rebels made your camp here. Honestly, when I look back on that time, it feels like limbo, almost as if I were in a state of suspended animation. I came alive the day I met you."

She had to look away as her eyes pricked at the sweet sentiment. "I know the feeling. It's hard to remember what life was like before you."

He rolled onto his back, tucking his wings away and pulling her onto his chest. "I had a thought today when I saw you with Charlie."

"She's a sweet baby. Strange but sweet. When I saw her hands pass through that orb, I just kept thinking she was truly the one from the prophecy. She's the baby destined to bring about Paragon's fall."

Sylas nodded. "I felt it too. But I felt something else as well."

Dianthe propped herself up on her elbow. "Tell me."

"I thought it suited you."

She quirked an eyebrow. "What suited me?"

"A baby."

A laugh cut through her throat like a bark. "If dragons could impregnate fairies, we'd have a dozen children by now. Goddess knows we've given it our best shot these many years."

His expression remained serious. "It doesn't have to be our natural child."

Something in his eyes melted her heart. "You're thinking about adopting."

He nodded. "When we were in Everfield, there were many children orphaned by the raids. There are so many. They are going to need homes."

She remembered their faces. The hungry look in their eyes. She'd wanted to do more for them at the time but couldn't. "A tent on someone else's island is no place to raise a child."

He scooped an arm under her and pulled her on top of him. "I didn't mean now."

"No, I didn't think you did."

"It's just that your vision of the future, Raven and her daughter playing in the garden, it made me think that one day this would be over. One day—maybe not this year, maybe not next year—but one day we are going to win this war. And when we do, it will be the first time since we met that we won't have the resistance tugging at our corners. We can have a home with a yard. Maybe a dog. There will be no more missions. No more dungeons."

"Sounds heavenly."

"It will be. And when we're there, in that place in the future, I don't see us being alone."

She pressed her lips to his. "Sometimes, Sylas, you are absolutely brilliant."

He narrowed his eyes. "I am?"

"You are. I never thought of it before. I've been fighting this war for so long. Since I was a child. I never pictured how my life would be when it was over. I can't see my own future. I never imagined something different for myself until now."

"What's your opinion of the picture I've painted?"

"I like it very much." She had loved holding Charlie. Whenever she'd encountered children, she'd always wondered wistfully about how it might be to have her own. Oh, how she could see it now, nothing more stressful than a tray of cookies in the oven. Children laughing in the yard. Friends and family. Celebration. Warmth and kindness. She wanted it all, even the dog. "Four."

"You like it very much for..."

"No, four, as in the number four. That's how many children we should invite into our home. When this is all over, of course."

He smiled as if she'd turned on a light inside his soul. "If it doesn't happen for some reason," he added. "If you change your mind or the world is turned upside down and it doesn't make sense, I love you, Dianthe, just as you are. You're enough. This is enough for me."

She straddled him and gave him a kiss she hoped he could feel in his toes. "I love you too, Sylas, and that will always be enough for me."

For that night, they had each other, they had love, and for as far as she could see into the future, he'd always be the treasure she'd found hidden on this island, her hidden dragon.

EPILOGUE

Colin had learned at an early age that life didn't often give him what he wanted. He'd never wanted to be the youngest heir to the Paragonian throne or to fight in the pits only to be made to lose again and again. He'd never wanted to witness his eldest brother, Marius, be murdered or know that it was his own wicked mother who was responsible for his death. He never wanted to lead a resistance whose goal it was to overthrow her.

But as he watched Leena working over her scroll, he thought she was his greatest disappointment. He loved her quite fervently. His dragon had marked her as a potential mate months ago. Yet it was not to be. Leena was a scribe. She'd taken a vow of celibacy in order to devote her life to chronicling the history of Ouros. And although he often suspected the attraction was mutual when they'd worked closely together, he'd never been so foolhardy to dream that she might break her vow to be with him.

"You're staring at me, Colin." Her bright purple eyes snagged on him.

He'd been watching her work in profile and had no idea she even knew he was there. Her dark copper braid lay over her shoulder, the hair pulled back from an elegantly pointed ear. She flashed him an innocent smile. "Do you need something?"

He cleared his throat. "It sounds like Raven, Clarissa, and Avery are having trouble translating the scroll. I was wondering how long your Quanling will allow you to stay."

"I go where the scroll goes. I suppose I will stay either until their translation is successful or you no longer have need of the scroll. I'll send a message to her to let her know the status of our mission."

He frowned.

"Does something about that make you unhappy?"

"It's just that... I need you... here." Part of him wanted to give in to his deepest desires and admit his unrequited love, to grab her and kiss her and show her his true feelings. But as the smile melted from her face, replaced by a look of pure confusion, he lost his nerve and added, "Clearly the crypt key is to a tomb in Rogos. You are the only one with any chance of helping us find the tomb and gain access to it. I would hope that after hearing about Eleanor terrorizing Everfield and Nochtbend, you'd be inclined to help us, if for no other reason than to ensure the ongoing freedom of Rogos to remain neutral."

Leena's uncommonly long lashes fluttered, and she squirmed in her chair. Her brow furrowed. "I think once the scroll is translated, I should return to Niven. I am sorry, Colin, but this time away from the temple has challenged my spiritual well-being."

He glanced down at his feet. "What's the freedom of Ouros compared to your spiritual well-being," he mumbled.

He thought she must have heard his snide remark, but she didn't respond to it. Instead, she swallowed hard and glanced away from him. "I am sure, if I have an opportunity to talk to my Quanling, that she will assign a replacement scribe to your mission. I am sure that whoever that is will help you as well or better than I can."

"I doubt that very much," he said, his eyes fixating on her lips.

Color climbed to her cheeks and Colin felt his dragon coil at the enticing pink blush. She was affected by him, whether she admitted it or not. He suspected with some amount of dismay that that was precisely why she wanted to head back to Niven as soon as possible. Well, he certainly wouldn't facilitate that plan.

"I must go back to my tent to meditate." Hurriedly, she rolled her scroll and placed it in her bag beside the others.

"I hope I didn't make you uncomfortable," he said. "I simply appreciate all you've done for this mission. I'll be sad to see you go."

She gave a shallow bow. "And I you, Colin." Her eyes locked on his, and he could have sworn he saw a spark of something there in their purple depths. "You have no idea the world you've opened to me."

"Oh?"

"I bid you good night." She bowed again quickly and hurried for her tent.

Colin watched her go, already formulating reasons in his mind why Leena and Leena alone must help with this mission, none of which involved his secret love for her. He only prayed her Quanling would go for it.

***

THANK YOU FOR READING HIDDEN DRAGON! IF you enjoyed Sylas and Dianthe's story, please leave a review wherever you buy books.

Colin's dragon has its jeweled heart set on Leena, but the elf scribe made a vow to her people and doesn't intend to break it. Still, there's only so much temptation any woman can bear. Things in Ouros are coming to a head. War has come, and Colin, along with his siblings, is at the center of it all. Can Leena resist the comfort of his embrace in what could be their final days?

Find out in book 8, THE DRAGONS OF PARAGON, available late summer 2021.

THE
DRAGONS
OF
PARAGON
THE TREASURE OF PARAGON BOOK 8
USA TODAY BESTSELLING AUTHOR
GENEVIEVE JACK

COMING SOON!

Award winning and USA Today bestselling author Genevieve Jack writes wild, witty, and wicked-hot paranormal romance and fantasy. Coffee and wine are her biofuel. The love lives of witches, shifters, and vampires are her favorite topic of conversation. She harbors a passion for old cemeteries and ghost tours, thanks to her years attending a high school rumored to be haunted. Her perfect day involves a heavy dose of nature and one crazy dog. Learn more at GenevieveJack.com.

Do you know Jack? Keep in touch to stay in the know about new releases, sales, and giveaways.

Join my VIP reader group

Fireborn Wolves

(Knight World Novels)

Logan (Prequel)

Vice, Book 1

Virtue, Book 2

Vengeance, Book 3

ACKNOWLEDGMENTS

As I close the seventh book in this epic paranormal romance series, I would like to again thank Anne at Victory Editing for her gentle guidance and careful eye. This series wouldn't be what it is without you.

Another big thank you to Deranged Doctor Designs for the fabulous cover art. They captured the look I was going for with this series perfectly.

And finally, thank you readers for trusting me with the hours you invest in my books. I strive to give you a memorable experience and hope you enjoyed this one.